Legend Of The Sparks

Ophelia Dickerson

Legend Of The Sparks

This is a work of fiction. The characters and events in this book are a product of the author's imagination and should not be construed otherwise. Any similarities to persons living or dead are coincidental and not intended by the author.

Copyright 2020 Ophelia Dickerson

ISBN: 9798698864196

Ophelia Dickerson

Other books by Ophelia Dickerson:

The Secret Life of Mom

Sucker for Blondes

Bombshell in Blue

Angel of No Mercy

She-Devil is Disguise

Acknowledgements:

No book is complete without its beta readers and other eyes that find the tiny points that I over look. I appreciate each and every one of my beta readers. Every one of them has made me a better writer. And then, of course, the ever insightful S.N. Thanks!

Prologue

11 years earlier

"You're such a slut, Becky Sue," Lucy jeered from her perch on the porch railing as she flicked her long dark hair back over her shoulder.

"Whatever. You're just jealous because Jed didn't ask you to prom." This was only the fourth time a similar insult had been hurled in as many days since their Jr. Prom. Becky Sue had tried to avoid Lucy, but no matter how hard she tried, it was impossible. They were in all the same classes, not to mention neighbors.

Tonight she'd given up trying and came over to hang out with Ray, Lucy's brother, like she always done. They'd all been neighbors and friends since she'd been old enough to walk.

But then Lucy had started to blossom out faster than Becky Sue and had continually flaunted it in her face. Becky Sue didn't care. She'd grown up under the teaching that brains were better than beauty. Her hometown only made it all the more clear. A majority of the women stayed home and raised babies. That was their life's work. But not Becky Sue. After she graduated next year she was going to college, from there the world was at her doorstep. Lucy's pettiness would be a thing of the past. Jed would be a thing of the past. She would be her own woman. She'd make her own future with no limitations.

"Would you two stop your caterwauling?" Ray asked as he unfolded his lanky frame from the steps of the porch and brushed his finger length hair back with his hands. "Jed ain't gonna marry neither one of you so I don't know what the fuss is even all about."

"Thank goodness," Becky Sue muttered under her breath. Jed may've been the hottest item in their class, but he had shit for brains and thought he was God's gift to women. Yes, she'd gone to Jr. Prom with him, she still wasn't sure what had prompted that bad decision, and everything she'd suspected he'd proven to be true. Luckily she'd been smart enough to see the signs coming and take the first ticket out. Lucy remained unconvinced that Becky Sue had not succumbed to his charms and ended on his long list of broken hearts and broke in bed.

"Come on Becky Sue, how about we go for a walk?" Ray offered Becky Sue his hand.

"Slut," Lucy spit as Becky Sue exited the porch.

"Bitch." This was how it was going to be. She'd been Lucy's friend once upon a time too, but somewhere in middle school, Lucy had become bitter towards her and as much as she'd tried to be nice, it seemed that Lucy was always looking for ways to put her down and best her. Lately Lucy'd been flat out vicious. This fluke with Jed was evidently the last straw.

She was done with trying. Done with nice. From now on Lucy could kiss Becky Sue's ass. Lucy had already cast enough doubt on Becky Sue's reputation since prom, she knew being nice wasn't going to get her anywhere.

Letting out a frustrated breath, Becky Sue tried to let it go as she allowed Ray to lead her along. She looked up into the clear night sky where a full moon drifted lazily. It was as if thousands of twinkling diamonds were scattered across a black velvet cloth, shimmering and sparkling light. She swatted a mosquito away from her face. This was the down side of the warming weather, mosquitoes, always mosquitoes and every biting bug that had ever been placed on the planet lived in these hills.

They walked in silence as Ray led her to his dad's barn behind the house where they'd often played as kids and now used as a sort of a hang out away from the house. It was then she noticed the warmth radiating from his touch. He'd always been like a brother to her, but lately she'd felt like something had shifted between them. Maybe it was the moon's phase. Maybe it was hallucinations from her woman's cycle nearing. Maybe it was raging teenage hormones. She didn't know. She just hoped that maybe Ray felt a little of the same because somewhere along the way she'd stopped seeing him fully as a brother figure and more as an attractive male.

Ray pulled out a key, unlocked the small barn door, and expertly flicked on a flashlight that was kept on a shelf nearby as he pulled her inside. They walked to their usual corner, the part partially blocked off from the rest of the barn where the hay was stored, and sunk down into the sweet smelling softness.

"You can't let Lucy get to you," Ray said, still holding her hand.

Becky Sue glanced down at their clasp hands wondering if she should take it to mean something or if it was nothing. She found she was over thinking everything these days. It was awful. She was as uncertain as she was certain. "I know. I try not to, but you see how she needles me. I try to drop the subject, change it, anything, but she always finds a way to circle around."

"I know. I just don't think she's ever accepted the fact that you're prettier and smarter than she is. I figure she despises you for it."

"I think the word you're looking for there is hate. She hates me, Ray. Wait, did you just say I was pretty."

He shrugged, the beams of the flashlights danced on the wooden walls. "Well, you know in a girl-next-door kinda way."

"You dummy. I am the girl next door."

"Yeah, but you're not just a girl next door, you're *the* girl next door."

"What's the difference?" Becky Sue felt the heat rising from their clasped hands trickle into her heart that was beginning to skip a beat.

"The difference is one I'm comfortable with because I've known her all my life. I know her inside and out. Her faults, her goodness. The other is a mystery.

She's not a kid anymore and suddenly I'm seeing it." He finally turned to her, the look in his eyes making her hold her breath, afraid to breath, afraid he'd meant it as a joke, afraid she'd wake up and it'd be another one of her crazy, vivid dreams she'd been having more and more.

His hand touched her face, tracing her jaw line. Her heart beat so loudly she was sure he could hear it too. She was transfixed by his blue eyes. Could this be real? Was this really about to happen? He tipped his head down to her, his hand sliding back into her hair holding her head, and touched his lips to hers.

Instant heat spread across her body. It took a second for her brain to catch up with her body, but as soon as it did, she kissed him back. It was everything the books and movies had portrayed it to be. There were fireworks, there was the foot popping, there were angels singing, everything all at once, as her senses were flooded with such powerful emotion and hunger that she moaned against the intensity of it.

Ray pulled back long enough to look into her eyes once more, searching. "Holy shit Becky Sue." And without hesitation came back with a hunger and need of his own that needed to be satiated and filled.

The night was warm, but the heat radiating between their entwined bodies was different. It was hunger and fire, earnest and longing.

Becky Sue thought she heard crackling, and opened her eyes, pulling away from Ray's kisses. If Lucy had followed them in there to spy on them she was going to kill her.

"What is it?" Ray whispered against her hair as he nuzzled her neck.

"I thought I heard something."

"It was probably just something shifting in Dad's shop."

She didn't mention her theory to him. It would completely destroy the moment. She tried to relax back into Ray as he kissed up her neck, his hands gaining confidence as he began to explore her body, but this time a flash of light reverberated from behind her eyelids pulling her back again.

"Becky Sue? Are you okay?" He mumbled against her neck.

Not really, but she couldn't tell him that. He'd misunderstand. He'd think it was him, but it wasn't. Was she afraid of something changing between them and this was her imaginations way of conjuring things that weren't there to distract her and pull her away?

"I'm fine. I think my imagination is playing tricks on me."

He quirked an eyebrow at her. But instead of answering, she responded by roughly kissing him, showing her mind she was in control and nothing it could do would prevent her from exploring this new road.

And it happened again. The spark of light, a quick flash and it was gone. She pulled back panting and grabbed the flashlight from where Ray had propped it.

Ophelia Dickerson

Before Ray could pull her back she strode to the single small window and shone the light out looking for Lucy. It had to be her, prowling around trying to find a way to ruin her evening. Nothing moved in the still night.

Ray came to stand beside her. "What's going on?"

"Haven't you noticed the flashes of light? I think your sister is out there prowling around trying to find a way to make trouble."

He peered out the window with her. "I don't see anything."

Becky Sue sighed. "Me neither."

"Maybe it's just the effects of my kisses on you." He grinned mischievously.

"I'll concede. Because if it's not I don't want to know what it is." She smiled back and ran her hands down his chest. He was fit and lean. Pleasing to the touch.

His mouth closed over hers, as he pushed her away from the window and up against the barn wall. She drank in his kisses. Again the light flashed. Her eyes popped open as a speck of light fell to the ground. She flinched in surprise. Was that a spark or was she seeing spots?

She forced herself to keep her eyes open as Ray kissed her. Another flash of light. This time she was sure it was a spark. It was nearby. Like…like it'd came from them. That was impossible. There had to be fire somewhere. But the barn was pitch black, minus the moonlight spilling in the window and the flashlight that Ray had subtly turned off, finally.

Could it be as the legends had said? Was it possible that Sparkers were real? Images from her youth filled her head from the stories she'd heard over the years. Blue rings of fire. Flamethrowers and animal shifters. No, that was impossible, wasn't it? She kissed Ray distractedly, but he hadn't seemed to notice her wandering mind.

Another flash of light caught the corner of her eyes. She tried to turn to look, but Ray caught her movement and pushed her in the opposite direction laying her down in the hay, half his weight on her. Parts of his body were crying out for her, swaying her mind from the flashes of light.

Ray was reaching for her shirt, when she caught the first whiff of something burning. She froze.

"What's that?"

"Huh?" Ray mumbled sounding perturbed she'd called a halt again to their make out session.

"I smell something burning."

He rolled to his side.

They saw it at the same time. A small fire had started near the spot they'd left moments before. It was gobbling up the hay and scratching at the walls.

"Shit!" They scrambled to their feet. Ray grabbed the flashlight, guiding them out of the barn, and didn't stop as he ran to the house to call for help.

Chapter 1

Ray

This was the worst possible idea the chief had ever had. How could he possibly expect him to go back to his home town and stay under the radar? Even the damn trees had ears and would spread gossip. And going back as a dejected, unemployed bum? It was nothing short of degrading. Was this the treatment he got for his latest promotion? Shit work?

When he'd called his mother, Mary Beth, to ask her if he could move back home for a while until he could get his life figured out, she'd been overjoyed. It made him feel a little shitty inside lying to her like that, but what could he do? And it wasn't like he was just lying to her he'd be lying to the whole damn town.

Ray turned down the winding driveway to his parents hoping that this wasn't a fruitless endeavor. He needed a way to blend back into the local population. Prodigal son returns home. He could hear Preacher Cooper already declaring that the Lord had brought another errant child home and when he left his mother would tell him Preacher Cooper's sermon the next week was how the devil had lured him away again.

A trio of hounds came bounding around from the back of the house baying as he put his truck in park. Nothing had changed. The house, the yard, the hounds. Nothing. Mary Beth bustled out of the house hushing the dogs. They quieted but danced close to his door. He opened it slowly as to not hit one. By the time it was opened his mom was there practically dragging him out of the truck.

"You're home! It's so good to see you." She wrapped her arms around him in what would've been a crushing hug had she been bigger than a mouse.

He hadn't been home since his divorce. Every holiday it was work, no matter if it really was or not.

"Hi Mom."

She felt his biceps and torso. "At least you've been eating good." He grinned down at her. They had no concept of gym rats here. "Bring your stuff on inside. I got your old room set up for you."

He'd had to make it look believable so had packed extra useless things. He grabbed two bags of clothes and followed her inside while the mutts danced around his feet nearly tripping him.

His old room hadn't changed a bit. The twin bed on the rickety frame was covered it the same sheets and quilt that had been on it when he left. He was reasonably sure his mom had washed it since then. He dropped the bags he was carrying in the floor and went out for more.

"Where's Dad? Or did you finally get tired of that ol' coot and throw him out?" He teased. That was one thing they had right, their marriage. He'd never heard an ill word against the other and as far as he knew neither had looked at any other since they started dating in high school.

"He's out in the barn. And you better watch that smart mouth or he'll lay a whipping on you.

Ray kissed her on the cheek. "It's good to be back." And to his surprise he meant it. Maybe it was the fact that nothing had changed. Literally, nothing. The only thing that was new was the newspapers piled on the coffee table, some of them were dated recently.

"Who's that fine fellar in here kissing on my woman?"

"Hey Dad." His dad walked up and shook his hand, pulled him up, and hugged him with the other hand. Chester wasn't much shorter than his son, but was barely half the girth, his chest was no comparison.

"It's good to have you back son." He grabbed his son's arm. "You haven't been laying 'round gettin' weak neither. That's good."

There was calculative look in his dad's eyes which probably spelled trouble for him. He'd be the hardest one to fool if Chester didn't make it a point to over look anything.

"I try not too."

"Here let me come help you get yer stuff in." He shifted the wad of tobacco in his mouth. Nope nothing had changed. Ray walked out the door followed by his dad. "So tell me what you've been up to out there in the big city? What's it like? Are the people as stuck up as I 'member?"

Ray smiled and shook his head. Good ol' Pop. He rarely made it off the mountain. His version of a "big city" was nothing compared to a real big city, but to him anything with a population of more than 1,000 people was too big and city for him. And so began the first fabricated lie laying the ground work for his stay.

His parents had wandered off after he had all his stuff unloaded from his truck leaving him to begin setting up his old room. The dresser he'd had as a kid was still there, but empty. He pulled at a drawer to fill in with his things. The knob came off in his hand. He spun the knob between his fingers wondering who was smart enough to get out of this town and who was still left.

He'd come across a couple guys he knew from here in Harrison, where he currently lived and worked. They'd grabbed opportunity when it came knocking just like he had. His sister, Lucy, was still living around here somewhere popping out babies left and right. They got along like oil and water, especially after she'd burned down the barn when he and Becky Sue had been inside. He'd never forgiven her for that and had barely talked to her since. Whatever had happened to Becky Sue anyway? She'd left for college before he left home. He thought he remembered a rumor once that something had happened to her mom and she came home, but she'd mostly stayed off his mom's radar, or maybe he hadn't really paid much attention to the gossip his mom shared when they talked occasionally on the phone.

Putting the knob back together, he tried to tighten it the best he could to be able to use it. He was still puttering around when Mary Beth called him for supper.

A pot of chicken-n-dumplings graced the table. His mouth watered. When was the last time he'd had his mom's cooking? Man had he missed this. He dove in like a man starved.

"Now that's what I like to see. A man eat. Makes him strong," said Chester.

"I've forgotten how good this is. I've been at the mercy of my own cooking for a while and frankly I just don't have the skill set to make anything like this."

"That's why you should remarry. I don't care how bad that girl broke your heart, no man should live alone like you do," Mary Beth declared.

He didn't have the heart to tell her his heart wasn't broken. He'd been deceived sure, but he'd figured out real fast what kind of lying, weaseling little bitch his ex had been and was in no hurry for a repeat. He'd had a couple of women walk in and out of his life since, but most of them couldn't cook, at least like this. But a man couldn't live alone without warming his bed sometimes. And sometimes the cooking had to take back seat to his other needs.

"Don't worry though. Now that you're back home I'm sure it won't take you long to find a good woman. As a matter of fact the phone's been ringing off the hook this evening. Gracious, I was barely able to cook. You remember my friend Barbara? She called. Her granddaughter graduated about two years ago and has been running wild ever since. She needs a good, strong man to take her in hand and settle her down. Oh and Vikki called. You remember Phoebe? I believe she graduated with you… or was she younger? Anyway, Phoebe's good for nothing husband ran off a couple years ago leaving her stranded with three mouths to feed. She could use a good strong man to help her out."

Buck tooth Phoebe? Was she being serious? The last he'd seen that girl she was skinny as a rail, freckle faced and scraggly.

"Mom. I'm didn't come back to get hitched right away. I need to figure out what I'm doing with my life first. I need a job."

"Hmmph." She huffed. "Seems to me like you would want to find a good woman to help you get back on your feet. Someone who would encourage you and give you motivation to do better."

He'd tried to make the chief understand this wouldn't work, but since he was the least likely to raise any red flags he'd been the one to get sent down here. If he could've only recorded this conversation and pass it to the chief, maybe he'd reconsider because something told him he'd spend more time trying to avoid matrimony than he would doing actual work.

"Settle down Mary Beth, I'm sure Ray will remarry soon enough. Don't push the boy. You don't want him to end up with another broken heart do you?" Chester patted his wife's hand and talked in a soothing voice. When had Dad become such a manipulator?

"No, I suppose not. I just know he'd be happier if he had someone at his side."

Ray did a mental head slap and hoped this assignment would be short so he could get out of this God forsaken town.

The rest of dinner smoothed out and ended well. Ray had just left his plate in the sink and walked out of the kitchen when he heard his dad's voice.

"Mary Beth have you talked to Becky Sue lately?" Ray slowed his steps trying to listen without being noticed. He'd wanted to ask about Becky Sue but was somewhere between being afraid she was married with five kids and having his mom match make them.

"No, why?"

"I need to talk to her and make sure she's planning on planting my watermelons again this year. I'm thinking to ask her to plant a few extras." Ray stopped just out of sight but within hearing distance.

"Well I need to go to the post office tomorrow. I'll stop by and talk to her."

Ray walked to his room musing. If he had one ally in this town it would be Becky Sue, at least if she was the same as she used to be.

He shuffled around a little bit and walked back out to where his mom was cleaning up dinner. His dad had just flipped on the TV. "I need to run into town tomorrow and try to pick up a few things. Is there anything you need while I'm there?"

"The only thing I was going to do was run to the post office and your dad needs to me to go talk to Becky Sue."

"I can do that if you'd like."

"That would nice."

He turned to leave the kitchen and glanced over at his dad. Chester looked his way and smiled. Why did he feel like he'd just walked into a trap

Chapter 2

There's a legend told in the hills of the Arkansas Ozark Mountains of a peculiar people known as Sparks, or Sparkers. They hold magical powers. It's rumored they can take on the form of an animal, a shape shifter if you will.

Now how to identify these people is a bit of mystery. They appear normal and walk among the general population. They may even believe they are normal. Some have stronger powers than others. Some are born with the power as a recessive gene and without the proper ignition will never know they are a Sparker. (This happens only if one parent is a Spark and the other is not. In this way, the Sparker gene can pass unnoticed from generation to generation until it eventually disappears.) If both parents are Sparkers the children born will possess their powers from birth.

There was a movement after the end of the Civil War to make the Sparkers extinct. It started after the Mayor's wife burned down their house in a fit of sparking rage after finding him in bed with the preacher's wife. The Mayor tried declaring a law that made it illegal for two Sparkers to marry and in an era of military rule and unrest, they couldn't risk running the error, being imprisoned, and sometimes relocated. The war hadn't helped the general population of Sparker's either, running down the male population like it did. While a Sparker may possess powers to take on a form of animal, and throw fire they are not immortal.

By the turn of the 20th century there were only a handful of known Sparkers remaining, the rest were either dead, or silent. The last, believed to be, local Sparker died December 20, 1903.

Becky Sue closed the book without finishing the introduction and replaced it back on the shelf. She knew the book forward and back, and more besides. Nothing but tales that rivaled Sasquatch and UFO sightings filled the pages. But the tourists loved it, that's why Uncle Melvin's book still sat on her shelf. Tourists.

On the next shelf were little figurines celebrating the legends of the Sparks. Animals hurtling balls of fire from their paws and feet. Some blowing fire from their mouth. Those were typically big sellers. Then there were figurines targeting the more romantically inclined. A boy and a girl came in three different classic romantic poses. In each one they were a fraction away from kissing, a blue haze representing fire encircled them, sparks flew in every direction.

Once upon a time, for a very short time, Becky Sue had entertained the thought that she might be a long lost Sparker. She closed her eyes and for a minute and let herself feel the breathless excitement she'd felt as Ray had taken her by the hand and led her to his dad's barn where they'd let the moonlight talk for them, whispering words of romance and sensual pleasures to come. Chills raced up her arm at his touch, despite the warm evening air. The fluttering of a hundred butterflies filled her breast and turned her stomach upside down. Waiting. Anticipating his every touch. His every breath.

When he'd finally gathered the courage to kiss her, a heat she'd never felt since, coursed through her body and had seemed to light up the night. Then she'd smelled the smoke. Within seconds flames were spreading across the barn, licking at the walls, threatening death and disaster. They'd run from the barn like the hounds of hell were after them. They didn't hesitate as they ran into the house to call the fire department, but in such a small rural community, the reaction time was too long and the barn had burned to the ground, exploding one of Chester's stills in the process. She'd gone home that night wondering if their kiss had ignited the Sparker in her. The next day Ray told her his sister, Lucy, had thrown a match in through a crack to scare them.

Becky Sue's bubble had burst. She wasn't a Sparker after all. It had only been a brief teenage fantasy.

She sighed and opened her eyes. She wasn't sure what had made her think about Ray after all these years. Maybe it was the longing for that rush again. Maybe she'd been lonely too long. If she ever found someone who made her feel the way Ray had that night, she wouldn't let them go so easily. She'd been just a dumb teenager who knew nothing about life, but had dreamed of legends and romance. So much had changed in the last eleven years, and yet, so little.

Her parents had divorced. Ray had moved off. She'd lost count of the number of babies born in that time frame, but the population was basically the same. The sane ones move away before the town sucked them in forever. And the economy of the little town still depended on the tourists. It always came back to the tourists.

Thunderhead was everything you'd expect to find in the rural mountains of Arkansas. Spring through late fall tourist would flock the mountains to canoe, hike, and collect trinkets and stories to take home to family and friends. The winter months showed the true make up of the town. Most businesses closed and folks wintered at home, except for the gas station.

There were more camp grounds surrounding the town than there were businesses inside it. Downtown consisted of an open city block that served as sort of a park complete with a couple of benches and some narrow concrete paths crisscrossing it.

The park was surrounded with crumbling brick buildings, most of which were built back in the 1920's. The only business not encircled in the town square was the Birdsong Motel, and even it had its back to Claire's diner.

Vernon's gas station was on the corner where the highway entered, on the opposite side of the road. It was typically the hot spot, but often times the tourists would want to stretch their legs and would wonder into the neighboring shops. On the end of the block opposite Vernon was Sam's canoe rentals, also a popular destination.

Becky Sue's shop was furthest from the highway, but facing it. She sold her handmade quilts, local souvenirs, and produce out of her garden, and sometimes in a good year jams and jellies she'd canned. She was also one of three business owners who carried Chester's Thunderhead tonic, a.k.a moonshine, which was technically illegal but with the revenue it brought in, it supported nearly a quarter of the town by various means from charity to taxes.

The other half of her building was Cindy's homemade candles, soaps, and lotions. Cindy was a good neighbor, mostly, that is for a grandmotherly type. Cindy's husband had passed away a year after Becky Sue had bought her shop. The woman had been lonely ever since and was constantly at Becky Sue's door chattering away or having her try a new soap or lotion she'd made. That was after three years of trying to set Becky Sue up with any unattached male she could find that was of age.

Thunderhead didn't have a lot of eligible bachelor options, and Becky Sue had politely turned down invitations from all of them. At the ripe old age of 28 yrs, she was the town spinster. Most the girls her age, especially those who hadn't moved off, were married and had three kids already, or were getting near it. It wasn't like she was a celibate spinster though.

Occasionally a rogue tourist would come to town and she'd get to practice her feminine wiles on him. But they always moved on and none of them had come close to bringing the heat that Ray had, which made her start to believe it'd been a teenage fluke of the imagination all the more.

She sighed as she propped the door open. The air was still a little brisk, but the sun warmed her skin. Spring was about to hit in full swing. Like flowers emerging after the winter, shops were beginning to open and tourists were starting to trickle in.

Life wasn't bad. She was content to make her quilts and tend her garden. She had meaningful friendships and she could support herself. Becky Sue was comfortable, if not a little bored on occasion. But every once in a while she wished she was a Spark, or at least had something spark in her life. And those times usually hit around spring when everything came back to life.

"Good morning Becky Sue," Cindy called out as she opened her door, propping it open with a brick to let the aromatic smells of her potions and lotions into the air to call the tourists in. "Did you hear who's back in town?" Her short grey curly hair was scattered across her head as the wind lifted it, making her look wilder than she actually was.

"No. Let me guess, Macy?" Macy was Cindy's granddaughter who'd graduated high school last spring only to fall in love with a passing tourist a week later. She moved out of town within two months of graduation. By Christmas she was already expecting her first baby. Becky Sue had been counting down months until Macy got thrown out in the cold and had to return home.

"Why ever would you say a thing like that?" Maybe because Becky Sue had become a cynic. There were no happily ever afters. Those only existed in fairy tales or in legends like the book Uncle Melvin had written about the Sparkers. "No. Ray is back in town. I ran into Mary Beth at the gas station this morning and she said he came in yesterday. Alone." Cindy gave me a side long look and winked. "Seems he's finally moving back home."

"Ray is like my brother." Her face screwed up into an are-you-crazy-look but somewhere deep inside a little voice called her a liar. He'd been her best friend growing up. They'd been almost inseparable, but sometime in their teens something had changed between them. They'd almost fallen for each other. But then there was the barn incident. Becky Sue swore she'd never let herself be disillusioned again. After that, they'd sort of drifted apart. Mary Beth, his mom, would stop in occasionally and share news of him and other gossip with her so she'd sort of kept track of him these last nine years since he left.

"Like doesn't mean is. You know it's perfectly legal to marry up to your third cousin. As a matter of fact, just last month Henry and Susie married and they're siblings by marriage."

"I heard about that." Henry's mother had passed away when he was at the tender age of eleven. Susie's father had run off with a hippy tourist when she was nine. Henry's father had married Susie's mother when they were both kids were hitting their teens. Technically there was no blood relation between them but that didn't detract from the fact it was still just a little weird.

"Just remember you won't stay young forever and you don't want to die a lonely old maid." She shook her finger at Becky Sue and her whole arm jiggled.

Yep, that's right. Don't want to be a lonely old skinny maid, because obviously men make you fat. It was inevitable. She'd seen it happen to nearly every single girl that'd stayed in town and settled down. Then all you do is pop out babies and all your energy is channeled into raising them. No self care. No business. No independence. "Yes, Cindy, I know."

"Oh, I almost forgot. I'll be over in a minute. I have a new soap for you to try. It's mint and lavender. I whipped it up last night. This should make you smell good enough to attract a man."

Great, now she stunk too. Cindy ducked back into her shop to retrieve the magical bar of soap that would end Becky Sue's spinster hood. Becky Sue briefly considered ducking out the back door, but she didn't run from anything, even Cindy. Or maybe she didn't run because she had nowhere to go and her mom still needed her here to take care of her.

A bench sat beside the large window of Becky's shop. She waited for Cindy there afraid if she went inside she'd never see the end of Cindy today. From her vantage point, she could see Vernon's gas station. There were three cars in the parking lot. A woman had a dog on a leash off on the side in the grass letting it do its business. A man stood off to the side of the doorway smoking. Another man was filling up the family car with gas. On the opposite side of the block, Sam was hooking up a trailer full of canoes, readying them to take out to the tourists. Yep, Thunderhead was waking from its winter nap.

Cindy bustled back out with a carefully wrapped soap square in her hand. "Here, smell it." She had it practically shoved up Becky Sue's nose before she could decline.

"It smells beautiful. I bet it'll turn into a bestseller."

"This one is for you. It'll do wonders for your skin too. It's one of the goat milk recipes I enhanced."

Becky Sue looked down at her skin. Did it need wonders done to it? Was it really that bad? Sure she was pale from being inside most the winter working on quilts for this spring, but it wouldn't take long for her normal healthy tan to return as she returned to her garden. In fact, she was planning to start planting her peas this week

"Thanks Cindy, I'll give it a try." Hey, it was something free she didn't have to buy, she wouldn't complain.

No, Becky Sue wasn't poor. She liked to think of herself as frugal. She worked hard and earned enough to take care of herself and help her mom a little. She'd been saving up for a vacation since she hadn't been on one since opening her shop seven years ago. If the next two years turned out good, she should finally be able to have saved enough to take the cruise she'd been dreaming about. "I better get in here and get to work. This quilt isn't going to stitch itself."

"What are you making now?"

"A patriotic themed star quilt."

"Oh, that should go good. You got your grandmother's talent that's for sure. She was a good woman. I see a lot of her in you."

Becky Sue gave her a half crooked smile. "Thanks." She darted into her shop, bar of soap in hand, and hoped Cindy would get a clue. Most days she didn't mind her and her chatter, but some days she just liked to be left alone. Today was one of those days.

Her mind whirled with questions concerning Ray's reappearance as she lifted her quilt already on the hoop and began hand stitching it together. She could only assume he was divorced now. Was he living back at his parents, or was his dad still pissed about the barn? Why, of all places, did he want to come back here? There were no real jobs. Most people worked for themselves or traveled to work in bigger areas, such as Harrison which was a good forty-five minutes away.

Becky Sue was deep in thought, fingers flying to and from the quilt leaving neat tiny stitches behind when footsteps in the doorway called her attention away.

"Hello," she set the quilt aside and stood to greet her customers. "How are ya'll today?"

The man she'd seen pumping gas was standing behind a woman roughly the same age as herself with two little dark haired girls in tow.

"Good." The woman eyed the quilts hanging on her homemade racks. "Are all these handmade?"

"Yep. If there's any particular theme or size you're looking for I can help point them out to you."

"Ok. Is it alright if I just look through them myself?"

"Sure." Becky Sue watched as the woman started looking through the quilt, occasionally fingering one and leaning over to whisper to her husband. Price consideration was usually the topic of discussion. She thought she charged a fair price for her quilts, but sometimes cheap tourists would try to barter with her. After explaining to them the cost of fabric and the time it took to make one, they would either give in and buy it at set price, or they'd leave empty handed.

The two little girls, aged somewhere between five and seven, began to play hide and seek in the panels of the quilts hanging near the floor. The dad soon got on to them and held one by each hand. They continued their shenanigans playing peek-a-boo around his legs.

Becky Sue smiled. She didn't mind kids most the time. It was usually the older ones that would come in, ice cream cone in hand, and touch everything as the ice cream slowly dripped onto the quilts that would piss her off. A little hide and seek never hurt anything.

After a few minutes she could see the dad getting as anxious as the kids to leave. The mom finally selected two twin size princess quilts and paid out.

The next few hours dragged by with only a shadow passing by the window once or twice. Becky Sue was just tightening the hoop after moving it again, when a familiar voice reached her ears.

"Afternoon Becky Sue."

She knew the voice but when she looked up she saw a stranger.

Chapter 3

Ray was no longer the gangly youth she'd known. He was compact, solid, muscled up. His brown hair was cut military style. His blue eyes were more piercing than ever.

"What're you doing here?"

The words sounded harsher to her ears than she meant them, but it was better to get straight to the point rather than beat around the bush or pretend to take an interest in each other's lives.

"What kind of greeting is that for the town's most eligible bachelor? Especially coming from the town's most eligible spinster." He walked up to the small counter and leaned over, grinning from ear to ear, to see what she was doing as he spoke.

Becky Sue looked down at her homemade clothes. *Most eligible spinster my ass.* In her home made clothes she looked more like a hybrid of something off of "The Little House on the Prairie" and a hippie, not an eligible bachelorette. But again, the homemade clothing helped with the tourist appeal. Once upon a time she'd have blushed and pretended to be flattered, but not now. Not with Ray.

"Most eligible bachelor, really?" The screw spinning in her hand made her look down at her hoop. She'd just tightened it too much and knocked the screw loose. Great, just what she needed, a near useless hoop. At least she had a backup.

"You're sarcasm is as sweet as ever. But yes, Mom has already had four calls checking my marital status, two of which had marriage proposals included for their daughters. You should hold off on that eye roll until you hear what I have to say."

She looked up and couldn't help but grin back. She'd been caught. Her friend Ray was home. Letting go of the hoop she moved around to the side of the counter to get a better look at him. He was more mouth watering delicious than Lydia's fudge. "Alright, I give in. It's good to see you again."

He opened his arms and stepped up to her. She wasn't really the hugging type, but she'd make an exception this once. He squeezed her tight against him. Reflexes and a small flowing fountain of relief at seeing him again demanded she squeeze back just as hard. The muscles across his chest were definitely new. And he smelled good too, like spices and exotic places. Things she only read about in books.

What was the appropriate time length for a hug? Becky Sue didn't know. All she knew was Ray felt good in her arms. Like home. It was as if he'd never left, and the barn incident had never happened. It made her feel warm and fuzzy, maybe a little too warm. Her body felt as if a heat lamp had been turned on, soaking up his body heat and possibly radiating some of her own. She felt his breath on her neck. Goosebumps raced down her arms, making the hairs stand on end. She shrugged off her reaction to the fact that she hadn't gotten any in a while.

This was the only other human being on earth who really and truly understood her, even after the long passage of time apart, she knew with a certainty she couldn't explain, that nothing had changed between them.

A sound in the door way broke up their embrace. She glanced over just in time to Cindy's look of shock before she turned and disappeared from the threshold.

"Well, looks like you won't have to worry about your eligible bachelor status for long. By dinner tonight I'm sure the whole town will have us married."

"Oh, I'm glad you mentioned that." He snapped his fingers like he'd just remembered something important.

"What? Marriage?"

"No, dinner. Mom said she hadn't seen much of you in a while and I should invite you over for dinner tonight."

"You know she's just as bad of a matchmaker as everybody else in this town, right?"

"Yeah, but I figured it'd be nice to have a chance to catch up. It's been a few years. After dinner I'll grab us a jug of Dad's moonshine and we can go hang out at the barn and tell tales."

"Now don't go calling it moonshine. We call it Thunderhead tonic now." She teasingly scolded. A confused look passed briefly over his face. They'd branded the moonshine for sale as a local tonic the year she'd graduated high school. "But you know, that doesn't sound like a half bad idea."

"Good. I'll see you about 6:30p.m. then?"

"You betcha."

He reached out and gave her a quick hug and walked out. His ass was so round and so perfect she just wanted to reach out and grab it. Had it always been that bubbly or had it come with the rest of his muscled physique? She caught herself drooling as he walked past the window, looked in at her, and winked.

Ray had turned into Adonis reincarnate. Becky Sue knew better than to let his new look sway her. It was a bad idea. A really bad idea. It would result in nothing but heartache if she gave in. But damn if he wasn't tempting.

No sooner than Ray had left and Becky Sue had returned to her quilt than Cindy came through the door.

"Becky Sue you better scoop that man up before one of these other women around here does. Honey, he looks good."

"I'm telling you, brother. We grew up really close."

Cindy put a hand to her voluptuous waist and gave Becky Sue a look that said she wasn't buying it. "And that embrace I just saw was sisterly too, huh?"

"Uh, yeah."

"He was nuzzling your neck, child! Don't you know anything? When a man that looks like that nuzzles your neck you better hang on and not let go."

Becky Sue gave an exasperated sigh. There was going to be no winning this argument. "He was not nuzzling my neck." Was he? Involuntarily she rubbed the chill on her arms.

"Are you cold?" Cindy's look was calculative and assessing.

"A little. I was buried under that quilt working and got all toasty warm, now that I've been out for a few minutes I got chilled." It was the best lie she could come up with.

At precisely 5 o'clock Becky Sue locked up her shop with a skip in her step. On most days she walked the half a mile to her house, but today she felt like running. She didn't. It would look too suspicious and the rumor mills that were already at work would roll into overdrive.

The only time she didn't walk to work was when it was raining, or she needed to carry more than a basket full of things to the shop. Technically she qualified as living in town, but her nearest neighbor was almost a quarter of a mile away. Her little place sat on about four acres, most of which was dedicated to her garden. Her house was quaint and decorated in homespun. Bits of thread clung to most the furniture and collected on everything almost as bad as dust. This was her sanctuary and creative cave.

"Sherlock, I'm home," she called out to her cat, a grey striped and slightly overweight ball of fur. Sherlock was perched on the back of the couch and halfway opened one eye, clearly unimpressed at her return.

She plopped down on the couch near him. "Fine if you don't want to wake up, I won't tell you what happened today." Both cat eyes opened. He yawned and stretched. "I thought that might change your attitude." Reaching up she scratched the back of his head while she talked. He relocated to her shoulder and began to purr.

Half an hour later she finally went and changed into jeans and long sleeve shirt. She grabbed a jacket and the keys to her little pickup truck on her way out the door.

Ray's parents, Mary Beth and Chester, lived back in the mountains. It was familiar stomping ground for Becky Sue, considering she grew up as their neighbor. Neighbor being a loose phrase as country folk usually couldn't see their neighbors through the trees.

The house itself was not a large affair, but for the area was it upper middle class. A porch large enough for a couple of rocking chairs covered the front. Ray sat in one idly rocking when she pulled into the yard and parked. Three beagles came racing around the side of the house, dancing, waggling their tails, and yipping at her door unwilling to let her out until she tossed them their treat she always brought when she delivered watermelons.

Ray stood and called the dogs. "Lucky, Duke, Daisy, come here." Still munching their treats, they obediently sauntered over to Ray where he reached down to pet each one. "I keep telling Dad he needs to lock these hoodlums up when people come over."

Becky Sue stepped from her truck. "No need. They're not gonna hurt anybody, unless you count getting licked to death." The dogs returned sniffing at her pant legs and hand. "Sorry guys, no more treats." They sniffed for another minute, finally decided she was telling the truth, and wondered off.

"Not everybody has a way with animals like you do."

"What's there to know? Feed them, treat them fairly, give them a little attention. It's amazing how little can go so far."

"If only there were more people in the world like you, Becky Sue."

"Yeah, you've been in the 'big city' too long. You've forgotten how folks are out here."

"Even folks out here can be bad." The tone of his voice caught her attention and she looked harder at him trying to read the things he wasn't saying. She walked up to the porch where he waited. He motioned for her to sit in the adjacent chair from him.

"Speak for yourself. Didn't I hear something about you going to jail a time or two after you left?" A look passed over his face she couldn't read. Why was he being so mysterious? This was one of the few things that had changed, she could no longer read most his thoughts.

"I'll tell you about it after dinner."

"I thought I heard somebody pull up. The dogs were going crazy. How are you Becky Sue?" Chester came out the door, leaving it half open, and shook her hand.

Chester was a postcard hillbilly. At 5'6" he was wiry, slightly shaggy grey hair, and round grey beard, piercing blue eyes like his son, and a firm handshake that revealed the strength of a man who lived mostly off the land. He was dressed in his customary overalls and plaid shirt. A lump in his thin cheek gave evidence of the wad of tobacco in his mouth.

"I'm good. How's the moonshine business?"

"Can't complain. I think my profits have doubled since I started making that watermelon hootch from your melons." He tucked his thumbs in the bib of his overalls. "By the way, you planning on planting watermelons again this year?"

"Oh, I might be persuaded. You gonna want your usual order?"

"Yep. I was thinking of increasing it, if you get enough. Them female tourists love the wine. As a matter of fact, the other day, I thought I was gonna get myself in a bind. They found one of them female tourists dead along side the crick. She had one of my Thunderhead tonic bottles on her. Turns out she overdosed on some high class drug instead. That's the only problem with them tourists. You never know what's gonna come floating along through this here town."

"Chester stop your bellyaching and ask that girl to come inside. I'm about to lay out dinner," Mary Beth called.

"Well, ya'll heard the boss. Looks like it's time to get our eats on." Chester turned and walked in. Ray looked over at Becky Sue and shook his head in a gesture that she took to mean, some things never change.

Becky Sue couldn't remember a time when the inside of this house didn't smell like bacon grease and raw grain alcohol. Today was no exception. The furnishing hadn't changed in the last ten years or so since she'd been there. The odd peach colored fake leather couch was draped with a burgundy colored afghan that she suspected was hiding the peeling parts of it. The burgundy colored recliner next to it listed to one side like a ship sinking at sea. The wooden coffee table was littered with newspapers and an empty glass jug that was guaranteed to have had some of Chester's homemade brew in it recently. The wood was a patchwork of discolored rings and gouges. A box TV sat across the room. It was probably the first TV the Burnett's had ever owned after they married thirty years ago.

The table was the same too. Only the sixth chair had been replaced with a mismatched one to the original set. A plate of fried chicken sat in the middle of the table on a crocheted hot pad accompanied by fried potatoes and beans.

They each took a place at the table, filled their plates, and spread local gossip.

After they sat and chatted for what seemed an appropriate time period after their dinner, Mary Beth got up and started to clear up the food and dishes.

"Becky Sue, would you be up for a walk?" Ray asked.

"That's a good idea. I'm just not sure I'm capable." She rubbed her full stomach. "I'm as stuffed as a dog tick that just fell off." She pushed back her chair anyway.

Ray stood and reached out a hand to help her up. "Come on you ol' tick, come hop on this dogs back, we'll go for ride."

She took his hand and allowed him to help her out of the chair. The warm rush she'd felt before at his touch flooded her veins. She dropped his hand like it was a hot potato.

"Don't forget this kids. It'll aid the digestion." Chester produced a jug full of a light pink liquid.

"Is it wine or that hundred forty proof rot gut you make?" Becky Sue asked as Ray reached out and took the jug from his dad.

"It's the wine. I know you gotta drive home tonight and don't want you to go getting all snockered."

Becky Sue followed Ray out the back door. When they were out of hearing distance from the house she said, "you know I'm doing a smell check on that before I start sipping?"

"You think Dad switched it out with his hundred forty?"

"Wouldn't surprise me. You noticed your mom didn't even blink. She just stood there humming like it was the most natural thing in the world to send your single son and a single female out into the night with a jug of alcohol. They're plotting against us, I'm telling you. I can hear their little brains. They're hoping we get drunk and sleep together so maybe I'll turn up pregnant. Then we have to get married. It keeps you from wondering off again. And they've made their match. It's been done more than once."

"Yeah, I know. So just make sure you don't seduce me." He winked at her then handed her the jug of watermelon wine to hold while he dug out his key and unlocked the side door.

"Somehow I just don't see that as a possibility. I mean after all, you've been in the *big* city. I'm sure I have nothing on those city women."

He turned and gave her a strange look before he flicked on the light switch to check the area then turned it back off. He flicked on the flashlight that was still kept near the door and led them over to a stack of square bales of hay and sat down.

Becky Sue sat down beside him. A sliver of moonlight fell on the dirt floor a few feet away. They listened to the sounds of the night. She thought this felt an awful lot like the night Lucy had burned down the barn, only cooler. She crossed her arms against the chill, her jacket lying useless in the passenger seat of her truck.

"You look cold," Ray said as he offered her the first sip from the jug.

"Not terribly." She took the open jug, sniffed it. Maybe it really was just the wine. She took a swig. Sweet warmth instantly made the chills disappear. She handed it back.

The jug bubbled a couple of times as Ray imbibed. He capped it and set it between their feet.

A hundred questions swirled in her head, but she didn't want to seem too nosy or accusatory. So she settled on silence. She knew if she was quiet long enough, Ray would talk. She didn't mind the silence either. She was used to it. Right now it was comfortable and calm.

One of the beagles began to bay, followed by the other two. She picked up the jug and made a couple of bubbles in it. Before she could set it back down, Ray took it from her hands. She watched as he put his full, sensuous lips where hers had just been and sipped the brew. A shot of fire went straight south through her. It was the wine. It had to be. She was too old to get all giddy about objects that had touched another's lips.

"It's been a while. How've you been?" Ray asked, setting the jug down.

He was trying to talk, but, like her, didn't seem to know where to begin.

"Good. The shop is going good. I've been making my garden a little bigger each year. Your dad buying my watermelons has helped. Mom has her good days and bad. What about you? I know you've got more to tell than me. Nothing around here changes very much."

He shrugged. "I don't know about that. I work. I go home. I go to the gym."

"I didn't want to ask, but what happened to send you back here. I mean with your job and all?"

"It's complicated."

"And?...Does it have to do with a woman?" She prodded.

He looked at her querulously. "A woman?"

"Alcohol? Drugs?"

"Becky Sue, what …" He seemed at a loss for words.

She shrugged. "People talk. Sometimes I hear."

"Look, I have no idea what kinds of rumors have been circulating around here about me, but I can promise you none of it's true. Unless of course it's that me and Betty Mae got divorced years ago. Otherwise I'm the same guy that left years ago that was your friend."

"The Ray that left here years ago was merely an acquaintance. A friend would've let me know they were leaving."

He hung his head for a second. "You're right. I'm sorry. I wasn't much of a friend. I'm not sure what happened. But you have to admit you became a little illusive yourself after Dad's barn burned."

Becky Sue opened her mouth to speak, but the words wouldn't come out. She didn't know how to go back and capture what they'd once had.

"Don't worry about it. It's over and the past is in the past. But tell me, do you still trust me? Like back when we were kids? Do you still believe in me?"

"Yeah." She reached for the jug, hoping to find the courage she needed to say what she wanted. "It might sound crazy, but ever since you walked into my shop today, it doesn't feel like a day has passed since years ago."

Moonlight bounced off his white teeth as he smiled. "If you're crazy, I'm crazy. I thought the same thing, but we men, we don't talk like that."

Becky Sue snickered.

Ray grew serious and glanced around like he was making sure no one else was listening. "Becky Sue, there's so much I need to tell you. You're the only one I got that I can trust completely." His tone of voice didn't match his words. It was matter of fact, not longing over missed friendship.

She sat up straighter and looked at him. This didn't sound romantic at all. Why would she even think there'd be any romance? She didn't want it. They'd tried it once and it didn't work. But why did it make her feel bad deep in her heart knowing there wouldn't be? "Ok, what do you need to tell me?"

"A lot has changed for me since I left."

"Obviously." For starters he was twice as hot now. He'd come back even more confident than he was before and there was a hardness about him that hadn't been there before he left.

"Betty Mae and I barely lasted two years after marrying. Long story short it was a mistake from the beginning." She could've told him that years ago, but she kept her mouth shut and let him speak. "I admittedly was a little lost and at odds with myself. There was no way I was coming back here, another whipped dog especially with no job, no wife, nothing to show for running off."

"What's different about now?" The words were out of her mouth before she could hold them in. He shot her a look that said if you'd shut up I'd tell you. She reached for the jug of watermelon and sipped. Maybe it would keep her from talking if she had something across her mouth. Thinking about things crossing her mouth, she wondered what Ray's lips would feel like and nearly spit the wine back in the jug.

For a full two minutes she choked and coughed while Ray just sat there and watched her. When she finally was able to catch her breath, she set the jug back on the ground calmly like nothing had happened.

"Are you still breathing?"

"I think so." It came out strained and rough, but she was able to squeeze out the words.

"You might want to lay low on that stuff. Dad still could've spiked it a little with his hundred forty proof."

Becky Sue glared at him, reached for the jug and stared him down the whole time as she lifted it to her lips. He didn't say a word. He just sat there and watched her with those eyes.

"Are you done proving your point yet?" The arrogant son of a bitch.

She leaned over in to him, their faces inches apart. "Yep."

His eyes fell to her lips, or at least that what she thought they went to. Something in the air shifted. Her heart kicked up its pace. She felt frozen in her place. She couldn't pull back, but she was afraid to move forward. They were breathing in sync, shuddering but steady. Their eyes locked and talked, covering more in those few seconds than they had all day. There was desire, discipline, regret, hope, a past, a future, and something much deeper. A pull neither could explain that tied them together.

Becky Sue pulled back first. Her imagination was running away with her and she had to stop it before she allowed her heart to get broke.

This time Ray was the one who reached for the jug, bubbling it five times in a deep long drink. In that moment she knew he felt it too. The danger of being too close, of being comfortable together but not knowing the waters they tread.

"I need your help," Ray blurted out after he set the jug back, but the words weren't from a man with a physical need that required a woman's touch.

"Ohhk. With what?"

"You remember what Dad was saying earlier about the body that was found a few days ago, the girl that overdosed?"

"Yeah…."

"I'm on assignment. There's proof that there's a drug smuggling operation running through here and since I'm the only one that wouldn't raise too many flags they sent me to gather intel. And I need your help blending back in. You're the only one I can trust Becky Sue."

Her mouth that had dropped open a moment before snapped shut. "Whoa, whoa, whoa, so you're saying you're like an undercover cop?"

"Basically. I belong to a special task force that specializes in investigations that are either too unnoticeable for local law to get involved in, or ones that the local law can't touch for one reason or another."

"And you need me to give you a cover story? You're good ol' friend that's the biggest sucker in the world. The town's most eligible spinster." The pieces to the story were crystal clear now. She was being used and had fallen hook, line, and sinker for it.

"Don't say it like that. You know damn good and well I could have my pick of women in this town to use as a decoy, but I didn't pick them. I picked you. You're smart. You're observant. You'd be a valuable asset. And… and I'd like to spend some time with you before I go back."

She wanted to be mad at him. She wanted to yell and scream at him for playing with her abominable girlish emotions. He'd even managed to make it sound like he really wanted their friendship back. She was speechless, afraid that if she opened her mouth the wrong thing would come out, or even worse, everything would tumble out in a jumbled mess. But she knew the only one to blame was herself. Her imagination had done the weaving and spinning.

Heat radiated from where his hand touched her shoulder. "Please."

How could she say no? Even if she wanted to, she'd say no and he'd look at her with those eyes that would peer down in her soul and he'd call her a liar and she'd agree to do it anyway. Giving a loud exasperated sigh to let him know she was doing this reluctantly she agreed.

Before she knew what happened his arms were around her. "I knew I could count on you. You're still my best friend in the whole world."

Her hands patted his back awkwardly in her twisted position. He held her like he wasn't letting go anytime soon, so she shifted to fit better into his arms. It may've been the alcohol starting to talk, but she didn't want to let him go either.

His head moved. Once again they were staring into each other eyes, his breath caressed her lips. A fire was starting low in her groin. Their lips touched, gently, unsure what the others reaction would be. Then his lips claimed hers with more force and passion. Her body began to hum. The fire was building in her chest. Her skin seemed to sizzle and crackle everywhere he touched her. His body began to hum. She jerked away. The look of surprise on his face was mixed with hurt.

"I need to go home. Sherlock will be missing me." She jumped from the hay bale and walked out without a backward glance. Avoiding the house, she walked the long way around to her truck and drove off as she tried to catch her breath and still her racing heart all while keeping the tears prickling at her eyes away.

Chapter 4

Ray

Ho-ly shit! If he hadn't seen it with his own eyes he wouldn't have believed it. Maybe there were perks to this assignment after all. The one thing this town had managed not to completely ruin was Becky Sue. At least not yet.

Inside he knew she was the same person he'd known way back. His friend, his companion. After all these years he knew he could still trust her. Okay, so things had gotten a little out of hand at the barn, but damn. What was he supposed to do? There was an easiness and comfort to the way they just linked back together effortlessly. And she was smoking hot. He remembered when he'd had a crush on her late in high school after she started developing curves, but not even that could compare to what he saw today. She was sex appeal in sheep's clothing.

She knew his bullshit too. When he'd walked into her shop he'd been stunned at the confident, self assured woman he found. She didn't fall for his usual smut. He was actually surprised when she agreed to dinner.

It wasn't in his plan until after he left her shop this morning to have her help with his cover, but as long as she was good, it would work out perfectly. It'd keep some of the other more wanton women off his back too, not that he didn't mind wanton but he preferred them without motive of making him settle down. And he'd get to spend time with his long time friend.

Just being around Becky Sue tonight had sparked things in his soul he'd forgotten were there. She'd brought life out of him long since repressed. She'd made his body hum for fucks sake! How did a woman make a man hum like that? It was like some strange electricity flowed through them and pulled them together, sometimes kicking and screaming and fighting, sometimes smoothly without a second thought. It was unnerving.

He stepped into the cold shower welcoming the chill to his body. He needed to cool off. She'd stirred a fire in him so hot that even now he wanted to find out where she lived and drive over there to plead with her to let him in, just once. He needed her like he'd never needed anyone in his life. If he could just have her once he'd calm down and be able to focus on what he was really here for.

Turning the water off, he reached out of the shower to grab the towel, only to see the shower hadn't helped. He was still at half mast. Damn.

Maybe she was a witch in disguise and had put a spell on him. There were plenty of old medicine woman stories that would support that theory. Yeah right, he didn't believe in that malarkey. He didn't believe in UFO's and aliens either.

Work. What he needed was work. He missed having a gym nearby. Normally when he was frustrated with a case, or life in general, he'd go to the gym and wear himself out until he could barely drive himself home and crawl into bed. Since that wasn't an option he'd have to absorb himself in his work.

The house was dark. His parents were already in bed. He left the door open to his room, rummaged through his drawer where he'd buried the case file, and opened it up. Paper clipped to the top right hand corner was a picture of a young woman. She had pixie cut strawberry blond hair, freckles across her nose, and barely looked 16. The top sheet was facts.

Name: Amy Lynn Drake

Age: 20yr

Marital status: single

Cause of death: overdose

Self inflicted or forced: unknown

Location deceased was found: Ozark Mountains, Buffalo River, approximately 3 miles from Elk Point Landing headed south to River Hollow.

Notes: died in company of friends. Possibly new experimental drug. All in company tested positive for same.

He knew the rest of the report on the next page by heart. Four friends were canoeing the Buffalo. They'd had a cooler full of beer, a couple of small bottles of

Thunderhead tonic (they'd swore were for medicinal use on their muscles from canoeing), and a couple small baggies of pot. Amy had coaxed them into trying something new she'd picked up that morning from a local man. After taking the first pill she'd claimed not to feel any effects and took a second within minutes. One of the guys claimed she'd tried to climb all over him before passing out, she then seizured and died. One of the girls claimed it had spoiled the mood. They'd been discussing sex of orgy proportions before Amy "pulled her stunt". The group was out of Missouri.

Closing the folder he closed his eyes as he thought about sex of orgy proportions with Becky Sue. That was much more pleasant thinking than a dead girl near the water. Becky Sue's body itself was a drug. Just thinking about the feel of her body and the way his reacted to it made his cock grow hard. He'd need a damn ice pack if he was going to ever sleep while he was in town at this rate.

He growled at himself, stood and began to pace. It was unsettling that they claimed a local had sold Amy the drugs and no one knew the man's name. He knew this town and the people, at least he used to. The fact that anyone local could keep it under wraps was a mystery in itself. The other troubling aspect of it was that once someone began to see the profits of the drug trade roll in, there was no turning back. It would only grow until it became a complete infestation.

It was time to nail this guy. Once he was able to pin point the seller, hopefully it'd lead to the producer and it would only take a small operation to bring them down. If this was only the pinhead to a larger operation, this assignment could last a long time and he'd be sent only God knew where. And for once he didn't want to go just anywhere and protect people he didn't know. He had people at home that needed his protection. Becky Sue needed his protection.

Just the thought of her name and the image of her smile made his cock respond. Dammit! He could rub it out himself but he knew it wouldn't be enough. His wrist would tire if he kept thinking of her. He trudged to the refrigerator to retrieve the ice pack.

Chapter 5

Mreow. A soft touch on her cheek. Pat, her nose. Pat, back to her cheek.

"No, Sherlock. Go back to sleep." Becky Sue pulled the covers up over her face in attempts to discourage Sherlock from waking her up any more. He walked across her body poking his nose at her hair, then walked back across.

Mreow. She could feel him sitting almost under her chin. A delicate paw pulled at the covers trying to find her face.

Rolling over to her back she gave in to the demanding ball of fluff. "Okay okay, I'm getting up." She tried to look at the red numbers on the alarm clock sitting atop her dresser across the small room. Was that 5:26 or 5:56? Who needed an alarm clock anyway with a cat around? She couldn't remember the last time she heard it go off since Sherlock had come along. Her eyes were heavy and gritty. She knew better than to drink Chester's home brew, but she suspected it was more than that.

Sherlock stepped delicately onto her chest, laid down, and purred. "Alright baby, let's go." He jumped off as soon as she began to move.

The sun was just beginning to turn the sky from a dusky grey into lighter tones. A light frost accumulated over night. Becky Sue stepped outside in her jogging suit and took a deep breath of the crisp morning air leaving Sherlock quietly munching his crunchies. She welcomed her morning run today more than most days.

After things with her mom had settled down, and she'd acquired her own place, she'd made it a point to run at least three times a week. It helped keep her stress levels low and her weight as well.

Mornings were her favorite time of the day. Most tourists weren't up this early. The town was quiet. No one peered out their windows when she passed by on the street. Only a few lights were on along her route. She knew each and every one and who was up, getting ready for work. That's why Ray needed her. She knew this town. The people. Their habits. She'd been the one to stay behind.

But did he suspect someone here was more than a pawn in a drug smuggling operation? Most the people in this town had barely graduated high school. They were simple folk, quiet, peaceful, content. None of them would be running drugs through here. Would they? She'd have heard of it by now, wouldn't she?

She was deep in thought when she rounded the last corner coming home. A pair of headlights temporarily blinded her before she could step off the road. The truck didn't slow. Most locals slowed and drove past her in the other lane. This one drove straight at her. She scooted over further and stopped at the ditch. Freezing her feet this early was not something she could appreciate. The red truck flew past without a flinch. She flipped them the bird, got out on the road, and picked her pace back up.

Damn tourist. It had better have been an emergency.

Between the run and the idiot driver she'd managed to not think about Ray for maybe a total of ten minutes. It bothered her that their bodies had seemed to hum. That had never happened before. She could chalk it up to an alcohol induced apparition, but she wasn't one to see things that weren't there, even intoxicated. She shook her head before stepping into the shower as if she could really shake the thoughts out of her head and wash them down the drain.

By the time she got to her mom's, who lived three miles up the highway, she'd managed to put most her thoughts about Ray and their weird alcohol induced chemistry to the back of her mind. The lights were on when she pulled in the drive. That was good. It meant Mom had managed to get up without help.

Becky Sue had been called back from her second semester of college when her mom, Kate, suffered a stroke. Becky Sue blamed it on the stress of her dad running off, but her mom refused to throw blame. She steadfastly insisted she'd done it to herself and was determined to make the most of it.

Kate lived alone and was basically wheelchair bound. Most days she could get herself out of bed and back in. On good days she could get in and out of the shower without help, and occasionally to a chair that didn't have wheels. It'd taken over a year and lots of therapy to get her to that point. But she was strong willed.

Becky Sue stopped by every day to make sure she was able to shower and get out of bed. Twice a week she would cook for the next few days. Sometimes in the peak of tourist season neighbors would help out by dropping food off.

"Good morning, Mom," Becky Sue called out so she'd know who was entering the house.

"Good morning sweetie." Her mom rolled to the doorway of the kitchen. Becky Sue walked over and kissed her cheek.

"You look perky this morning. Feeling good today?"

"Yes, I am. I'm not so sure about you though. I would think that after having dinner with the Burnett's last night you'd look radiant this morning, but in truth you look like you could use a long winter's nap and a bowl of soup."

Becky Sue hadn't told her mom about the dinner, but should've known it would get out. Undermining the gossip vine in this town was dangerous.

"Oh come on. Not you too. You know Ray is like my brother. You lived next to the Burnett's until," she waved her hand because she hated to say it, "until the divorce and your stroke. They're our friends. Am I not allowed to go eat dinner with friends?" Her voice was rising, but she couldn't seem to stop it. Exasperation oozed from every pore. Exasperation with the town gossips. Exasperation with herself.

"Don't go getting all wound up on me young lady. I was just trying to be polite and stay in tuned with your life."

Becky Sue sighed. "I know, Mom. I promise when I start dating someone you'll be the first to know. I went over to the Burnett's last night because I haven't seen Ray since before I left for college. We caught up a little, but I don't know how long he's even going to hang around."

"What did he tell you? Mary Beth seems to think he's back for good."

Becky Sue shrugged. "Nothing really. I guess it's just the impression I got from him." She should've kept her mouth shut, but she had to quiet the matchmakers in this town before she lost her mind.

Her mother gave her one last assessing look before she rolled out of the doorway. "I'll go get in the shower if you have time."

"Go ahead. I'll inventory your food situation."

A cursory evaluation of the pantry and fridge indicated that a trip to the grocery store would be in order in the near future. In all the trips she'd made to Harrison for Mom's therapy and grocery shopping, she'd never run into Ray. In fact, she'd barely thought about him any time she went. It was funny how life worked sometimes.

Becky Sue left her mom's after making sure she'd cleared the shower, drove back to her house, parked her pick up, and walked to work. She unlocked the back door and set her lunch box down on the shelf under the counter.

The patriotic star quilt was still folded neatly on the table awaiting her return. She estimated only seven more hoops to go before the quilting part was done. Every time she finished a quilt she felt accomplished. She was looking forward to finishing it in the next couple of days. She needed something to keep her grounded.

It was still a few minutes till open, so she walked around with her little duster, tickling the dust off the shelves and making sure everything was neat and tidy. As she moved down the center aisle, Uncle Melvin's book caught her eye again. She set the duster on the shelf and picked up a copy of the book and flipped it open.

Another problem is the carrying of genes. Sparkers have a special gene that carries their power. It is held to the trait of blue eyes. A Spark must have blue eyes to hold any power. This is why some children who only have one Spark as a parent do not inherit the Sparker's powers.

A Spark may also lose their power if a Quell takes it from them. While a Quell has no power of their own to speak of, they are quite efficient at completely diffusing a Sparker to the point where they cannot retain any of their abilities and become normal. Some say the Sparker may still pass on the gene to their children if they have been diffused, but there is no evidence to back this up.

Becky Sue shut the book and returned it to its place on the shelf. She'd forgotten about the Quell. There was even less written about them than there were the Sparkers. She picked up her duster. It didn't matter. It was all just fun stories to tell the tourists, another selling point to draw interest to the town.

After the dusting was complete, she unlocked the door but didn't prop it open this time. Clouds covered the sky and the breeze carried a chill. This afternoon she might regret not driving, especially if the clouds opened up like they threatened. She should've paid more attention to the weather, but she was abnormally distracted. It would cut down on the tourist traffic too giving her even more time to work on her quilt, and more quiet time to think about things she shouldn't but she might have a solution for that.

A peek outside and there was no real movement yet. She walked over to Vernon's and bought a newspaper from the outside dispenser. Vernon waved to her through the window. She waved back and hurriedly turned away before he could corner her like everyone else.

Becky Sue wasn't very good at keeping up with current events past what the gossip vine provided, which usually was more than what was told in print. If there were things she didn't know about in the paper it was usually because it didn't pertain to her as it happened in other communities. After talking to

Chester and Ray yesterday though it seemed like it was maybe a good time to start keeping up with more official news.

She hadn't even made it back across the street from the park to her building when Cindy popped out of her shop, smiling and eagerly waiting for her to get within talking distance.

"Good morning, Becky Sue. How was your date?"

This was quickly becoming a mute point to argue. "It was fine."

The smug look on Cindy's face was more of an I-told-you-so. "So Ray's home to stay? When are you getting married? How many kids do you think you'll be able to have by the time your thirty five?"

Becky Sue looked up to the sky, concentrating on her breathing before she turned, smiling, to Cindy. "You know we didn't discuss marriage so I doubt we will, but we think we can squeeze in about four kids in the next seven years."

She left an open mouthed Cindy staring after her as she walked back into her shop. Let the gossip mills chew on that for a while, she smirked to herself. This could be fun. Why didn't she think of this years before? The look on Cindy's face had been priceless. For once, she'd left the woman speechless. Granted it wouldn't last for long, but she could enjoy it for the next few minutes.

Less than ten minutes later, the phone started to ring.

"Becky Sue's handmade quilts, how can I help you?"

"You can start by telling me what exactly it is you and Ray are planning on doing. You haven't eloped with him have you?"

"Cindy called you didn't she," Becky Sue asked her mom. Maybe stirring the gossip mills wasn't so much fun after all.

"Of course she did. You failed to mention any of this to me this morning when you were here."

"Mom, look. I was just mouthing off. None of its true. First thing this morning Cindy cornered me and started her interrogation. It was the first thing that popped out of my mouth."

"Becky Sue Hocking, I taught you better than to lie. Why would you do that to poor old Cindy and me, your own mother!"

"I'm sorry. I didn't think about it being a lie. I just wanted to be left alone. Everyone is always trying to match make for me and I'm tired of it."

The bell above the door jangled. "I gotta go Mom. A customer just came in."

"Alright. But I don't want to hear about you lying any more, you hear me?"

"Yes mother."

"Love you."

"Love you too." She returned the phone to its cradle and greeted her customer. Maybe Ray had it figured out. Maybe moving to a bigger area was the answer. Nobody to match make. Nobody to scold her if she let slip a little white lie. But then again if she left, she'd have to take Mom with her to care for her. If her Mom was dead, she wouldn't have to worry about caring for her either, but then she wouldn't have to worry about half the problems she had anyway. It was a vicious cycle and she didn't want her mom to die anytime soon, even when she was being a pain.

Amazingly enough, Cindy had made herself scarce. Becky Sue assumed she was in no hurry to be made a fool of again which made the day surprisingly quiet and slow feeling. She could guarantee that her mom called Cindy back and told her it was all a lie.

That's why when the bells above her door jingled again sometime later she jumped and pricked her finger with the needle.

"Hello, how are you today?" She called out without looking up as she tried to stop the pinprick of blood on her finger.

"I'm good. How about you?" Ray had crossed the short distance through the shop and leaned over the counter.

"Oh, it's you."

"You don't sound excited to see me."

She shrugged noncommittally.

"I would think someone you were planning to have four kids with in the next seven years would get a more enthusiastic greeting."

"You've got to be kidding me. How did you hear about that so fast?"

"Mom sent me over to pick up some soap from Cindy and she asked me about it. It seems you have a lying problem and I should probably choose differently if I'm going to settle back down here."

Becky Sue laughed outright then. Ray grinned at her. "I'm so tired of these old buzzards always trying to match make. I could've been married fifty times over by now at the rate they're going."

His face turned serious. "That's okay. It'll help serve our purpose."

Yeah, our purpose. Strictly business. But it appeared she would have to act the love struck spinster after all. She glanced over at the newspaper she'd picked up this morning. It'd been a waste of fifty cents. There'd been nothing of interest in it today, no new updates about the girl who'd overdosed and basically everything past that was irrelevant.

"Well, what have you got in mind to start with?"

His mischievous grin was back, his eyes sparkled. "First, we have to make believers out of the town's people that I'm now courting you, so they believe I'm here to stay, to keep my cover. Just in case any of them have heard rumors about my real job. If they think I'm settling back down they won't think I'm still active."

She was having trouble getting excited about this. "Alright, what do we need to do? Go have sex in the park?" She gestured out the window.

"Maybe nothing quite so blatant and drastic. I was thinking dinner at Claire's tonight. But if you want to speed things up a bit you could let me spend the night at your place." He winked.

"Keep dreaming, big boy."

"Becky Sue." She looked directly at him. "Relax, have some fun with this. You're the only one I could pull this off with, and don't worry, no matter what, we'll always be friends."

"Yeah, I know." But after he was gone again, she'd be the one picking up the pieces of her broken heart if she relaxed too much.

He walked around the counter to where she sat. "You're the best." He kissed the top of her head and a spark of static electricity pulled a few hairs straight up. Then he was gone.

Chapter 6

Claire's diner was practically empty. The rain shower an hour ago had definitely put a damper on things, but the rain could do nothing to squelch the town's gossip vine.

Claire herself seated Becky Sue and Ray near the window. She was putting them in full view of the town so no one could say the rumors weren't true.

"I feel like one of Bill's pieces in the display window," Becky Sue whispered to Ray as soon as Claire was out of earshot.

"Keep whispering like that and you will be." Point taken.

Becky Sue didn't bother looking at the menu. She knew it by heart. Ray glanced at the front, flipped to the back and set it back down.

"Literally nothing has changed," he said.

"Nope."

"You think I could convince her to run a special once a week just to try something new?"

"You'd give the poor woman a heart attack."

"Who had a heart attack?" Claire asked as she walked back with their drinks.

"No one had a heart attack. We're just talking theoretical," Becky Sue said.

"You should stop talking about theories and stick to facts. That's probably why you're not married yet Becky Sue, all that college got to your head and gave you too many ideas." Ray sat there grinning at her. She looked at him and hoped he could read her mind. *Do you see what I have to deal with here?*

"Ya'll ready to order?"

"I'll have the country fried steak with the mashed potatoes and okra. I sure have missed your cooking Claire. Ain't nobody cook okra like you do. " Ray said still smiling. He was turning his charm on Claire and she was falling for it. No wonder Becky Sue wasn't married yet, she could usually spot these bullshit lines a mile away.

"I'll take the Cajun chicken with a loaded baked potato and corn."

Claire wrote down her order then leaned over and whispered in her ear, "come by sometime and I'll teach you the secret of how I cook the okra. It's a sure fire way to catch that man just in case you run into trouble."

Becky Sue almost choked. Claire ambled off to the kitchen, probably to instruct the cook on how exactly to make Ray's okra.

"What was that all about," Ray asked.

Becky Sue repeated what Claire had told her, but could barely contain her laughter. Ray grinned.

"I honestly can't tell a difference in her okra and anyone else's."

"You're such an operator."

"I got skills. How do you think I made it so far?"

"Yeah, you got so many skills you're back here again." She said it without thinking. "Nevermind."

They managed to make small talk over the rest of dinner without Becky Sue blundering any more. Claire looked like she was trying to stay a discrete distance away, but Becky Sue felt she was hovering on the edge of hearing distance, hoping to pick up a morsel to share on the gossip vine.

"Thanks for dinner. It was good."

"You're welcome. Would you like a ride home?"

Becky Sue looked out the window. The sun had set and she'd walked over, straight from work, to meet him. At first she thought to refuse, but remembered the truck that nearly ran her over that morning. "Sure, I'll take you up on it."

Crawling into his Ford F-150 felt a drastic change to her little Chevy s-10. All she had to do was tell him it was the old Briggs place and they were to her house before their conversation started back up.

It didn't feel right leaving such a pleasant evening so early, and for all their talking so far, Becky Sue felt like there was a lot Ray wasn't telling her because of eavesdroppers.

"Would you like to come in," Becky Sue asked, opening the truck door.

"This isn't a ploy to get me drunk and take advantage of me is it?" He grinned.

"No. I don't usually keep any of your dad's special in stock."

"You know if I come in, tomorrow our mom's will be on the phone with each other planning a wedding right?"

"Good point." Becky Sue went to get out.

Ray killed the engine. "Too late. You already invited me in."

Becky Sue opened the door and Sherlock was in his customary spot on the back of the couch. He opened one eye, realized she wasn't alone, then stretched and jumped down to come investigate.

"Ray this is Sherlock Holmes. Sherlock this is my friend Ray."

"Hi Sherlock." Ray bent down and scratched behind Sherlock's ears. "You're a friendly little guy."

"Sherlock is the only one I can talk to and not worry about it getting spread about town. He's pretty good company."

"Where did you get him?"

"Actually he found me. It was maybe a year after I moved in here and he wondered up shortly after the fourth of July. I thought he was somebody's pet that'd been scared by the fireworks, but nobody claimed him. He must've been a tourist's cat and they lost him. He's been here ever since."

Ray walked over to the couch and sat down. Sherlock followed him and jumped into his lap.

"I don't know if I've ever seen him take to anybody else quite like that though," Becky Sue observed.

"You have many people over?" The look Ray gave her wasn't asking about friends and acquaintances. He was asking about men.

She shrugged noncommittally. It was none of his business. "Sometimes, but I'm not really much of an entertainer."

He picked up a piece of thread that clung to the couch, rolling it between his fingers distractedly. "No, didn't think you were the type. You seem married to your work, like me."

"I guess, but sometimes I try to get out and live a little."

A skeptical look said he didn't believe her. "Have you thought about what you're gonna do once your mom passes? I know that's why you've stuck yourself in this town and haven't moved on. There's nothing really for you here."

Becky Sue paused. "I haven't really thought about it. I have my business."

"I know the whole town thinks you've officially hit spinsterhood for good despite the fact they keep trying to find you a husband. You don't strike me as the type that would stay single forever."

"I've dated a few times, just haven't found anyone who fits me."

"I'm not talking about sex. I'm talking about an actual relationship."

"And what do you know about real relationships? How many times you been married since you left?"

"Once." Becky Sue stopped short. She'd heard rumors a couple times that he'd remarried.

"Let me rephrase that, how many women you been with since you got divorced? How many of them were real relationships?"

"It doesn't matter. We're not talking about me. I've shown I can be marriage material before."

In other words he couldn't count the number of women that'd crawled into his bed and he kept trying to deflect her questions by poking at her.

"How did we get on this subject anyway? Neither of our love lives matter. Right now we're just working on making a good cover story for you and giving you an alibi if you need one, right?" She wanted to know more but at the same time she didn't. Talking about her lack of love life was depressing enough without having to hear about what she suspected his was.

Ray gave her a look that said he understood everything she wasn't saying. It unnerved her.

"Wait before we change the subject, I have one more question."

"Shoot."

"If we're supposed to be *together*, how far do we have to go? I mean, is it enough that the rumor mills are working overtime right now? Or do we like have to kiss in public or something?"

Ray covered the last foot and a half of space between them, convincing Sherlock his time was up. The cat jumped to the floor and sauntered off. "Do you want to kiss me in public?"

His eyes searched her face, rested on her lips, and slowly wondered down her body. A searing heat trailed the path of his eyes. Why was it so sexy the way he looked at her? She really needed to get out more. This kind of reaction to Ray was bad. It was nothing but a catastrophe in the making.

"I just want to make sure I do the job right. I've never had to be anyone's cover before." The words came out softer, more sensual than she expected.

The warmth of his body touching her was making it hard to concentrate on their conversation. She wanted to touch him again. She wanted to explore his body. She wanted to see what kind of reaction she could evoke from him. The heat of her body called out for his.

"Why don't we just play it by ear and see how it goes."

His lips were inches from hers. His breath a soft caress. This was bad. It was all going to be a big mistake.

"Would you like to see how I'm going to set up my garden this year and how I'm going to squeeze in more watermelons for your dad?" Becky Sue asked jumping up before she could fall for his sensual pleasures that seemed to lurk just beneath his skin.

The stunned look on his face was quickly erased.

"Sure." It sounded more confused than interested.

They walked out the back door into the night. A full moon lit the yard like solar powered lights. A few trees kept the parts closest to the house dark, but beyond that it was mostly open. Each year Becky Sue had expanded her garden little by little.

She pointed out different areas where she would plant squash, tomatoes, peppers, corn. "And I think this area here is where I'll have to till more to plant the extra watermelons." After pointing, she dropped her hand to her side, accidently hitting Ray's leg as he was standing too close.

Her feet were rooted to the spot, she was afraid to turn. She could feel his energy and heat radiating into her skin, even through her light jacket.

"Becky Sue." The way he said her name, she knew she was in trouble.

She turned to him.

Moon beams bounced off his blue eyes. She was captivated. Without another word, he wrapped his arms around her. Their eyes locked. There was no running. No turning away. She was trapped in that fiery blue gaze. He lowered his head, his face hovered inches from her as he paused. She forgot to breathe. Then he kissed her. The familiar heat she felt with him hit instantly. Her body started to hum as she met his earnest kiss with her own. His body was reacting as violently as hers. Her skin sizzled and sparked at his every touch. She reached for him and felt the static beneath her finger tips.

A flash of light to her closed eyes pulled her back. "What was that?"

"What?"

"That flash of light?"

"Think one of your neighbors is out here with a flashlight spying on us?"

"No. It wasn't that kind of light."

"Meteor shower?"

Becky Sue looked up at the sky. Ray took the opportunity and kissed her exposed neck.

Sizzle, pop.

No meteors.

His kisses were calling her back. His lips gently prying her mouth open to welcome his tongue. She gasped at the heat flooding her body. If he didn't stop now, she'd take him here in her back yard.

Sizzle, pop.

Becky Sue's eye flew open again just as a small flicker of light faded from her peripheral vision. It was like the barn incident all over again, only this time she was reasonably sure Lucy was nowhere around.

"Did you see it?"

"See what?" Ray's voice was husky and clearly annoyed.

"That spark?"

He looked around. "It was probably a spark from your neighbor's chimney. Otherwise the only other thing on fire around here is you."

Before she could open her mouth to argue he was there. Tasting her. Breathing in her scent.

He was too inviting to worry about what might be catching fire, as long as it wasn't her house. He was hard in all the right places. As soon as she felt the hardness beneath his zipper, she knew there was no turning back tonight. She clamped her eyes shut. Maybe the sparks she saw were the stars behind her eyelids as he made her heady, dizzy. Weak and longing.

Sizzle. Sizzle. Pop.

Ray's fingers trailed around her stomach beneath her shirt and slipped into the waistband beneath her work skirt. They slid into her wetness. She moaned, but it came out more of a purr. This was torture. She wanted him. She wanted him with every fiber of her being. She needed him inside of her and she needed it now.

Sizzle. Pop. Pop. Pop.

She slipped her hand to the waist of his jeans and opened the button. She was half afraid when she undid his zipper something might get stuck, he was so hard. He moaned. It sounded like a low growl. Her breathing was rapid, frantic with need.

Clothes were quickly pushed aside. She was on the ground, his hand cradling her head. He lay sprawled atop her. She couldn't breathe. Couldn't think. All she knew was need. His body was humming and sizzling, eagerly pressing between her legs.

She felt the tip of him touch her. He eased inside. She sucked in a great gasp of air as he filled her.

He felt better than she could've possibly imagined. There was not a space left untouched. She was frozen, rigged, afraid to move. Afraid to break the spell. He began to thrust gently inside her.

Pop. Pop. Pop. Pop.

Was this what ecstasy felt like? Like birds were singing. Like a warm breeze blowing. Floating on a cloud of intense pleasure.

Pop. Pop. Pop. Pop.

She dug her fingers into his back and buttox, prodding him to dive deeper, harder. She bit her lip, afraid to cry out in pleasure, afraid it would wake the whole neighborhood.

Pleading and begging, she pushed him harder. His breathing was rapid in her ears, ragged and ruthless. She didn't want this to end but she needed release. She was teetering on the edge of a great abyss, longing to fall head first into it.

Feeling him finally release, triggering her own response. Lazily she opened her eyes as she tried to catch her breath. A blue glow encircled them. It bobbed and danced like flames deep in a fire. It moved gently, blocking out the rest of the world.

She blinked. It was still there. She lay there staring at it, wondering if it was real. She blinked again. Nope definitely not a sex haze or mirage.

Ray sagged heavily against her. His body still crackled. A spark shot off from between them and landed in the grass. She flinched.

"What is it?" He stirred. "Holy crap!" He'd finally opened his eyes.

He scrambled off of her. As soon as they parted the fiery blue haze disappeared.

"What just happened?" He was looking around frantically, pulling his pants up and buttoning them.

Becky Sue took in the surroundings. A small circle where they'd been laying on the ground had singe marks. It was impossible wasn't it? Surely she was seeing things. Her imagination was running wild again.

"Do you see what I see?" She asked pointing to the burnt grass in a perfect circle.

He followed her finger, his mouth hung open. They looked at each other.

"It looks like we're the fabled Sparkers and we just flipped the switch."

Chapter 7

"What? How? I thought those old stories were nothing more than old timers telling a good yarn and it just grew out of proportion." Ray hadn't taken his eyes off the circle.

"I didn't really believe them either, but there was one point when I was young that I almost considered the possibility. Do you remember that time when we were teenagers in your dad's barn and the whole place burned down after we kissed?"

Ray finally tore his eyes away from the burnt grass. A light seemed to go on inside his head. "I remember. Are you saying we're the ones who actually burned down the barn?"

Becky Sue motioned to the ground. "I'm gonna say it's a pretty good possibility."

"Wow," he said as he sunk down onto the back steps. "I'm-I'm, I don't know what to say? What do I do?" He held his hands up to examine them in the moonlight. "I'm a Sparker."

She grinned, walked over, and sat down beside him. "It's a lot to take in isn't it? At least I don't feel like such a lunatic anymore."

"Yeah. How are you not freaking out right now? I mean we have these incredible powers and you're sitting there all calm and shit about it."

Becky Sue shrugged. "This week I've picked up Uncle Melvin's book a lot and been reading bits and pieces and thinking about it more. And...I guess I always felt like I was different. Maybe its women's intuition that I knew something was off. It makes me feel a little bit better about the barn incident though." Ray looked at her like she'd lost her mind. "That means Lucy didn't burn it down, and honestly, I thought you were just making up the story about Lucy because you didn't really like me after all."

"I really thought it was Lucy. I never would've believed it had you told me it was from being a Sparker. And I did like you, but after that you just seemed different and I thought you had found somebody else." Ray's eyes bore into hers, pleading his misunderstanding. A weight that she'd carried around for years lifted. Everything she thought had been real and true.

The moon seemed to smile with her. The radiance was almost as bright at the sun itself. Reaching over, she pulled him to her and kissed him hard and deep.

Suddenly she jumped up.

"What? What is it?" Ray asked still sitting on the steps, still looking confused.

"We better be careful. I don't want to burn my house down with the sparks."

"Oh, I didn't think of that." He stood, deep in thought. "But what did they use to do? Surely they didn't have sex outside all the time? I don't remember any stories about Sparkers burning their own houses down."

"You got a point there. We need to do some research on how this whole Spark thing works."

He stepped to her side, wrapped an arm around her, and breathed onto her neck. "Or we could learn by trial and error."

She felt the heat that didn't have much to do with being a Sparker, but had everything to do with having this hot man next to her, touching her, breathing on her. "We'll probably have to do some of that too. With the passing of generations not using their powers, ours may have weakened, mutated, or changed."

"Uh huh." Ray wasn't listening. He was leaning in to her, brushing his lips against hers. It was hard to concentrate and focus on what she was trying to say. He was warm and inviting.

"I'm not seeing or feeling any sparks," Becky Sue said.

"What?" Ray pulled up short. His eyes opened and looked at her, hurt. "You're not liking it?"

"No, that's not what I meant. Before, we had sparks flying while we kissed. Ours bodies hummed. Everything was… static. I'm not getting any of that this time."

"Do you think we burned out our power before we had a chance to use it?"

"I don't know."

Curiosity was overcoming their need for each other.

Ray waved his hand around in a magician's abracadabra.

"What are you doing?"

"Trying to see if I can throw fire."

Becky Sue raised an eyebrow. "Would you mind aiming away from my house?"

He looked up. "Oh sorry."

Ray danced around like every super hero and cartoon character they'd ever seen, throwing this hand or that, trying to find his fire within.

"Maybe there's a trick to it," Becky Sue suggested.

He stopped dancing about. "Maybe."

"Why don't you take a break before you hurt yourself and come in? I think I have some apple cider I could warm."

Inside, Becky Sue went to her kitchen to warm the cider while Ray made himself comfortable on the couch. Through the open doorway, she could hear him talking to Sherlock. She smiled.

After warming the cider, she poured them each a cup and walked into the living room. At the doorway, she stopped dead in her tracks and blinked hard. Something was wrong with her eyes. There were two grey striped cats on the couch. One of them was looking around in fright and bewilderment, trampling a pile of fabric. Had the Spark ignition done something to her vision?

"Becky Sue! I did it!" The cat who looked lost a moment before began to talk in Ray's voice.

She shrieked splashing apple cider all over herself and the floor.

"It's me, Ray. I think I look like Sherlock."

"How'd you do that?"

Ray the cat sat down and swished its tail back and forth. "I don't know actually. I was just talking to Sherlock and poof. I'm fuzzy." Holding out a paw, he began to groom himself.

"Umm, instead of licking yourself would you like to change back and help me clean this up?"

"Sure." He sat and swished his tail some more. Sherlock eyed him from his perch on the back of the couch, a low growl in his throat, clearly unhappy about having a new cat in his domain.

"Any time now."

"I think I'm stuck. I don't know how to undo this."

"Seriously?"

"Seriously."

Becky Sue cursed under her breath, walked back into the kitchen, set the cups near the sink, grabbed a towel and began to mop up her mess.

Ray the cat walked over to her. "What're we going to do?"

She sat back on her heels and looked at him. "I don't know. How do you manage these things?"

He didn't answer. Instead he sat and stared up at her with his big blue cat eyes.

"Oh stop it. I can barely stand it when you look at me like that when you're human." A cat smile made his whiskers twitch.

She shook her head. "You're impossible." Then she picked up the soaked towel and stood. "I'm going to change."

"Yeah, but now I'm a cute, fuzzy kitty. You can't resist me."

Becky Sue walked to her room and began to strip.

"Why are you watching me?"

Ray the cat sat in the doorway. "Because I can."

She threw her shirt at him, managing to cover his head for a second before he walked out from under it.

The next morning Becky Sue awoke to Sherlock curled up against her neck and purring. Absently she stroked him for a minute.

"Keep petting me like that and I'm going to get a kitty hard on."

She jerked straight up in bed. "Ray! Holy crap I forgot." The real Sherlock stirred at her feet and gave her a look through slatted eyes. "You don't know the half of it baby," she said to Sherlock giving him a quick scratch between his ears.

"Do you think you can behave while I check on my mom this morning?"

"Maybe, but I wish you'd hurry and help me back to my human form because I have an itch that no matter how much I lick, really needs you to fix it."

She glared at him, "not my problem."

Becky Sue turned into her mom's driveway at eight sharp. The lights were on. Kate was up.

"Good morning, Mom."

Her mom sat in her wheelchair next to the couch, arms crossed, her blue eyes flashed daggers, a look of pure dissatisfaction on her face. "Anything you need to tell me?"

"Umm, like what?" Cold dread and fear raced through her. Here came the storm.

"Like why Ray spent the night at your house? I thought I raised you better than that. At least be engaged before you start having him sleep over!"

It was obvious she'd already had at least one phone call this morning informing her Ray's truck still sat in Becky Sue's driveway. In broad daylight. How scandalous!

Becky Sue didn't have the heart to tell her that she'd slept with other men that she was far from being engaged with before. "It wasn't like that."

"Enlighten me."

She opened her mouth, but nothing came out. How could she tell her that she and Ray were Sparkers? That he'd turned himself into a cat and couldn't figure out how to get back. Her mom wouldn't believe a word of it.

Her shoulders sagged. "Maybe it was."

Kate wheeled closer. "I know you're full grown, but that doesn't mean you can't listen to your momma. I'm telling you child, you better not be letting that man sleep over again until you're properly engaged otherwise you know what kind of reputation you'll get don't you? That's right. You'll be the town slut instead of eligible spinster then nobody will want to marry you. Why buy the chicken when the eggs are free?"

"Yes, Momma." She felt like a scolded kid again who'd gotten in trouble for something her brother had done that she was blamed for. She couldn't explain. Who would believe her? And did she really want the townspeople to know if she held any strange power? So she took the lecture and reminded herself of whom she was now.

Kate wheeled off to shower. Becky Sue double checked the fridge and cupboards again. A new casserole sat in the fridge. It looked like one of Cindy's. She bet they had a time of it chit chatting when she came by to drop the food. Too bad Cindy hadn't waited. Today would've been much better for gossip.

"I'm not mad at you. I remember what it was like being young." Becky Sue looked up from the old newspaper she'd been reading. The shower had seemed to calm her mom down. "But you can't allow passion and a few nice muscles to let down your guard."

"I know, Momma."

"Come give me a hug and get going. I'm sure you have lots to do today."

Becky Sue gave her a hug and kissed her cheek. "Bye Mom, love you."

"Love you, too."

***

"Help! Help!" Ray's voice greeted her ears at she reached for the door to her house, mixed with angry, growling cat noises. "Get off me you tub of lard cat. No, Don't scratch my face. No. Help!"

Becky Sue rushed inside. Two grey striped fur balls were rolling around on the floor. One was clearly attacking the other.

As soon as the door opened, the cat, presumably Sherlock, disengaged himself from the fight and shot out the room.

"Thank goodness your back. What took so long?" Ray the cat asked, rolling over onto all fours. "Are you okay? You look a little shaken."

"I'm fine. It's nothing. Just my mom being Mom. What's with the cat attack?"

"You were taking forever and I was getting really hungry and thirsty. I tried getting a drink of water out of the sink, but I couldn't even jump up on the counter. I was really thirsty. I looked all over trying to find a place to get a drink other than Sherlock's water bowl, because let's face it, that's just gross. I couldn't find anything! I finally gave in and took a drink out of his water bowl and he attacked me! I'm still working on this whole four legged thing and couldn't figure out how to defend myself."

Becky Sue choked back a giggle, but the more she tried to hold it in the harder she laughed.

"It's not funny."

She could barely catch her breath she was laughing so hard. "It is from where I'm standing."

"Ha, ha, ha."

When she finally caught her breath she asked, "are you ready to go to work with me now?"

"As long as he's not coming with, yes." He pointed a dainty grey paw in the direction Sherlock had disappeared.

"No, you're safe."

A short while later they pulled into the side parking area to Becky Sue's shop. After Ray refused to be walked down the road like a cat, she agreed to take her truck. If Cindy saw her sneaking in the back with cat in hand, there were bound to be more questions and more lies to cover them up.

"Here, start reading Uncle Melvin's book and see if you can find anything helpful, while I duck over to the library." She picked a book off the shelf and put it in front of the Ray the cat, who she'd set on the counter.

She was half way to the door when he called to her. "Uh, I hate to tell you this, but I'm not very dexterous with these paws. I can't get this book opened."

Doing an about face, she walked back. Ray was pawing at the side of the book with no success.

"I can see how helpful, you're going to be." She took him off the counter and put the book away. "Just look after the shop while I'm out."

"Now that, I can do. Nobody will get out of here stealing anything without having to deal with the claws of fury." An exorcism didn't look as strange as Ray trying to do a ninja cat in a cat's body.

"Just don't talk to anybody, alright?"

"You're taking all the fun out of this."

Becky Sue didn't bother to reply, but unlocked the front door and let herself out. She crossed the street cattycorner to her shop where the tiny town library shared a building with Lydia's bakery.

**

Ray watched Becky Sue walk out the door. Being a cat wasn't so bad. There were all kinds of advantages that were inappropriate for a human to do. Like following Becky Sue to her bedroom and watching her undress. His cat body began to purr at the thought of her naked body. It was a good thing she wasn't in here. This would be hard to explain. At least when he got a boner he could hide it better than this purring sound.

He was walking around trying to figure out how to make it quit when the door bells jangled. He stopped instantly on alert. The purring stopped too. Huh, interesting. Backing into the corner he watched as Cindy from next door bustled in.

"Becky Sue," she called out. She looked around sneaky like, like maybe she suspected no one was here when there was no answer.

Cindy walked around the counter and scanned through a stack of papers before putting them back. She quickly searched through other loose papers before turning away to take a quick peek into the closet before leaving.

At first he'd thought to ask her what she was doing here, but he didn't really want anyone to know about his secret weapon, well if he could ever figure out how to shape shift again. Being stuck as a cat forever would put a real drain on his life right now. He pattered to the window and jumped up into the sill to see what she'd do next.

**

"Good morning, Mrs. Collin's," Becky Sue greeted the lady behind the desk with long white hair, glasses perched at the tip of her nose and dressed in calico. She'd been the town historian and librarian for as long as Becky Sue could remember.

"Good morning Becky Sue. What can I do for you today? I have some medical books on pregnancy and a newer one, *What to Expect When You're Expecting*."

"What?" She was momentarily thrown off track. There was nothing this town didn't know. She was sure word of Ray staying over had covered most the town by now. "No, no, no. I'm not pregnant." The look Mrs. Collins gave her was skeptical like maybe she just didn't know yet. "I've actually been a little bored and started reading Uncle Melvin's book about the Sparkers. I was wondering if you have any more information about them."

After one more look at Becky Sue's waistline, she said, "I have a diary from the mayor's wife, you know the one who burned down his house when she caught him cheating. She was supposedly a Spark. I think that's probably it. There's not much written about the Sparkers. Most of it is urban legend."

"That's what I figured too, but I've been finding it entertaining."

Mrs. Collins rose and walked down an aisle mumbling something about finding men entertaining too. Maybe she could convince her mom to move to an assisted living facility and get the hell out of this small town. Keys jangled. The old lady retrieved something from the one shelf shielded by glass where all the rare pieces were kept.

"Now, I'm assuming you want to take these with you since your shop is supposed to be open today?"

"That was the plan."

"Well, technically these books aren't supposed to leave the library, but I'll let you borrow them if you promise to bring them back at the end of the day."

"Okay. If I don't finish them can I come back tomorrow and pick it up again?"

"I suppose. You've always been a reliable girl. Although lately there's been some rumors to counter that." Mrs. Collins stared at the old relics. There were three relatively identical books. The outer edges of the pages were yellowed with age. The binding was the color of dirt. Scroll work had been etched around the cover, but now was barely visible.

"I promise I won't harm a page and I'll bring it back to you at the end of the day."

Grudgingly, Mrs. Collins began to log the diaries in to the outgoing books. Becky Sue glanced around. Nothing much had changed since she'd been here last. The display of "new" books were at least ten years old. The same reading chair that she'd sat in as a kid was off to the corner.

"Here you go. Have a good day." The older lady stretched out her hand with the diaries in it.

She took the books and practically ran back to her shop.

The bells above the door jangled as she entered. "I'm back."

Ray the cat walked out from behind the counter. "You have nosey neighbors, did you know that?"

"Yeah, what's new?"

"Cindy was over here looking behind the counter while you were gone. I'm not sure what she was looking for, but whatever it was she didn't leave with anything."

"What on earth would she be looking for?"

"You tell me." His cat eyes bore into her. Then it hit her. He was thinking like a cop. Did she have anything someone would consider dangerous, like information? Not likely. And Cindy involved in the drug trade? No way. It had to be something unrelated and stupid. Maybe Cindy thought she and Ray had married and was looking for a hidden marriage certificate. That sounded more Cindy's speed.

She shrugged. With the current exception of Ray the cat walking around her shop she was probably the most boring person in town. Still, less and less was making sense these days.

"Did you figure out how to get me out of this feline fiasco yet?"

"No, but I'm hoping this has some clues." Becky Sue held up the diaries like a trophy.

"Me too. What's that?" He was staring intently at her book hand.

Becky Sue flipped her hand over. A bright, different book was at the back. What was this? *Double feature: The Complete Guide to Child Birth, How to raise successful children.* That sneaky old lady. Oh well, she didn't have time to go back and return it now. It'd have to go back at the end of the day too. She smacked her forehead with her palm. "Ugh, apparently old Mrs. Collins slipped it to me because the whole town seems to know you stayed at my house last night."

Ray burst out laughing. It was comical to see a cat laugh with its mouth wide open, but even that wasn't enough to crack Becky Sue.

"You better watch it or I'll lock you in a closet, or even better a cage."

"Lighten up. It's not every day you get to be the talk of the town." Ray rubbed his fury body against her leg and purred. She walked past him around the counter and put the books down. "But I sure wish I was a human again to help you and get back to my intel gathering."

Just then the bells above the door jangled. Cindy waltzed in.

Chapter 8

There was a sharp intake of breath and shuffling sound on the other side of the counter. Becky Sue resisted the urge to see what Ray the cat was doing instead focused on Cindy.

Cindy's attention was momentarily distracted when she opened her mouth to speak, freezing her orifice in a strange, contorted scowl, before turning back to her. "You got mice in here?"

"Why? Are you having problems with them?"

"Heavens, no. I just saw something move in the corner when I walked in."

"Oh. I brought Sherlock with me today. He's been a little out of sorts lately. I wanted to keep an eye on him."

Cindy turned to the quilt racks where most of Becky Sue's work hung and cooed. "Here kitty, kitty. Come here Sherlock."

Becky Sue watched her, wondering what Ray would do, but just as Cindy turned Becky Sue saw a naked foot poking out, before pulling up behind the quilts. Oh shit! Ray was back to human... and naked.

"He probably won't come out if he's hiding. He's not particular to people he doesn't know, especially since he's not feeling himself."

"Hmmph." Cindy waited another few seconds and when no cat appeared she turned back to Becky Sue. "Have you tried that new soap I brought you yet? It's great isn't it?"

Becky Sue felt the little wrapped rectangle on the shelf under the counter and pushed it back further, just in case. Cindy's soap bar hadn't left the shop.

"It's very nice."

"Have you been getting many sales yet? I think the tourist season is a little slow in coming this year. Does it feel like that to you?" Sometimes that woman could talk without taking a breath.

"I haven't seen a difference yet."

"No, I don't guess you would." It felt like a jibe, but Cindy waved a hand like it was nothing. "But that's not why I came over. I came to ask if you knew anything about a strange blue light near your place last night?"

"A blue light?" Her reply was distracted. She had to get Cindy out of here, but the woman wouldn't shut up. Having a blue light around her house was the least of her problems. She had a naked man hiding in her shop, during business hours no less. Wait, blue light? Oh crap. Someone had noticed.

"Yes. Ira was telling me this morning that there was some strange blue glow coming from near your house."

"It was probably her cataracts. You know her eyes have been getting worse again but she refuses to go get her glasses changed or do that cataract surgery her doctor's been trying to get her to do for the last few years."

"She didn't have any trouble identifying Ray's truck at your house. Are you sure you didn't see anything?"

Becky Sue shook her head.

"Well I'll keep my ears open and if I find out what it was I'll let you know." With that she turned her bulk and sashayed out the door, the bells jangling a happy tune behind her.

Becky Sue hurried to the window checking for any more people. "It's safe to come out now."

Ray crawled out from behind the quilt rack in all his naked glory. Becky Sue struggled to not stare at him. He was a beautiful man, sculpted in all the right places. She turned away.

"I didn't think she was ever going leave."

"Me neither. How did you get back to human form?"

"I have no idea. One minute I'm standing there all furry, the bell jangled, the next I'm on hands and knees like this."

She smirked.

"What're you laughing at?" Ray asked, not in the least amused. Becky Sue laughed harder. "Go ahead and laugh, but how am I supposed to get out of here like this? I don't have any clothes here unless you thought to bring them. The whole town will see me and tell on you."

That brought her up short. "You're right. Where are your clothes?"

"At your house, I think." He walked around the counter to hide as best he could from anyone looking in the window.

"That's great. Just great." Suddenly Ray's predicament wasn't so funny anymore. And to add chaos to trouble, she was having trouble concentrating and figuring out what to do with him so near. He was turning her to mush. Her body called for his. She couldn't look at him otherwise it'd be her undoing.

Sniffing Becky Sue leaned over close to him. "You smell like a cat."

"Does the cat smell turn you on?"

"No."

"You're not fun. Where's your sense of excitement and adventure." He snaked an arm around her, drawing her close to his naked body. She had to look at him now. The heat radiating from his body was hard to ignore. The look in his eye changed from playful to looking like he was contemplating eating her for lunch. She felt him flick against her leg. He leaned in to kiss her. She stiffened.

"I'm not risking burning down my shop for you."

He froze, his shoulders sunk, and he dropped his hands. "Alright, you win."

As soon as his hands were no longer touching her body, she felt the emptiness. Why of all people did it have to be Ray? Had their long term friendship been a result of the pull of the Sparkers to each other? Was their sexual attraction a result of the Sparker gene that flowed through them? Or was it the real deal, no magic in play? She pushed the questions to the back of her mind. Right now she had to focus on getting him dressed before someone saw him and ran them both out of town with the scandal.

"Why don't you stay here? Hide in the closet if you have to. I'll run to the house and grab your clothes. It shouldn't take more than a couple minutes."

"Do I have a choice in the matter?"

"Sure, you could streak down the road to my house and retrieve them yourself."

"I'll let you go."

"Thought so."

Becky Sue walked out the back door, hoping Cindy wouldn't see her leave. She returned without incident and gave Ray his clothes.

After a quick discussion on what the next step was, they agreed to let Ray go home and shower before he came back to start helping research their powers and all. Becky Sue made herself comfortable, grabbed the diary off the top, and began to read.

May 6, 1867

After the war ended we all knew life would never be the same again, but I don't think anyone expected it to be like this. Many of the townspeople are struggling to survive. Will this struggle ever end? The few men who made it back seem to be at a loss. No one seems to know what to do. My husband, the great and "honorable" Mayor Cletus T. Buford, has turned into a puppet, dancing and singing to whatever tune he's told. As long as he's not having to worry about making decisions he's free to gallivant around and do whatever he so pleases, which appears to be taking to bed any willing female.

Yes, I've mentioned this before, but I have yet to have any proof. I have thought to follow him in one of my animal forms, but he knows I can shape shift so will not make a move unless he does not suspect. I have debated the animal much, but I'm sure that is the only way I will catch him and make him answer. At first I thought to become a horse. I would blend in well with the rest, but then I run the risk of being captured and stolen, or worse, branded. Cletus would also notice an out of place horse among the rest and would suspect me of spying.

I have thought to become a mouse, but it is so small I'm afraid I would have trouble keeping up, or worse, getting trampled. I've thought to become a bird, but a singular lone bird watching constantly would put him on alert.

If I knew for sure he would bring them home, I would become a cockroach and watch from the cracks in the wall. But he is crafty. I think he has each harlot in a different place. But mark my words, I will find out and I will destroy him.

Winifred Buford

Bells above the door jangled.

"Becky Sue Hocking, you better show your face. You have some explaining to do."

Becky Sue grinned as she poked her head over the counter at her best friend, Maggie. "What is it?"

Maggie was 5'4", skinny as a post, curly brown hair sprung out of her low ponytail giving her a wild look. Two year old, tow headed Tucker sat on her hip, his face dirty from a recent feeding, or possibly eating dirt, it was hard to tell with him.

"I'm always the last one to know anything around here anymore. I can't even hear it from the horse's mouth. Instead I have to hear it from the horse's mother." Maggie waved her free hand.

"Maggie Ann what are you talking about?"

"You! I'm talking about you!" She walked up and leaned on the counter and smiled mischievously, her voice lowered. "So how's he in bed?"

"What?" Her mind was scrambling to keep up. Then it hit her. "I haven't had him in my bed."

Maggie quirked a disbelieving brow at her. It was true. Ray hadn't been in her bed, at least in human form.

"Fine. At least tell me what's going on between the two of you. I haven't got a phone call or anything. Then your mom calls me this morning asking what I knew about the two of you." She set Tucker on the counter. He immediately began to reach for the pens and anything else he could get his hands on. Maggie magically produced a toy from her diaper bag/purse and gave to him.

"You know everything in this town gets exaggerated, and I've been busy with the shop opening back up and getting ready to do spring planting." Maggie's expression said she wasn't buying it. "Anyway the day before yesterday, Cindy tells me Ray is back in town. That same day he stopped by with an invitation from Mary Beth for dinner. I went to dinner at the Burnett's. After dinner Ray and I talked a little. Nothing deep. In fact, he started running his mouth. I got mad and left early. Yesterday he came by to try to mend fences and asked to take me out. We ate at Claire's. We're having such a good time I invited him in when we got to my house. We watched a little TV and he fell asleep on the couch. End of story." Why couldn't she have thought of that when her mom cornered her earlier? And why had she felt the need to lie to her best friend? Maybe because the trust was too unbelievable, even to her own ears.

Maggie reached over and grabbed a pen out of Tucker's hand before it made it too his mouth. "Well for him just sleeping on the couch you sure have a nice glow about you this morning." She looked like a teenager, eagerly waiting for the juicy details.

Becky Sue unsuccessfully tried to keep down the blush rising to her cheeks. "Okay, guilty. We might've kissed a little." A little understated considering the fire ring they'd left in their wake.

"I knew it! So are you two a thing now? Is he going to stay here? Are you going to move to Harrison if he goes back?"

"We're just going to hang out and see where it goes." She wasn't ready to admit to Maggie that their relationship was a farce. And after his assignment was over, she didn't want to have to play the broken hearted girl who got dumped for the city. Even if she did get left with a broken heart, she wouldn't admit it to anyone because it'd inevitably get back to Ray and to him they were just play acting.

"Yeah, I know how that goes. It goes straight to bed. I can tell you that now. How do you think I ended up with these kids?" Just then she looked over Becky Sue's shoulder and pointed. "You're such a liar! You little hussy." She followed the accusing finger. There sat the child birth and rearing book.

She rolled her eyes. "No, no, no, no. I went to the library this morning for a book and Mrs. Collins heard the same rumors you did and slipped this to me before I realized what she'd done."

Maggie busted up laughing. "Oh my lord, that's hilarious. Who knew old Mrs. Collins was so sly."

"I swear this town is so screwed up." Becky Sue picked up the offending book and tucked it under the counter before anyone else she knew came in and spotted it.

"Where are your other two by the way?" Becky Sue asked as she halted Tucker's pen grabbing and tried to change the subject.

"Out in the square playing. Oh, the other thing I was going to ask you before I got distracted was, did you see that strange blue light last night somewhere over near your house?"

"I heard about it, but didn't see anything."

"Yeah, that's right. You were busy watching TV, huh?" She winked.

Just as Becky Sue opened her mouth to answer, the door burst open. Maggie's other two tow headed kids raced into the shop.

"Mom, I'm bleeding."

"Levi hit me."

Levi's nose was gushing blood. Becky Sue reacted first and grabbed some tissues from under the counter and passed them to Maggie. She tilted his head back and plugged his nose with the tissues.

"I'm going to have to leave and take care of these wild things. Don't be a stranger and call me. No more leaving me in the dark." Maggie grabbed Tucker off the counter after rescuing another pen from being eaten and ushered her crew out the door.

Becky Sue smiled as she watched them leave. They were like tiny whirlwinds. They blew in and they blew out just as fast, never stopping to linger. She grabbed a cleaning rag and mopped up the few drops of blood Levi had trailed in.

Once again she returned to her chair and opened the diary. She scanned the next few pages as Winifred detailed the struggles of the town and her internal debate on how to catch her cheating husband. Nothing to point her to how to use her powers though.

Only a couple of tourists came in while she read. The season was early. She wasn't worried.

"You're back fast," Becky Sue greeted Ray as she put the empty food container into her lunch box. He walked up to her and she could smell his freshly showered body. It smelled of earth and spice and maybe a hint of something heady and wild, something untamed and free. She caught herself before she inhaled deeply. His shirt was fitted and tucked into his jeans. She wanted to free it and rub her hands across his chest, down his hips, into his jeans. Stop. Focus. These thoughts were making her too warm in all the wrong places.

"I'm anxious to find out how to use these incredible new powers we have. And I don't want to be stuck in the body of a house pet again. Have you found anything?"

"Not really. I found out that Winifred Buford, you know the mayor's wife that burned down their house after catching him with another woman, was in the form of a cockroach when she caught them. Past that, she really hasn't gone into how to use the Sparker power."

"Are there any other books that you know of about the Sparkers?"

"Other than what we have here? No."

"Are you sure we can't touch and kiss here?" He said closing the distance between them, his hand snaking around her waist to draw her to him. Their bodies touched. Heat filled the last cool places. Her hands instinctively reached out for him, her fingers trailed tiny circles on his back tracing the lines of his muscles.

His mouth was inches from hers. His breath caressed her face like the sighing of a gentle breeze. His blue eyes held her captive. She couldn't breathe. Couldn't think. She wanted him bad, but not bad enough to let all her hard work go down in flames. "So help me if I see one stray spark, you're out," she whispered huskily.

Hungrily his lips came down on her, leaving her breathless. His tongue thrust and parried. He tasted like sunshine and freedom. She pulled into him, craving his every touch. Trying to draw from him the same need she felt.

Bells jangled. She pushed him away, breathless as she was. Three tourists entered, the man who walked in first pretended he hadn't caught them about to claw each other apart.

"Afternoon. How're ya'll today?" Becky Sue greeted cheerily.

They mumbled some semblance of reply.

"I think I better so sit out back on the step." Ray said in a low voice taking one of the diaries with him.

"Good idea."

The three tourists walked around the shop, picking up things that struck their interest. Becky Sue tried to tuck her stray hair behind her ears to keep from looking like an untamed hillbilly.

The teenager that was part of the three, picked up Uncle Melvin's book, read the back, then flipped through the pages. She turned to Becky Sue. "Are any of these stories true?"

"Well the mayor's wife did burn their house down, whether she was a Sparker or not is debatable. But there's documented proof of the house. Let me ask you this. Do you believe in Bigfoot?"

"Yeah."

"Okay then you'll probably enjoy it. There's some colorful characters in it."

The girl looked to her mom who was listening to the conversation for approval. She nodded. They looked around a few more minutes before purchasing the book and leaving.

Becky Sue poked her nose out the back door to check on Ray. He wasn't there. She looked around for a lizard or caterpillar or some other random thing he could've accidently changed himself into, but the diary was gone too. Crap. Mrs. Collins was going to nail her to the wall if she misplaced one of them.

She walked back in fuming and bewildered. Where did he go? Why would he take off with something so valuable and not give her notice? Had something happened to him? Had some of the people from the drug ring he was investigating kidnap him, or worse? She was really beginning to worry.

Pacing to the big window at the front of her shop, she spied two men on one of the benches in the park square. One of them was Ray, diary in hand. The other was no one she recognized, which made him a tourist. Even from here she could see the man was good looking. He looked like he spent a lot of time outdoors. Tanned, rangy, dark hair, broad shoulders. Ray pointed towards her shop. The man turned. She ducked out of the window back to her place behind the counter. She didn't know what Ray was pointing for, but she didn't want to be caught staring.

Back in the diary, she tried to read, but was too busy wondering what Ray was talking to the tourist about her or her shop to concentrate.

A little bit later, Ray walked in through the front door. He didn't speak until he got close enough she could hear him whisper. He was tense. "Is there anybody in here?"

"No."

"I think I just picked up a lead about the drug running." He relaxed a little, but seemed to be full of nervous energy.

"Oh? That's good, right?"

"Yeah. I told him my girlfriend was making me read this old diary to find some magic to help in bed. He said he knew a better way to magic rather than an old book. Bam, just like that he tells me how to get in touch with someone to make a purchase. How would you like to go fishing?"

"Fishing?"

Ray grinned. "Fishing."

Ray left an hour later to get ready for their fishing trip. They were no closer to having an answer on how to use their powers.

**

A Sparker? Who in the hell would've thought in a million years that it was a real thing. But how cool was that? If he could just figure out how to harness and use his power he'd be unstoppable. He could climb to the top and barely blink. He just had to figure out how to keep his clothes on… literally.

And damn it, if Becky Sue wasn't a distraction. He'd already faced the firing squad that was his mother when he'd come home earlier over his staying out all night with her. He'd played it off as falling asleep watching TV on the couch. It wasn't like he could've done a whole lot when he was in cat form anyway. They didn't need sleepovers either. Just the thought of their pre-sleepover encounter had his blood rushing hot and his cock straining in his jeans. She'd been fiery and wanton. Willing and wet. He'd known they both felt attraction for each other since their rekindling, but what he'd found was beyond what he could've hoped for. His attraction for her wasn't dimming each time he touched her, like it often did with others, instead each time he was near her he almost couldn't help but touch her, partly for the thrill it gave him, partly to see if she was really real.

He didn't like it. He didn't like it at all. He felt bewitched. Open and exposed. He'd always played his cards close to his chest, but with her it was different. She knew him down to his stone cold heart. And now she was melting it.

Frustrated he slammed the door of his truck after he got out and winced. He needed to relax and calm down or he'd explode ruining everything, including his job, Spark or no Spark.

He slipped into the house as quietly as he could. Mary Beth was sitting on the couch in front of the old television.

"Why are you coming into this house so stealthy like?"

"I didn't realize I was being stealthy." She gave him a look of disbelief. "Will you be home for dinner tonight?"

"I don't plan on staying out all night, but don't hold dinner for me either. I was thinking to go out fishing and don't know when I'll be back."

"What kind of fishing you doing?"

"I was thinking to go over by Ashburn."

"Oh, that kind of fishing."

"What kind did you think I was talking about, Mom?"

"Don't be questioning my motives. Just remember you're not getting any younger."

He shook his head and went to his room to hide. If he survived his assignment here, he could survive anything.

**

Ten minutes before her usual shut down time, Becky Sue locked up her shop and walked back over to the library to return her books.

Mrs. Collins was still seated at her desk. One of the town's old timers was browsing through an aisle of books. Becky Sue set her stack on the desk, the double feature for expectant mothers on top, silently letting Mrs. Collins know she'd been called out.

"Are you sure you don't want to keep this one a little longer, dearie." Mrs. Collins held out the offensive book to her.

"Positive. I have no use for it." She said it loud enough that the other patron would hear so when she left and they talked about her, the woman browsing would hear the answer straight from the horse's mouth.

"Will you be back tomorrow for the diaries again?"

"No. I read enough. Thank you."

**

It'd been years since he'd been out here, but nothing had changed. Just like the rest of the town. He pulled into Roy's Bait and Tackle.

He opened the door to the shop and frowned. Jed Turner was sitting behind the register with a bottle pressed against his lips.

Jed jerked the bottle quickly out of his mouth, somehow managing not to splash himself with the contents.

"Well, well, well if it isn't Ray Burnett, back from the dead."

"Hi, Jed. How's it going? It's been a while."

"Sure has. Don't seem to affect you none though." Jed sneered while eying him like he'd just taken something from him and was debating how much to fight to get it back.

Once upon a time Jed had been the golden boy. The one all the girls in town fawned and swooned over. He'd basked in the glory and played fast and loose with it all. Ray noted the absence of a wedding ring. No surprise there. Jed had never grown up. In this town there were only 2 reasons to not be married. One was if you'd just divorced, there was an unwritten time frame of supposed bachelorhood, and two was if the town was done with you, including its women, which was no small feat. He'd bet money that Jed fit into the latter category.

"It has, it's just not as visible as you'd like, but I didn't come here to talk about how I'm aging. I have my girl coming up soon and plan to do some fishing. Dropped by to pick up some lures and bait."

"I'll bet you are. Let me know if you need anything extra to help with your girl. I got just the thing."

Just then a customer entered. Then another. Business was picking up. Ray looked around the store for a minute to listen, but nothing else suspicious came up.

"I'll be back later, Jed." He waved and walked out.

Surely Jed couldn't be the brains behind the operation. He was too willing, and too drunk, to run an operation. That meant there was a bigger fish out there he had yet to find.

He drove down around the campground, not really sure what he was looking for. Nothing stood out. He parked his truck and grabbed a fishing pole. He needed a reason to be watching people on the water pass by.

The sun was starting to set when he finally reeled in his line. His bucket was empty. Every fish he'd caught, he'd thrown back knowing he didn't have the time to clean it. Although a fish dinner didn't sound so bad. Mom could cook fish like nobody else, but now was not the time. He had work to do.

He knew it was too much to ask for a simple, easy, in-your-face solution. On one hand it'd be good to wrap this job up nice and tidy like, but on the other, the more time here meant more time he could spend with Becky Sue. He smiled to himself, threw his gear in his truck, and started meandering back to the bait shop to meet her.

**

It was a twenty minute drive, part curvy highway, part dirt road, to the Ashburn campground. It was known for its fishing mainly, but also canoeing and hiking trails. It was probably the most popular among the tourists.

She parked her pickup in front of Roy's Bait and Tackle, located next to the campground entrance. Last she'd heard old man Roy had cashed in and turned the business over to his son, Jed. She'd seen Jed last summer. He'd looked like life had chewed him up and spit him back out. It was almost a shame that someone who'd been so good looking and popular in school would end up with the short end of the stick in life. That is if he wasn't such a sleaze ball. She felt dirty every time she looked at him after their train wreck of a Jr. Prom together.

Ray's truck was already in the lot, but there was no sign of him. Becky Sue was in no hurry to rush inside and find him either. After a short debate on whether to go in or not, she convinced herself it wasn't a big deal.

"Well, well, well, if it ain't the little sweetheart herself. What brings you to my fine establishment Becky Sue?"

One look at Jed and she knew he was drunk. His face was rudy red, his hair was disheveled and looked like it hadn't seen scissors or a brush in some time. He scratched at his stomach. His shirt looked like it hadn't seen laundry soap in a year. Ray glanced up from inspecting a lure.

"There you are honey. I was wondering what was keeping you." Ray walked up and kissed her lightly on the lips. So this was how it was going to be.

"Sorry to keep you. I had to check on Sherlock and change."

"Well don't that beat a pig on a stick," Jed interrupted. "Little sweet Becky Sue hooked up with wild man Ray."

Becky Sue glared at him. Ray squeezed her hand and spoke before she could. "Yep. She's mine alright. I've done put my wild ways behind me and started to think it's time to slow life down a bit." He slipped an arm around her. It was warm and inviting. If this was going to be how they're going to have to act for a while, she was a goner. "I had her come out here with me today to try to loosen her up. She's so uptight. I've been trying to get her to relax more. She works too much."

Jed leered at her. "Good luck with that. I tried to loosen her up once and it didn't work, but that was before I really knew how. Now I know a secret way to get women to beg for it from me. If you have any trouble let me know and I'll share it with you."

Becky Sue tried to keep her expression innocent and beguiling, when all she wanted to do was tell the sleaze ball where to stick it. When Jed had taken her to the Jr. Prom he'd assumed that going to the dance was also consent to take it further and when he'd tried make his move she'd bloodied his nose. As for now, she couldn't see how any woman would want to touch him with a ten foot pole.

"I'll keep that in mind, Jed. Here, what do I owe you for these lures? And you got any liver?"

Jed produced a tub of liver and rang them up.

Becky Sue followed Ray through the campground gate and around to the fishing area. They found a spot where no one could come up on them and listen easily.

"Is Jed your lead?"

"Unfortunately, I think so. He was too far gone today to get much out of him, at least reliable information. I don't think he's capable of running an operation the size of what we think this is either. He runs his mouth too much and can't control himself."

"So what's the plan?"

"Tomorrow I'll come back early and tell him you're a tight old spinster who doesn't give easily," he grabbed her boob and pulled her to him for a kiss, "and ask him about his secret. Talk him up a bit. See what he knows."

"Hmm I don't know if I like being the 'tight old spinster'. Might give me a bad rap with the male tourists. You know I like to snag one for a good time at least once a year if I can."

"Why you wanna go look elsewhere when I got everything you need, and more, right here?" He took her hand and placed it on his cock. It was hard and burned with heat. Her body responded in kind instantly. She hated that she was so attracted to him. He brought out the worst in her.

Except for the being a Spark thing, that might be kind of cool. But other than that all he did was bring out the animal. All she wanted was him inside of her, filling her with his cock. Stroking her wetness.

He pulled her to him and kissed her again, this time with a little more tongue. She wanted to pull back, to slow down, but she had no restraint when it came to his call. Dropping his fishing pole beside him, he took her with both hands, one holding her to him, the other exploring under her shirt, rubbing her nipple until it was sharp enough to cut ice. His fingers danced down her stomach, under her waist band, and into her wetness. She moaned a low, feral sound. He bit her lip.

"You're ready and waiting aren't you?"

"I have no control with you. You bring out my worst."

He laughed a low throaty sound. "If this is your worst, I'll take it. I don't want you any better." With that he slid a second finger into her wetness. She gasped and arched her back. His lips trailed down her neck. She needed him bad. She needed him now. And if he didn't quit the next person that came along would find a sight they didn't quite expect to see on the banks of the river.

He nipped at her nipples through her shirt. Her insides were wound up tighter than a banjo string. If this was how he wanted to play, two could play at this game.

She let go of her fishing pole, braced herself on her elbow, and used the other hand to massage him. It was already hard, but at his touch it grew harder. She slid her hand into his pants. The tip of his cock was wet. She massaged it with her thumb.

"Becky Sue, I swear you're going to be the death of me."

It was her turn to give a throaty laugh. It felt good to dish out what was given. Let his sex scream at him for release like hers was.

She stroked his length firmly. He bit her ear. "Stop. Mercy. Stop. By all that's good, don't make me take you here for the whole world to see."

His hand retracted from her.

"You started it."

A mischievous grin played on his lips. "I can't help it. You're my weakness. Like the forbidden fruit. Since I found out I can have you I can't seem to get enough. I just want to be inside you and not come out."

"Sounds like a bad spot to be in." But she felt the same.

"Should we take this to a little bit more private spot?"

She extracted her hand from his pants and kissed his lips. "Somewhere not too far I hope."

They quickly packed up their fishing gear and stowed it in his truck.

"Where to Napolean?" Ray stood next to her, heat rolled off his body.

Only a small part of the campground was visible from where they stood. It was easy to envision all kinds of little nooks to slip away into, but they needed to not be noticeable, or able to catch anything on fire, just in case the blue flame peeked again.

She snapped her fingers. "I know a place. I'll direct you." They climbed into his truck. She scooted to the middle so she could play with him as he drove down the road.

Chapter 9

The next morning Becky Sue awoke to Sherlock patting her face, at least she hoped it was Sherlock and not Ray again. She saw only one cat so she felt safe in assuming it was the real Sherlock. Today was a running day, but she didn't feel like it. She'd gotten plenty of exercise with Ray yesterday, once when their fishing trip had ended abruptly and then again before he left to go home last night. So far nothing else had burned and the sparks of fire had seemed to disappear. She hadn't quite figured out what to think of that. Had their powers evaporated as fast as they'd shown or did that only happen when they received their powers?

Sherlock ran ahead of her as she walked through the house to check his food and water. She topped each off and crawled back in bed. Maybe mornings were over rated.

Thinking sleep would come back easily was a mistake. She lay there tossing and turning until finally she gave up. Her brain was awake.

By the time daylight broke she'd managed to knock out some household chores that'd she'd been slacking off of for a week. But as the sun begun to rise higher, her thoughts turned to Ray. He was planning to go back to Jed and try to find out more about the drugs. She didn't like the fact that he was going alone, but he was the professional. She had to trust that he could do his job without getting in trouble, or worse. In the meantime, all she could do was worry until she heard from him.

After checking on her mom, she walked to work with her mind made up to focus on working on the patriotic star quilt. Theoretically it should be done by next week. But theories only work when there's no distractions, and Ray was a big distraction.

She hated that she felt so gullible. So attracted to him. She also knew nothing would ever come of it. It would never last. He'd go back to being the good guy saving the world and she'd stay here, tucked away in her little mountains, sewing and passing town gossip. Maybe if she could figure out if she had and how to use her new powers life might hold a little more interest around here. She sighed as she unlocked the front door to her shop, at least she could enjoy him being good in bed while he was around.

The quilt was coming together nicely. It wouldn't take long to sell. She was deep in concentration, making each little stitch count in the overall design when the door bells jangled jolting her, making her prick her finger. She bit back a curse and squeezed it to stop the blood.

"Hello. Doing alright today?" Becky Sue called out without looking to the door.

"Hi. I'm fine. How about you?" The voice that spoke was all male and smooth as butter. She whipped her head around before she could set her quilt down. There stood the mystery man Ray had been talking to yesterday on the bench. He was even hotter in person.

She blinked before catching herself staring. "I'm good. Can I help you find anything specific?"

Sultry. That's the word she would use to describe his eyes. Long, thick beautiful lashes swept across his dark brown eyes like a veil giving him an exotic look. His lips were full, but not overly dramatic. His face was all hard points, chiseled and tan. She couldn't look away if she tried.

"Actually, yesterday I was talking to a guy, I think it was your boyfriend, and he was telling me some local legend stories that sounded interesting. Said you had a book in here about them."

"Boyfriend?" She asked dumbly.

"Yeah, probably just under six feet, body builder, short brown hair. I think he said his name was Ray?"

"Oh, oh him." Pull it together girl, you're losing it.

"He's your boyfriend right?"

"He's my... we're just... it's complicated." If this beautiful male specimen in front of her was interested she'd deny she ever knew Ray if that's what it took to get him into bed. Screw Ray with his you're my best friend, be my undercover girl friend. She wasn't getting any younger and nature was calling. The attraction she felt towards Ray was probably just a spinoff of sharing the Spark with him anyway. A relationship couldn't last just because of some strange, old magic gene they shared. Besides she was like any other girl. She wanted romance and excitement, not the scared for your life excitement that was bound to come with Ray, but the excitement of being found by someone and learning about them and them about you.

He smiled, showing perfectly straight, white teeth. "I see." Leaning against the counter he let his eyes linger as they took in her homespun look. For once, she wished she'd have worn jeans and t-shirt like a normal person rather than her homemade broom skirt and top. He didn't immediately run for the door, so that had to be good.

"You're looking for a book right?" She sounded like a brainless rock. What was wrong with her this morning?

"Yeah. Something about shape shifters. It sounded really cool."

"I know what you're talking about." Walking around the counter she retrieved Uncle Melvin's book off the shelf.

She hadn't heard him move, but she could feel his presence next to her before she saw him. "This is it." Handing him the book, she felt his energy and the air seemed to be sucked out of the room. Breath. Slowly. In, out, in, out.

At 5'9" she was no shrimp, but he towered over her. He was easily over six foot tall and all lean muscle.

Where Ray was built like a chiseled brick, he was built like a bow string, taunt and wiry.

"So what do you know about these legendary people? Have you read this book?"

"I've read it. I don't believe it. There are some stories in there that have a grain of truth to them that've been recorded, like the mayor's wife burning down their house." Hold up, don't get yourself tangled too deep in a lie. He knows Ray was reading one of the diaries yesterday. "Actually me and my friend have been arguing over whether the legends of the Sparkers were real or not. I borrowed some books from the library to prove him wrong the other day, but he's determined to prove himself right. I mean who really believes people can change into animals? Or throw fire like Spiderman does his web? I can see how some cute parlor tricks could make people believe the fire throwing thing pretty easily, especially back then, but now? No way."

"I think it'd be cool if people could change into animals. Just think of the possibilities!"His eyes lit up and for a minute she wanted to tell him they could. But she didn't. She had to protect their secret. At least until this drug ring was busted. She'd read enough of Winifred's diary to know the dangers of the opposition knowing too much about the powers.

"It would be kinda cool I guess," she conceded, "but unrealistic."

"You're boy's right. You're not any fun." She wasn't sure if he was teasing or being insulting.

"I can be fun, but my *magical powers* are a little more realistic." She was flirting hard, but she couldn't help it. Her insides were coiled and taunt, the heat from his body a couple feet away was driving her crazy.

"Oh? And what magical powers do you possess?"

The bells above her door jangled. It was Ray.

Mr. Hottie saw Ray. "How much do I owe you for the book?"

As soon as he was out the door Ray asked, "what was that all about?"

"He came in on your recommendation for Uncle Melvin's book on Sparkers."

"Seems like there was a little more than that going on." Ray actually looked and sounded jealous.

"Um, no." Because he hadn't even told her his name or given her his phone number.

Ray only looked mildly pacified.

"What'd you find out?" Change the subject before the interrogation went further.

"Jed's not the ringleader, that's almost for certain. He's just small fish."

"No surprise there."

"How do you feel about going camping? I need a way to keep an eye on Jed. An alibi and a pair of extra eyes wouldn't hurt. I think he'll lead us somewhere."

"Yeah probably to the nearest place he can find liquor."

"What do you say?"

"When?"

"Tonight and probably a few more days."

"What about my shop? I can't just close down."

"Just sleep at camp, hang out in the evenings, and come back to do your normal day stuff." He made it sound so simple.

"Is there another option?"

"Not really."

What the heck? She figured her chances with Mr. Hottie were over anyway. Sherlock would probably think she abandoned him. Her mother would probably end up moving in so she could keep an eye on her wandering daughter. The town would probably turn it into their honeymoon after they eloped. Chump change for busting a drug ring, right?

"Fine. I'll do it."

"I knew you would. You're the best." He brushed his lips across hers briefly. She refrained from reaching out and pulling him in. It would just be one more catastrophe in the making if she did. "Couldn't do it without you. Just come out after work. I'll be out at the campground somewhere."

He disappeared out her door as fast as he'd blown in.

She didn't feel like the best. She didn't feel like much of anything. It was easy for him to say meaningless words when he didn't have to stick around and be held accountable for them. It didn't work that way for her.

Becky Sue was still sulking when Cindy popped in. "You sure have a long face for having so many men in here this morning. What's wrong, you and Ray have a fight? Was it over that gorgeous tourist that was in here? Was Ray jealous?"

"What? No." Her brain scrambled to keep up. Would Ray be jealous if she went out with Mr. Hottie? Would she even care if he was? "This is my thinking face. You caught me deep in thought."

"Mmmhmm. Thinking bout them men. Well, I just came over to drop these cookies I made last night. I'm glad I decided to bring you some. Men like their women curvy, and honey, you need some curves."

Great. Just what she needed, more positive outlook on her life. But she was right. At least there were cookies. Cookies made the world better. She accepted the cookies and Cindy breezed back out the door.

Surprisingly, the rest of the day passed uneventfully. Becky Sue locked up her shop and walked home to check on Sherlock and pack her things. She should call her mom and let her know where she was if she needed her. But she didn't. Maybe by some super cosmic power word of her and Ray camping out wouldn't get to her mother for a few days, and even if it did, it was easier to deal with it after the fact.

The Ashburn campground was practically identical to the other half dozen or so scattered around. The only thing that made this a more popular site was the cabins and the fishing. The water here was deeper than much the rest, and even during the long waterless days of summer, there was still swimmable water and fishing.

Becky Sue drove through the gates just as the last rays of light were disappearing on the horizon. She drove around and checked each camp section methodically for Ray, finally finding his truck parked outside a cabin. This wasn't what she expected.

She knocked on the door.

Ray opened it and pulled her inside. "You're just in time. I think. Were the lights still on at the bait shop when you passed?"

"I think so."

"Good. Come on." He stopped as he reached for the door. "Where's your stuff?"

"In the truck."

"Why?"

"I thought you said camping. Not cabin. I was just making sure before I hauled it out."

He shook his head like she was impossible. She followed him out the door and into his truck.

"So what are we doing?"

"We're going to follow Jed and see where he goes."

"Was he less drunk today than yesterday?"

"I don't know. I didn't check."

"Don't get too excited then. He's probably headed straight home to a beer or a bottle."

They turned out of the campground just as Jed's truck pulled out from the bait shop. They followed him for several miles. Jed drove down the road like grandpa

Sunday, crossing the double yellow a couple of times before turning off onto a side road in the middle of nowhere.

"Told ya he's headed home."

Ray drove past the turn off then turned around and doubled back. Jed may've been drunk but that didn't mean he was delusional enough not to know he was being followed.

"He lives here?"

"Yeah."

"How far up is it to the house?"

"Less than a mile, I think."

"Neighbors?"

"Not since old man McCoy died."

Ray parked the truck off to the side of the rutted dirt road in the deepest shadow he could find. "We'll walk from here."

With a full moon a few days earlier, it was still bright enough to see, mostly. The road began to lightly ascend.

"Are we going to be hiking uphill the rest of the way," Ray whispered after it felt like they'd walked a mile uphill.

"I don't remember."

The road veered to the left before leveling off some. A small light shown through the trees. They slowed their pace.

"He have any dogs that're going to give us away?"

"I don't know. I don't make it a point to keep up with him."

"As much as that information would be helpful, I'm glad you don't keep up with him that well." He grabbed her jacket and pulled her in for a kiss. Like every time before when he touched her fire seared through her veins.

"Don't start something you can't finish." She meant it for the moment, but realized she was talking about more than just a kiss and sex.

He kissed her again, a little harder and with a little tongue. "I don't plan on it. Just not here."

A small, dilapidated house sat in the center of a clearing. Light was coming from two of the front windows. Off to the side a single wide trailer house was falling in on itself. Most the roof was caved in. the front door was missing. Only half the windows remained. While it would provide good cover and get them close to the house, she didn't want to go anywhere near that place in the daytime, let alone in the dark.

They skirted the edge of the clearing trying to get a better look. Only Jed's truck was parked in the yard. No dogs raced around the house to eat them or blow their cover.

"Sure would be nice to know how to use our powers that way we could walk right up to the front door and he'd never suspect," Ray said.

"I'd become a lizard. That way I'd crawl right up to his window and peek in." She smiled as she pictured herself as a lizard peering into Jed's window. "Did a cloud just cross the moon? It got dark suddenly."

"What're you talking about? Becky Sue? Where'd you go?"

"I'm right here. I haven't moved." She reached out to poke him, but something was covering her. "What the …" She felt a moment of panic. Then she realized she was standing on all fours. "Oh no."

"What happened?" Ray's whisper was concerned.

A small pinprick of light was to her left. She moved towards it. It got bigger. She was free. Except she'd nearly ran into a tree. No, not tree, blades of grass. She looked down at her body. It was shiny in the moonlight. Her tail shimmered blue. "I'm a lizard." Her clothes lay in a heap next to her. She'd been trapped under them when she changed. "And I'm naked."

Ray was tall. Really, really tall from where she stood on the ground. He looked down in the general direction of her voice. "I don't mind the naked part. Where are you?"

"Don't move. You'll step on me."

"Wave or something so I can see you."

"Wave? Are you crazy? Hold still for a minute."

She looked at her little lizard feet. Here goes nothing. She climbed onto his shoe, up his pant leg, as soon as she got to his shirt he started to squirm.

"Don't wiggle. You'll knock me off."

"You're tickling me."

"I can't help it." She scrambled on to his shoulder.

He turned his head to her and smiled. He was huge. "There you are. Cute. I like the new look."

Becky Sue rolled her eyes. She was a little breathless. That'd been like climbing a hundred foot rock wall.

"Well, now that I'm a lizard I might as well make myself useful. Can you get me up closer to the house? That's a long way for somebody with such short legs." She felt the vibration in his body as he held in a laugh. "Glad somebody thinks this is funny."

He crept up to the side of the house and set her on the small porch. She scaled the nearest wall of peeled paint and peered in the first lit window. It appeared to have been a kitchen at one time, but was littered with empty food packages, beer cans, jugs from Chester's home brew, bait and tackle boxes and roaches. It was disgusting. Did roaches and lizards get along? She hoped so.

She made her way over to the next lit window. Jed sat on an old run down love seat. The original color or pattern was beyond faded and covered with stains. He was staring intently at the TV. A beer can looked like it was about to tip out of his hand. Was he passed out drunk yet? He wasn't moving.

She sat and watched, waiting for something to happen.

"Psst. Becky Sue, can you see anything?" Ray whispered from the side. She shook her little lizard head. "Can you find a way to get inside and go check it out?"

Scrambling off the window sill, she ran across the porch to where Ray hunkered down on the side. "He's in there on the couch. Looks like he's gone for the night."

"Can you find a way in and check it out? See if you can find anything?" He asked again.

"Are you kidding? There's roaches and spiders in that house bigger than me! And what if I flip back to my human form by accident and he catches me? Then what?"

"Chicken."

"No. I'm a lizard. I'm scared and I run."

"Alright, we'll go check the other windows and if we don't see anything we'll leave."

She crawled back onto his shoulder as he snooped around the house. Nothing seemed unusual given the little they knew of him. No bags of drugs were stacked in the corner of any of the rooms.

"Go check one more time then we'll leave."

"You're gonna make sure I make up for not running today aren't you?"

Ray grinned. Becky Sue took off across the porch and peered in the window one last time. Jed hadn't moved. She raced down and back to Ray's shoulder.

"No movement. Let's go. I'm tired of being a lizard now. I'm ready to be a human."

"I'm ready for you to be human too. I had plans for us tonight."

She could just imagine. She closed her eyes as he walked and pictured herself naked under him, his cock rock hard plummeting her.

All of a sudden she felt herself falling. She caught a shriek of surprise before it came out. Ray grunted. She hit the ground, hard. They were nearly to the edge of the clearing. The cool blades of grass tickled.

"I'm human! I'm human again!" Becky Sue lay in the grass where she'd fallen off Ray and examined her hands, her arms, her legs. "And I'm naked!" She crossed her chest with one arm and covered her lady parts with the other.

"Yeah." His eyes raked her. "You could've given me a little warning though before you turned yourself back into a human while you were on my shoulder."

She giggled at the image that came to her mind. Naked woman on his shoulder and him toppling like a lego tower.

"Sorry I didn't realize I was going to do it."

"How'd you do it?"

"I'm not sure, and can we have this conversation after we find my clothes? Please."

"Do you have to put your clothes back on?"

"Yes. I'm freezing."

They crept around to where she thought she'd changed into a lizard, all the while glancing over her shoulder hoping Jed didn't wake up and decide to look outside.

Chapter 10

"What's our next move?" Becky Sue asked Ray he drove them back to the campground.

"To get you out of those clothes again." He placed his hand on the inside of her thigh. Every time he touched her there was heat, but was it because she wanted to bed him or was it their Spark energy connecting?

"I mean with your assignment. Jed looks like a dead end. What's next?"

"I don't think Jed is a dead end, but he's not big fish either. We need to keep an eye on him from the time he gets up to the time he sleeps at night. I'm sure there's a thread there to follow, we just have to figure out how to pull it."

"So what you're saying is you're going to be following around a drunk pervert who spends most of his day smelling like dead minnows until something happens?"

He crinkled his nose into a disgusted face. "Basically, yeah."

"You know, suddenly your job doesn't sound so fun and exciting anymore."

"Why do you think I brought you along?" He squeezed the inside of her thigh and rubbed his fingers over her pants between her legs. She jabbed him hard in the ribs. "I'm kidding, I'm kidding. But this may turn out to the most fun surveillance work I've ever done."

They turned into the campground. Becky Sue retrieved her overnight bag from her truck and followed Ray inside. When she'd come in earlier she hadn't been able to really look at the place. She did now as she set her bag inside the door.

It was warm and cozy. A cold fireplace took up most of one wall. A sturdy wood framed couch with double stuffed cushions lined the side near the door. A TV across the room shared a wall with one doorway that looked like it might be a kitchenette. The final wall featured a doorway to a bedroom and a nature painting.

Ray appeared out of the bedroom in sock feet. "Why don't you bring your stuff in here and then we can relax on the couch for a little bit together."

Becky Sue emptied her bag, laying her clothes out in attempts to avoid wrinkles. By the time she made it to the couch, Ray had a bag of popcorn made and was flipping through channels.

She sat close enough to snitch popcorn, but far enough to keep the heat from building between them, which was probably a lost cause, but she had to try.

"What do you think about this animal shape shifting stuff? Did you figure it out when you were a lizard," he asked, still absently channel surfing.

"Not really. I've been thinking it through, but don't know if it's really how it works or not."

"Shoot. What do you think?" He sat there all ears.

"I think it has something to do with wishing you're an animal and/or possibly visualizing it, because I remember visualizing myself as a lizard peeking through Jed's window."

"What about coming back to human form?"

She fought down a rising blush as she remembered what she had been thinking when she suddenly felt herself falling. "Same. I was picturing myself like this." More or less.

"Like that or like this?" He closed the gap between them, leaving the popcorn behind, and wrapping his arms around her.

"Close enough." The heat their bodies produced was intense. His touch invigorated her. Made her feel invincible. She could take on the whole world, as long as he was connected to her. Maybe that's what attracted her to him was the feeling of power he gave her. That and there was some unexplainable pull to him, that she'd always felt, a closeness and kinship that she didn't have with anyone else. Perhaps it was the blood of the Sparker in them that pulled them together.

He kissed her slow and gentle. She relaxed into him, enjoying the feel of his hard body pressed against hers.

"I wonder if we can turn ourselves into animals and have sex," he suddenly said as he trailed kisses down her neck.

"What?"

"Do you want to try to shift into animals and have wild animal sex?" His voice was husky, sexy, dripping with temptation.

"Uh, what did you have in mind?" he reached for her boob, and twirled her nipple between his finger. The warmth between her legs was already intensifying.

"Well, I like doggie style. How about if we start simple and try it as dogs first and see how it goes?" He bit her lip as a hand slipped into her wetness. How was she supposed to tell him no?

"I... guess." He nibbled his way down her neck before pulling her shirt up over her head. She had no idea what she was doing, and didn't really care as long as it got him inside of her, soon.

She pulled his shirt off and reached for his pants at the same time he reached for hers. Stretching out across the couch, she pushed at him to enter. She could feel his cock pressing against the edge of her, teasing her. Was she to resort to begging? She nipped at his ear again and nibbled down his neck. He was so warm. His scent intoxicated her.

Thrusting her hips upward she begged for him to enter. He gave in. She grabbed his ass, prodding him deeper. He suckled her left nipple, twirling it around on his tongue, making it hard enough to cut diamonds. She was clenched down on him. It wasn't time for gentle and easy. She needed hard and wild. Her breathing was already ragged and irregular. When bodies were in tuned with each other so well, foreplay was just a word in a book somewhere.

"Whoa, whoa, whoa, slow down. I thought we're going to have a little fun with this," he breathed into her ear.

Ah, crap. She had no willpower to argue. She was too needy.

He slid out of her and sat back. "Are you ready?"

"As ready as I'll ever be. What kind of dog are we going to be?"

"What?"

"What kind of dog? We probably need to be the same breed because if you end up a big dog and me a little or vice versa, this may not turn out so well."

"I didn't think of that. How about a beagle?"

"I can do that."

"Want to take my hands?" He held out his hands to her. They were thick with layers of muscle. She studied his sausage fingers. No wonder they felt so good massaging her feminine parts.

They clasp hands. "On the count of three. One, two, three. I wish to become a beagle."

Becky Sue pictured Chester's little beagle, Daisy, and opened her eyes just in time to see a tongue going straight to her face. She turned her head away as the licking persisted. Had it worked? The beagle on the couch next to her looked a lot like Lucky, another of Chester's dogs. He was wagging his tail happily.

"Nice fur coat you got there," said the dog in Ray's voice.

Paw, claws, fur, the works. They'd succeeded. Ray licked her face again and surprisingly she was still wet and willing. She turned around showing him her ass.

Two paws touched her back, lost balance, fell and came back. After several failed attempts, Ray said, "I think we're going to have to try this on the floor. I can't keep my balance."

They jumped off the couch. It was her turn to lick his face. Her tongue against his fur felt rough and overly textured. He rolled over on his back. His cock hung out. She licked it. He let out a low moan that was half howl. She licked it faster. It got harder. He was panting. His back feet kicked in gleeful pleasure. He flipped back over onto all fours. She turned her back to him again.

This time his aim was straight and true. He entered her wetness and filled her. Her moan came out more howl. His cock increased in size inside her. It pressed against every wall. Thick. Full.

He danced around, his back legs unsteady, as he rammed deep. She kept them balanced, four feet on the floor.

"Damn, I didn't know doggie style could feel so good," he panted. "You're like a wet rubber band around me. Tight and wet as hell."

He came in record time. She felt every pulse on every wall.

"Holy shit." She released as he throbbed inside.

As they caught their breath he tried to pull out. He pulled again. This time it tugged on her femininity too hard. She whimpered. She was wrapped too tight around him. His cock was too large to pull out. "I can't move."

"I know and it feels so good, as long as you don't yank too hard," she breathed airily. His cock flickered inside as it thought about getting hard again.

"I don't know if I have it in me for another shot right now. Especially if I stay in you like this."

"Then I think we better get back to human form. From what I've seen of dogs humping we could be stuck like this for a while."

"Alright. Count of three again." She nodded. "One, two, three. I wish to be a human again."

Becky Sue envisioned what she looked like naked, on her knees, Ray behind her, inside.

Fleshy hands gripped her hips. She felt looser, saturating wet. Ray slid out.

Straightening up, she took in his near perfect body. "That was... interesting. But I think I like to feel your flesh better than your fur."

He pulled her to him, sliding his fingers inside her as he did, kissed her and breathed out, "this was amazing." He wiggled his fingers. "I don't know if I've ever felt anything so tight. I'm also pretty sure I haven't cum that fast since I was a teenager."

A throaty laugh erupted from deep inside her. "Serves you right. Next time I'm going to find an animal that bites off the males head after mating."

"You mean you'd do this again?"

"Maybe... if you can persuade me." She pressed her lips to his and probed his sensuous mouth with her tongue.

"You really are an animal aren't you?"

"Just wait till I figure out how to use my fire powers." She bit at his lip.

His cock was hard again pressing against her leg. He lifted her up by her ass, wrapping her legs around him, and carried her to the bed.

**

It was criminal to have to get out of the warm bed next to her, especially at this hour. The sky hadn't even begun to turn grey in the wee dawn hours yet, and here he was crawling out of bed to go follow a drunken idiot who was selling drugs on the side. Maybe he should go with a tried and true method of roughing him up to spill the beans about his supplier, but just the thought of putting his hands on Minnow Breath repulsed him.

He stopped long enough to drink a cup of coffee, grabbed some protein bars to keep him going the rest of the day, and left the cabin.

Now that he knew more about how to shape shift he was anxious to try it out as he watched Jed today. He pulled off the road a little past the turn off to

Jed's place and parked his truck. Glancing around to make sure no early risers were wandering about, he hid his keys, chucked his clothes, and thought bear.

As he ambled up the road he briefly wondered what would happen if someone shot him while he was in bear form. Would it kill him like a human or would it depend on the caliber like any normal bear? Maybe he should've picked something less hunted, but he wanted to watch Jed piss his pants when he caught sight of him

The walk up the hill was strenuous for a fat bear, but once he reached Jed's he checked the perimeter of the house for light and sound. Everything was quiet. He ambled back to the edge of the tree line and sat. The perk to being a bear was it was more comfortable, and warm, sitting on the cool ground than as a human.

Staring into the dark was taxing. His eyes grew heavy as he waited for movement. The first rays of sunlight began to touch the land. The only thing keeping his eyes open was the coffee he'd drank and even still it was a struggle. The warmth of the sun on the cool air was making him sleeper. He stood and walked the perimeter of the trees. Nothing moved. He made his way back to his place and lay down.

He was just beginning to drift off when the front door opened. Raising himself on all fours, he started toward Jed. Jed's hair was a mess. He took a deep swig out of his bottle he was carrying as the door closed behind him.

Smacking his lips and appearing satisfied and relaxed, he opened his eyes to his surroundings. His eyes grew round and he yelped at the sight of the big black bear ambling his way and darted back into the house. Ray turned around and walked back into the woods a short distance before Jed could return with a gun. He needed to change into something smaller and less noticeable. In an instant, a small lizard had replaced the bear.

Scurrying to the nearest tree he climbed up around the ground debris and grass in time to see Jed walk back out looking wary, shot gun in hand. Ray the lizard grinned. Being a Sparker was rather fun.

**

The next morning Ray's side of the bed was cold and empty when Becky Sue reached out for him. The sun was already up and rising. She'd slept in later than she expected. After a quick check of the little cabin and no sign of him she figured he was watching Jed.

Pulling into her mom's a few minutes behind schedule, she hurried inside. "Morning Mom," she called out.

Kate didn't appear in the doorway. A sound from the back of the house sent her to the bedroom. Her mom was still in bed.

"Morning Mom," she repeated. "Late morning, or rough morning."

"Rough. I'm stuck in this bed and you're late."

"Sorry, I over slept." She went to the side of her mother's bed and started working with her to get her up.

"That's not surprising after your night." Becky Sue shot her a look. "Don't act like you don't know what you did. I know you're out sleeping with Ray again."

Becky Sue groaned and rolled her eyes.

"I don't know why you act like you're so surprised I know these things. I keep telling you, you can't plant the corn till you buy the farm." Her mom didn't seem to be struggling as hard as what she expected her to be. Moving her hadn't slowed down her tirade.

She pushed her wheelchair into the bathroom and began to set up everything for a shower while her mom droned on about never being able to get married after being a harlot. There was no use arguing. She couldn't explain her reasons. Ray's cover had to be believable. Apparently it was. Not that she was innocent by a long shot of the things her mother accused her of, but those were the chances she was willing to take. Besides if she ever got around to marrying it was highly unlikely it would be a local, therefore her reputation would be a moot point.

Kate pulled back the shower curtain, hair dripping, her lecture wound down, "well young lady what have you got to say for yourself?"

"Nothing."

Her mom gaped at her, taken aback at her nonchalance. After that brief interlude she started all over again on how she raised her daughter better, blah, ba-blah, blah.

Today she didn't linger. Tuning her mom out could only go so far.

Sherlock gave her a dirty look as she opened the front door, when she stopped by to check on everything at her house, and grabbed her lunch before heading to work. She left her pick up at home and walked, hoping it would help dissipate some of the crumminess she was feeling.

Was everything she was doing worth catching some drug traffickers? Maybe. Could she have done it without getting so intimate with Ray? Probably, but being with him had sparked her powers and given her new abilities she didn't know she possessed. But did she have to keep doing it? Most likely, for the simple fact that she couldn't turn him down. There was some strange, unexplainable pull to him that she couldn't ignore. If it was only the Spark power that connected them, she should cut her ties and be done. If it was more than that she needed to know sooner rather than later.

A couple hours working on her patriotic star quilt, and Becky Sue was only slightly less sulky than when she'd come into work. Normally the calming rhythm of stitching back and forth, in and out, would relax her mind. But not today.

Cindy had already been by with her usual dose of daily gossip, which, no surprise, was about Becky Sue herself and Ray. What was she thinking going out to the campground with him? We're they already engaged? Had they eloped? She'd mostly just let Cindy burn herself out asking questions before she left without any new juicy pieces of gossip, other than Becky Sue was being tight lipped.

The jangle of bells above the door startled her out of her melancholy trance. The hot guy with no name strode through the door. He was so at ease with the world. The fluid motion of his body made him seem more relaxed. Where Ray was like an army of marching ants, powerful and pushing forward without thought, the man with no name was like a smooth flowing river, gentle with an undercurrent of power.

"Afternoon, can I help you?" She set her quilt aside.

His face brightened when she appeared. "I just came by and talk to you."

"Oh, ok." She didn't feel flattered often, but this time she did. A stranger desired her company, without a seeming ulterior motive. Maybe.

"That book I picked up yesterday is really interesting. I'm already half finished with it."

"Good." She didn't mind talking books to this creature that was so easy on the eyes.

"You're a local, born and raised here, right?" She nodded. "Can you tell me any other stories, besides what's in the book? You know, little stories that only locals know. Everywhere I travel I try to find out about local legends, the wilder and more farfetched, the more it hooks me. It's my weakness." His smile was bright, touching his eyes, his teeth straight and white.

"Let me think for a minute," she said trying to get her mind off his broad shoulders and bronzed muscles.

"By the way my name is Phoenix." He held out his hand to shake. His hand engulfed hers and she didn't have the smallest, most feminine of hands. His grip was firm and strong. Blood rushed to all the wrong places at his touch and the hair on her arm stood up sending mixed signals through her body.

"Phoenix? As in the legendary bird?"

He gave her an impish grin. "Yeah. My mom is a little eccentric."

"It suits you though. Is that what prodded you into exploring legends?"

"You know I hadn't thought of it that way, but I guess you're right. It started with my name and I've been a legend hunter ever since."

"That's cool."

"What's your name?"

"Becky Sue."

"Nice to meet you, Becky Sue."

His warm brown gaze was distracting. He was mysterious and friendly, but at the same time he felt untouchable. She couldn't put a finger on why. Was is because of Ray? Nah. Was it because she felt separated from the general population now that she knew she was a Spark? He was watching her. What had they been talking about? Oh yeah, Sparker stories.

"Alright. You know about the Indian removal in the 1830's?" He nodded. History was kind of her thing and it made her heart do a little happy dance when she could talk history to someone who was familiar with the same things.

"The story goes that a band of Cherokee were coming through the area headed to Oklahoma from one of the eastern states. Back then these mountains were barely populated with more than deer, bear, snakes, well you get the picture. Anyway, this band of Cherokee got lost in the mountains and winter was coming in early that year. Their leader was ready to set up camp along the river in hopes of waiting it out and surviving on the good hunting when they came across a white family living here. It just so happened that this family was full blooded Spark. There were four girls and a boy. The boy was only a tot. If my memory serves me correctly, the oldest girl is the one who spotted the Cherokee first and went with her father out to meet them. The oldest girl offered to serve as a guide although she had never been out of the mountains before. She took the form of an eagle and led the little band of Cherokee over the fastest, easiest route to Oklahoma. When they arrived, one of the chiefs was so grateful that he proposed a marriage between her and his oldest son. She accepted the proposal and became part of the tribe. She was the first known Spark to intermingle with the Indians." Phoenix stared at her like he was waiting for more.

"I wish Uncle Melvin had put that story is his book. It would've sounded a lot better. He has a way of making the simplest story have so much life, color, and detail."

"I don't know. It sounded good to me." He was smiling at her again. "Do you know more stories?"

Her mind was racing with stories of the Sparkers she wanted to tell him, if he would just keep smiling at her she'd tell him stories all day. "Yeah, but you'd probably be here all day if I told them all to you."

"I wouldn't mind." He checked his watch. "But I have to go meet my friends soon. I know you said you were in a complicated relationship, but would you consider having dinner with me and tell me more stories."

Dinner? Had he just asked her on a sort of date? How could she ditch Ray for a couple hours? "The only place to eat here is Claire's diner." She was stalling as her mind raced, looking for a way to make it happen.

"We could go there if you like, but I was thinking something more casual. Like at my camp. I'll handle the food. "

Did he just offer to cook for her too? "That might be a nice change. Where are you camped?"

"It's not at any of the camp grounds. It's along the river. We'll have to take the canoe to get there."

Interesting. She'd be completely at his mercy. But who was she kidding? It wouldn't be bad. She might even be able to avoid the gossip if she could duck out unseen. "How long are you going to be here? I've already promised to help a friend tonight." If he was really interested he would wait. Ray also needed to be handled ahead of time.

"Was planning on hanging around a few days. How about tomorrow?"

"Tomorrow is good for me." Her shop was closed the day after that so everything should work out beautifully. They worked out the details for her to meet him at Elk Point Landing an hour after she closed shop.

If her mom ever caught wind of this she'd never hear the end of it. Kate would see it as seeing two men at the same time. Not as one a friend and one a potential mate. She'd crap her pants.

Chapter 11

Becky Sue pulled up next to Ray's truck at the cabin he'd rented. The windows were dark. She fished the extra key out of the cup holder and opened the door. The sound of small feet scampering, running through the dead leaves were the first thing she heard. She looked around trying to identify the source. Whatever it was was coming in fast.

A squirrel shot out of the woods at full speed from the corner of the cabin.

"Oh good, you're here. Open the door. We gotta hurry." It was Ray.

The fluffy tail twitched impatiently out of the corner of her eye as she fumbled the lock, opening the door. Ray the squirrel shot inside. By the time Becky Sue made it in the door and found the light switch, Ray was back to human form. His naked body disappeared inside the bedroom. She couldn't help but notice how his muscles moved when he walked.

A few seconds later she was still mentally drooling over his body when he reappeared completely dressed. "Let's go. Jed was about to close shop."

Another night of following the drunk pervert. How romantic. She mentally kicked herself. She wasn't here for romance. She was here to help catch a drug dealer. Besides she had a real date tomorrow night with a man that might actually enjoy her company.

Ray pulled out of the campground, just as a pair of taillights faded in the distance. The bait shop was dark and Jed's truck was gone. He sped up just enough to keep the taillights in view hoping it was Jed.

The route was the same as the night before.

"This is getting us nowhere," Becky Sue said watching the taillights turn off once more towards Jed's place.

"It will. It's all about timing." He sounded confident.

"Have you been watching him all day?"

"Yep. I left while you were still sleeping, came out here and have had him under surveillance all day. Not that he knew it. I've been perfecting my animal abilities."

"Oh brother."

He parked in the same spot as the night before. They exited the truck and he began to take off his clothes, tossing them back into the truck.

"What are you doing?" She whispered.

"Changing. What does it look like? I'm thinking wolf would be good for tonight's work."

"Sounds like a good way to get shot if he sees you too."

Ray stood in only his underwear as he turned to her. "He's not gonna see me. Trust me. That man's been drinking since he opened his eyes this morning. I can't believe he drove himself home."

She didn't respond. She was too busy looking at him in all his naked glory as he slid his underwear down and tossed them on top of the rest of his clothing. Maybe it was the animal instinct that now resided in her that made her want to take him right then and there at the truck.

He became a beautiful red wolf, built like a leader solid and strong, in front of her eyes. She stared not actually having watched the transformation before. It was mesmerizing and quick.

"Come on what are you waiting for?"

"Umm.." He padded around the front of the truck and sat at the front passenger wheel well looking up at her. Even his wolf eyes were blue and seemed to glow in the night. Before her mind could wonder too far, a cloud rolled across the moon, blotting out the light.

This was as good a time as any. She quickly stripped her clothes and made the transformation into a she wolf.

"Looking good, sexy." Ray panted near her ear.

"You know, I think wolves are one of the animals that kill their mate after they do it," she said as she trotted past him.

Without another word, Ray took the lead at a casual trot.

"This hill isn't so bad with four legs," Becky Sue commented half way up.

"I keep telling you this animal thing can be pretty handy."

"I'm sure it'll be very handy to have now with your job."

"Yeah I'm pretty pumped."

They stopped talking at the edge of the yard. Jed was already inside, lights were on. Creeping through the tall grass they checked the perimeter.

With heightened smell it was easy to detect Jed's unique scent. It was rank and almost gagged Becky Sue. An opossum had come through recently.

"Why are you panting and drooling all over me," Ray whispered.

"Huh? Oops. I smell the deer that came through earlier and I can practically taste them. I'm hungry."

"Way to bash a guy's ego. I thought it was because of me."

"Nice try." A different hunger was beginning to stir in her stomach even as she said the words. Ray's scent kept drifting her way. It was wild, untamed. It promised satisfaction and created need.

With an understanding that seemed natural, they split up and sniffed the yard, front, back, and side trying to determine anything unusual.

"Find anything?" Ray asked when they met up at the edge of the woods.

"A rabbit, deer, opossum, Jed and trash. Although Jed and the trash are about equally nasty. You?"

"About the same. There was one more scent that I kept catching that was distracting me." He edged closer to her. "I just figured out what it was too." He licked her face with his wolf tongue.

"I have a date tomorrow night," she blurted out, hoping to stop them for they started puppy humping in Jed's yard. It was a catastrophe waiting to happen.

"Oh really? With who?" His voice sounded surprised, maybe disbelieving.

"A tourist."

Silence covered them much the same as the cloud had covered the moon and kept it hidden. Ray abruptly declared it was time to go.

They trotted back to the truck. Ray took the dominant lead. When they reached the truck, he transformed back first and began to dress quickly.

"What's his name?"

She transformed back to human.

"Phoenix."

"That's a place not a name." Ray started the truck. Becky Sue kept to her side and didn't scoot to the middle like the night before. "What's he look like?"

"Not everything fits inside you're little bubble of how you think it should be." She retorted. "He's the guy you were talking to the other day about the Sparkers. In a way you sent him to me." His face crinkled in a grimace. Mistakenly, she'd thought he would be happy for her that she'd found someone interesting. That didn't seem to be the case. He was acting a little jealous and it made her uncomfortable. For the first time that she could remember in their friendship, she felt there was something to hide from Ray.

"You're kidding."

"Uh, no. Why would I be kidding?"

Ray shook his head.

"What? You didn't like him? You gonna play big brother now and tell me not to see him." He opened his mouth but before he could say a word she continued. "You've been out of my life for years. You can't just show up and start telling me who I should and shouldn't see. I'm grown up. I can handle myself."

"I've noticed." His face was a mask. His words stated flatly. She wasn't sure how to respond to that.

"Don't worry. I'll still play this little game with you and help you catch these criminals, but when you're gone again, I want the chance to have a real life with real relationships."

He remained silent as they pulled back into the campground.

Often times the silence between them was comforting and easy, but not tonight. Tonight it was charged with nervous energy, uneasy, tormenting silence.

She grabbed an extra blanket and pillow and curled up on the couch.

"What are you doing in here?" Ray walked into the living room and crossed his arms as he looked down at her.

"Sleeping. What does it look like?" She closed her eyes to punctuate her point.

"Come get in the bed. I promise no funny business."

She cracked an eye. Was that a smart move? No. Did it sound a hell of a lot more comfortable than this couch? Yes. While the cushions looked fluffy and soft her hip was sitting on a wooden support piece.

"Promise?"

"Promise."

She sat up and sighed. This was a bad idea, especially if she wanted to pull away from Ray, but she was tired and a comfortable bed was a weakness.

Grabbing her pillow and blanket, Ray followed her to bed and crawled in beside her. She rolled over, back facing him. Undeterred he draped his thick arm across her side, his solid, chiseled chest to her back, his breath in her ear. If she was going to have relationships with other men, this shouldn't feel so right, but it did. Don't jump the gun. So far Phoenix only wants you to tell him stories. She hoped he wanted more than that because she needed someone to pull her away from Ray. He was too comfortable. He was too everything and all it would lead to was heartache. She wasn't willing to risk the hurt. She'd watched her mom self destruct after her dad ran away and it had left a bitter taste in her mouth.

**

She was being cold towards him and he felt it. He couldn't blame her really, but that didn't mean he liked it either. He'd made her no promises. They were just friends helping each other out, in work and play. That was it. But even as he thought it, he knew it was a lie. There'd always been something special between them and it had only evidenced itself more when he'd come back again. It was like they'd never had interrupted years of no communication.

He shook his head trying to rid himself of thoughts of her as he flew over the treetops. Even the cool air beneath his wings as he floated couldn't keep his mind straight, but he had to pay attention or else he'd pass up Jed's house. Being a bird had its advantages, but it definitely brought a different perspective to the land from the air. He tried to focus on the feeling of the weightlessness his expanded wings gave him and enjoy it.

Jed's house came into view. Ray circled around and landed on Jed's truck. This morning he'd decided to leave his truck at the cabin and go in shifted form to keep the risk of exposure down. He was pretty sure he had a good handle on this animal thing, at least enough to not get caught with his pants down in public. Granted the whole bird thing had taken him a minute to figure it all out with flying and all, but after taking a deep breath and tapping into the instincts of the bird it was fine.

He didn't expect to see any movement this early, but he flew around to the windows to check. Nothing. He floated over to the tree line to watch from the branch of an oak. It was a good thing heights didn't make him skittish so much anymore like when he was a kid.

He'd slept an extra hour before starting today, hoping to be able to stay more awake and alert today, but it had been troubled especially knowing that she might leave if he so much as touched her wrong. It was nothing short of self torture keeping her close. He prided himself at self control, mostly after noticing how well he did after starting this job, but Becky Sue was like nothing he'd encountered before. An anomaly. Now she wanted to go with that Phoenix character and nothing about that sat right with him.

His mind roiled as he sat thinking on the branch watching the dark empty house. Dawn couldn't come soon enough.

**

The next morning Becky Sue woke to a cold bed. Ray was already gone again. She must've been sleeping harder than she thought to not have noticed when he left. Maybe it was because she'd lain there half the night talking herself down. Sleeping next to Ray so intimately was torture. She fought with herself not to touch him, not to give in to his touch, his lips. It was exhausting. She was exhausted.

The energy it would take to deal with her mother this morning felt more than she could bear. Wasn't there anyone else she could call to go in her place? She had no explanations, reasonable or otherwise. All she could do was hope that Kate wouldn't find out about Phoenix until Ray was long gone.

Lights were off inside her mother's house again. She frowned. That wasn't a good sign. Was her mom deteriorating and she hadn't noticed?

"Mom? Good morning." She went straight to the bedroom where Kate lay in the bed. "Mom is anything wrong? Do I need to take you to the doctor? This is the second day you haven't been able to get up without help."

"I'll tell you what's wrong. My daughter. Do you know what she does? She goes gallivanting around with a divorcee like it's the most natural thing in the world. He waltzes into town and my daughter jumps straight into his bed. Do you know what that makes me look like? A bad mother that's what."

Becky Sue exhaled loudly. "Nobody thinks you're a bad mom." Kate huffed. "So can you, or can't you get out of bed by yourself? Are you trying to punish me, because I'm not a kid anymore." Exasperation filled her voice. She could only fight so many people at a time and she was at her quota.

"Of all the ungrateful, self centered, selfish people in the world, I didn't think you were one of them." Her mom began throwing the blankets off her as she shuffled around in the bed trying to position herself to get out alone.

"You know as well as I do that if I keep helping you you'll lose strength. You've got to be able to do it yourself or you won't be able to keep living alone." She ignored the tirade. For once in her life, she wanted to be selfish. She wanted to run away from this town and do something for herself without having to worry about anything or anybody else. No helping good friends, no helping her mother, just doing things she enjoyed, alone.

Still grumbling about ungrateful children, her mom got up and wheeled into the bathroom for her shower.

Becky Sue checked the fridge. She needed to get to a store soon, or cook some food, but time was suddenly an issue. Maybe she could drop a hint to Cindy or Mary Beth to bring a casserole by.

She swept and spot mopped the kitchen before flopping back on the couch to wait. Her eyes were heavy. She laid her head back and closed her eyes picturing herself on a warm sunny beach with lots of sand and hot, tanned men in tight, short swim trunks next to the water. The waves gently rolling in and out, splashing the men, making their bodies wet and glisten in the sun. She could feel one of them staring at her, devouring her with his eyes. He had the body of Adonis, but she couldn't see his face. The sun was too bright. But there he was, warm full lips on hers. He was inviting and felt familiar in her heart. She blinked. It was Ray.

"Becky Sue?" Her mom's voice broke into her dream. She startled.

"What?"

"Were you asleep?"

"I didn't think so, but maybe." She couldn't even get away from Ray in her dreams. It was definitely time to get out.

"I've never known you to fall asleep sitting up like that. You're not getting your sleep at night. See that's what I've been trying to tell you. You need to leave that man alone. He's bad for you."

"Yes, Mom. There's food in the fridge. I'll try to make sure to get something over here for tomorrow." Just agree and keep walking, right out the door to the truck.

As she unlocked the door to her shop, she wondered if everyone was going to turn on her today. Mom, Ray, Sherlock. Her cat had tried to bite her toes letting her know his displeasure at her being gone so much before trying to bolt out the door when she left. All she wanted was a real, sort of, date. If Phoenix stood her up today she was going to say to hell with it, go home, forget Ray, forget Phoenix, and be content to stay in her house alone with Sherlock and not even try to interact like a normal human.

The hours ticked by slowly, leaving plenty of time to sew, think, and over think. A few customers had dribbled in and out. Nothing exciting. By closing time, she had one hoop to go before binding the edge of the patriotic star quilt. She'd be able to finish it Monday easily, unless Spring Breakers overly flooded the area and kept her busy. But that would be alright too. Any kind of sales meant money in the pocket.

**

Ray sat outside Jed's bait shop occasionally shifting positions to be less noticeable, but it was unnecessary. Jed had yet to start nipping at his bottle, which was a bit unusual considering what he'd seen so far. He'd been at the shop for a couple of hours already. He felt in his bones that something would happen today, he just couldn't point to what.

Deciding he'd been hanging out as a bird too long, he changed into a squirrel when no one was there. He's just scampered around the tree made himself comfortable when Phoenix came into the bait shop.

Just the thought of that character hitting on Becky Sue raised his blood pressure. He didn't feel outmatched, or jealous, it was more a protective instinct. The man gave him an ill feel in his gut and he didn't like it. Years ago he'd have said gut feelings were a fake, but he'd learned in his current line of work to trust his gut. Rarely had it steered him wrong.

Ray watched as Phoenix approached the counter. He leaned in from the tree branch trying to listen, but the window wasn't spilling any of its secrets. Just then, Phoenix cocked his head toward him. His dark eyes seemed to bore right through, like he could see his humanness through the body of the squirrel. Ray twitched his tail and scampered up the branch toward the tree before turning back again.

There was something off about this guy and he didn't like it. He didn't like it all. Sure he looked all touristy and causal in his cargo pants and fishing style vest over his shirt, but he didn't read right. Where was he camped? He'd checked the register and grounds here earlier. No sign of him. He was like a walking shadow.

He waited, watching carefully from his perch. On his way out the door, Phoenix turned one more time and stared straight at him. Ray froze, unsure what he should do. Phoenix turned and left. Ray sagged across the branch. He needed to pull records on Phoenix as soon as possible, but the earliest chance he'd have would be tomorrow because somewhere in the last few minutes he'd decided that there was no way in hell he was letting Becky Sue go out alone with this guy unaccompanied.

**

Nervousness wasn't something she was accustomed to feeling, but at first glimpse turning into Elk Point Landing, her stomach turned queasy. Daylight savings time going into effect last week didn't help either. The sun always set earlier this side of the mountain, and darkness wasn't particularly her friend.

Only three vehicles were parked in the area. No one was in sight. Not even Phoenix.

This was a bad idea. She glanced in the rearview mirror. Should she just leave now? What did she really know about this guy other than he was handsome and charming? He could be another Ted Bundy for all she knew. Maybe she shouldn't have been so willing to come out here. Maybe she should've risked dining at Claire's.

This was all Ray's fault. If she wasn't his dumb cover then she wouldn't have to be skulking out here in the woods with some guy she barely knew his name. She reached for the gear shift to put her truck in reverse only to look out the window and see Phoenix in the yellow glow of the single bulb hanging outside of the small rust colored brick bathroom. She left the truck in park and reached for the backpack she'd packed for the trip. Extra change of clothes in a plastic bag in case they tipped. Flashlight, mini first aid kit, couple bottles of water, another jacket, a knife with a 10" blade, and an extra pair of shoes also in a plastic bag completed her emergency kit.

Phoenix saw her exit the truck and waved to her. She locked it and put the keys into her backpack.

"Hi, are you ready for a little trip?"

"Sure." She smiled up at him.

"Here let me take your bag." He shouldered her backpack and led her to the water's edge where his canoe was pulled up on the bank. "Why don't you hop in the front. I'll steer from the back."

"Will you be able to catch your stop in the dark?" Doubt crept into her voice as she noticed the lack of light. A light stirring of leaves nearby from a small animal pulled her attention momentarily away. A squirrel ducked behind a tree. Crazy rodent.

"Having second thoughts?"

"Not about this, but since you're not from around here, it was just a thought." She shrugged turning back to the conversation.

"I hung a lantern out at the edge of the water." At least he wasn't dumb.

He took her hand and helped her into the canoe. His touch was cool but sensuous. The tips of his fingers caressed her wrist, warming her blood. Tossing in her backpack, he pushed the canoe out into the water, jumping in at the last second. The squirrel made a mad dash for the canoe and jumped in right before Phoenix.

"What the ...?" Phoenix said noticing the squirrel. He grabbed for it. The animal dodged him. Becky Sue tried to keep them straight as he kept after the squirrel. She couldn't see what he was doing behind her, but felt the light rocking motions from him moving. She hoped it wasn't a rabid squirrel. If it bit him it could be bad. Finally a light splashing sound followed by a gasp and the canoe settled out.

Night sounds filled the cool night air as the moon played peek-a-boo behind some passing clouds. Rain was coming in the forecast, but not tonight. She felt like she was in an old movie where the boy and girl were floating along in some kind of boat while the music played a song about falling in love.

"Have you thought of more stories to tell me?" The movie illusion shattered. No one was falling in love. She was a fixture of the local population. A storyteller brought here to entertain.

"Yeah. Have you finished the book already?"

"Yep." If he was nothing else he was dogmatic.

"Did you like it?" The soft sounds of their paddles dipping into the water was soothing.

"I did. I had a question though. In the beginning it mentioned something about the Quell, but nothing else was said about them. Why?"

"I'm not really sure. I think the only power they were supposed to have had was taking away the power of the Sparkers, but other than that they didn't really pose a large threat, at least not as big as banishment. The Sparks power wasn't any good after the mayor's law went into effect anyway, so the Quell died out faster than the Sparkers did I guess."

"Makes sense. I guess both became practically useless. Have you ever done any genealogy research to see if you're related to a Sparker?"

"No. But then again I guess I never really thought the legends had any truth to them."

"It would be cool if they were true, wouldn't it?"

She shrugged, smiling into the dark, her secret safe. "I suppose it would be."

A light appeared to the left. "Is that your camp ahead?"

"Yes it is."

At the thought of a warm campfire, her stomach decided to remind her she was hungry.

"What are you fixing for dinner?"

"Squirrel stew. I hope you like it."

Chapter 12

A shudder ran down Becky Sue's back as an image of Ray running up to the cabin last night in squirrel form flashed through her mind. She was starting to see boogey men everywhere. Phoenix couldn't know that she and Ray could shape shift, let alone know he'd been a squirrel recently.

Phoenix pulled the canoe out of the water behind a stand of river bushes. It wouldn't have seemed like he was hiding it had the dark foreboding followed her as she stepped from the canoe on shore. Chastising herself for reading too much into a perfectly nice guy she straightened her shoulders and pushed the disturbing thoughts from her head. Still, she gripped her backpack tighter knowing the knife she carried was near the top in case anything happened.

He took the lantern off the branch where it hung and led her along the bank. The ground sloped upwards. Within a few feet they were on rock, making their way upward on a narrow path. The rock opened in a low, wide crevice. Phoenix ducked inside. Becky Sue followed under the low hanging, before standing up in a small cave. It was maybe twenty feet in diameters. A curtain hung in the back, she assumed for his sleeping area. He set his lantern on a small outcrop of rock.

"You're not afraid of being out here in the woods with me alone are you?" He asked as he turned toward her. She hadn't let her death grip on her backpack loosen.

"No. I'm perfectly capable of handling myself. I grew up in the woods of these mountains. Nothing much scares me." She might've thought he was camping with friends and not alone, but that was okay. One less person to run their mouth to a local and start another gossip chain about her.

"Good." He turned toward the cold fire. "Would you mind helping me gather some firewood? I'm sorry I don't have any gathered. I was going to do it earlier, but got distracted. I only have enough to start a small fire."

"Sure." She set her pack against a rock wall, dug out her flashlight and slipped her sheathed knife into the waistband of her pants.

When she returned with a small armload of firewood a small fire was burning easily in the makeshift fire pit.

"That was fast."

"Yeah. I have a confession. I like to play with fire."

"Seems you have a knack for it." Although knack wasn't the word she wanted to use. It was like a magic trick. She'd never seen anyone start a fire that fast and have it going so good. Off in a shadowy corner sat a neat stack of firewood. She ignored the chill in the air. Maybe his friends had collected some and he didn't know it.

"It's my job to know fire."

"Oh?"

"I'm a firefighter at home." That explained a lot.

He began building the fire with small branches she'd brought and others lying nearby. He produced a metal grate, setting it over the fire. Out of his ice chest he pulled little baggies of precut vegetables and a jar of meat that he dumped in a pot of water. The meat was the right color and consistency to be squirrel.

Becky Sue settled into a fold out chair content to watch Phoenix cook.

A cricket crawled up her leg. She flicked it off. Was that muttered cursing?

"Everything alright? Need any help?"

"I'm good. Just waiting for it to boil before I put the lid on it." He grinned back at her. Why did she think he was muttering under his breath?

Another cricket, or maybe the same one, crawled back up her leg. What the heck? Was this place infested with crickets? She was about to flick it off again when the fire flickered and a glint of blue flashed from the cricket. Getting the cricket in her hand, she held it up to look at it better in the poor light. Blue eyes flashed at her.

"Ray?" She whispered, hoping Phoenix wouldn't hear. The cricket winked. She glared at it. "I'm going to kill you. So help me." She was furious. Ray was spying on her. He was in her hand, she reared back to throw him not caring if he got hurt, when Phoenix turned to her.

She made like she was stretching, yawned, dropped Ray to the ground, and debated stomping on him.

"Tired already?" Phoenix asked.

"No. Just feeling lazy."

"Too lazy to tell me stories?" He pulled another fold out chair next to her and sat.

"Nah. I can tell stories in my sleep."

"Good. I want to hear some stories."

"Alright. Have you heard about how the Sparks helped the South in the Civil War?" He shook his head no. The whites of his eyes gleamed bright against his dark pupils and face. He was dark and mysterious. She wanted to know more about him. Was he married? Did he have a girlfriend back home? Was he interested in more than just her stories?

"As you probably know Arkansas was highly divided in loyalties to both sides of the war. However, most of the Sparkers sided with the South. They felt their land was being invaded. So just like many young men of the day, they signed up and went off to war. You won't find their stories in any of the history books because many times once their commanders found out their special powers they were sent in as spies. No records exist. How many battles can you think of where

174

the North should've won because of sheer numbers and force, yet the Confederates routed them?"

"A few."

"Why do you think that happened? The Sparkers. There were quite a few in the day. When a commander would find out there was more than one Spark in his command, oftentimes he would split them up and send some to companies and commanders around the state, or send them to the hotter spots of the war. The Battle of the Wilderness, it's rumored that Longstreet had a Sparker in his command there. Legend has it that the Spark shifted to an Eagle and rained fire balls down on Hancock, adding to the smoke and chaos. Unfortunately, it backfired when Longstreet was wounded by one of his own men."

"That sucks." Phoenix was leaned over toward her in his chair, hanging on every word.

"Yeah. Not all the stories have happy endings. Sometimes the magic backfired. Sometimes a Sparker would lose it and go out of control, burning things or fighting in certain animal forms until it was killed."

"Do you know any stories about the Quell?"

She sat back in her chair to think. Their arms touched. There was no shooting sparks or rushing of heat transferring bodies like there had been with Ray. There was only a giddy school girl sense about it, like sneaking out of the house at night. Looking down she noticed a cricket on her shoe. Ray. Kicking him off would attract attention. She had to pretend he wasn't there.

"I think there's only one story about the Quell that I can think of and it dates back to the Civil War too."

"Tell me." He was like an eager child ready to devour anything he was told.

"Like I was saying, Arkansas was highly divided. Now most the mountain folks knew the Sparkers were sided with the South, but the Quell had sided with the North. There's a story, that I think has almost been forgotten for lack of retelling, that another spy, a Quell, worked for the North. She was a beautiful woman, with deep brown eyes, a perfect figure and thick, dark hair. She lost her husband early in the war. One of the first casualties. Soon after, she disappeared. The next anyone heard of her one of the boys back on leave said he'd seen her when they were near a Union camp. After the war, some of the remaining Sparkers had lost their powers. They blamed it on the hardships of war, but some secretly believed it was because this beautiful Quell had come and taken their powers from them. They just wouldn't admit it to their families."

"What happened to the woman?"

"She never returned."

"You're a really good story teller." Phoenix's hand covered hers. Maybe he really was interested in more than just her stories. His brown eyes gazed into her soul. She caught her breath, hoping he wouldn't see to the magic she held deep inside. While she wanted to touch him and let him hold her and whisper sweet nothings in her ear, she didn't want it be known that she was a Spark. A legend in her own rite.

Cricket.

Ray the cricket was climbing up her leg again. She feigned nonchalance and pretended not to see him, choosing instead to stare into the flame of the fire. The smell of the stew wafted to her, tantalizing her senses.

Cricket.

She was going to kill him. Would it be bad form to throw him on the ground and stomp him right then and there? Would it hurt her powers or bring bad juju to her?

"You know what else interests me?" Phoenix asked stroking her hand with his thumb. She turned to him. "You."

Cricket.

"Me?" Opening her mouth to ask why, she thought better of it, and snapped it shut.

"I don't get it. How's a girl like you still unmarried?"

Cricket.

She should be getting lost in those dark brown soulful eyes, but instead she was distracted knowing Ray was in her lap staring her down. "I'm going with the shortage of men around here."

Cricket. Cricket. Cricket.

Now Ray was laughing at her.

Phoenix smiled. "That explains it partially, but what about the tourists that comes through? Don't you ever meet any of them?"

"Every once in a while I'll meet an interesting one. But they always return home. No one wants to stay and right now I'm stuck here. My mom is disabled and I'm the only one to care for her."

"Couldn't you take her with you?"

Becky Sue thought of all the reasons that wouldn't work. It would be a short in coming catastrophe. And putting her mom in a home was out of the question.

Cricket.

"No. It's complicated." Refusing to look down at Ray, she kept her focus on Phoenix. She should be leaning into him letting him kiss her by now, but she couldn't. Not with Ray watching. Instead she found herself acting aloof and only passively interested.

"For living in such a small town in the middle of nowhere, you sure seem to have a complicated life. I thought it was supposed to be simple out here?"

"You have no idea."

Cricket. Cricket.

Reaching her free hand down, she tried to cover Ray so he couldn't watch her. He jumped out of reach. Phoenix felt her shifting.

"Are you getting cold?"

"No, just hungry." Her stomach rumbled in affirmation.

He grinned. "Let me see what I can do."

Phoenix poked in the pot at the stew. Becky Sue looked for Ray as soon as Phoenix's back was turned, but Ray was nowhere to be seen. Shit. She knew he was somewhere nearby. She could feel him.

"I don't like this guy. There's something off about him." Ray's voice was whispered in her ear. Glancing to her right, there he was, perched on her shoulder.

She rolled her eyes and shook her head, afraid of getting caught whispering back.

"I'm going to look around. I have no doubt you'll keep him busy while I do." His voice held a slight bite. Was he jealous?

**

Ray jumped out of reach before Becky Sue could stop him. He couldn't believe she was being so dense. Bounding down to the cold rock floor of the cave, he made it to the mysterious sheets hanging against the wall. Who camped in a cave anyway? How did an outsider know of its existence? That was the question that really bothered him. The cave wasn't something most tourists would notice. It was tucked up a good twenty feet or so from the water, the opening small and partially hidden by small trees and brush growing out of the rocks. He either had an inside person who knew the area well, or he'd made more than one trip through this town, mostly likely several.

On little cricket feet, he wiggled under the curtain. At first glance it looked ordinary enough. What was with all the secrecy? He needed a higher vantage point. The only problem with being a cricket was he was too small. The view of the world from a half an inch, at best, was skewed. He tried to hop onto a canvas bag lying nearby. He was too little, not enough bounce.

He spied a cast off rock. That he could manage, but it still didn't bring him high enough to get the full picture. Frustrated as he was, he was unwilling to give up. He was tempted to shift into something larger, but he couldn't risk it. Phoenix knew. He didn't know how he knew, but he knew. Phoenix nailed him as a squirrel. He wouldn't be surprised if Phoenix didn't know he was here now. They were in a dance of playing knowing-not knowing. It was... eerie to say the least after just finding out about his powers himself a few days ago.

Ray bounced and climbed around slowly making his way upward to a good view. Who knew he could use zippers and strings as leverage? Being able to shape shift gave him slight illusions of invincibility. He might've caved into the notion had he not seen too much.

**

Where did he go? She thought she wanted him gone, but not being able to see him was more distracting than having him there under foot.

"It's almost done. If we let it simmer a few more minutes it should be good." Phoenix resumed his seat beside her. "So tell me. What's this with you and Ray?"

Hearing his name come out of Phoenix's mouth sent a shiver through her that had nothing to do with the damp air despite the fire's valiant attempt to warm the inside of the cave. It was just a prick of conscience knowing that Ray was here, listening somewhere. Becky Sue waved the question off. "We've been friends since forever. We grew up as close as siblings, maybe closer. Once upon a time we almost became romantically involved, but nothing ever came of it." It was possible she was trying to convince herself of this more than him. "Now that he's back the whole town thinks we should get involved."

"What do you think you should do?" The way his dark eyes pierced her soul the more she wasn't sure what to say, so she went with what she wanted to believe.

**

Ray reached a peak of decent surveillance. He took in the camping gear. It seemed a little excessive, especially since a tent was unnecessary. The sheer number of random canvas sacks, baskets and other similar things were out of place. Maybe he'd sent his friends out for the night and there were more actually camped here.

No. There was only one sleeping bag laid out and no space for others.

He'd kept his ears tuned to Becky Sue's conversation and when he heard Phoenix pin her with the question about them, he paused, no longer seeing what was around him.

"It's not happening. He'll find a job soon enough and be gone again. I have to stay here and take care of my mom." At least she remembered to keep his cover.

Was that really how she felt or was she just trying to impress this douche?

"And long distance relationships or moving isn't in the picture then, huh?" Phoenix asked her.

"Nope."

Ray jumped from his perch, landing hard on the rocky ground. He was pissed as hell. How could she not think that they had something special between them? Her body had hummed for him and his for hers for fucks sake! What did she think this was? Some kind of throw away fling?

He'd always been the one to walk away from any relationship. He didn't like being on this end, especially with Becky Sue. Apparently their years of friendship meant nothing either.

He stormed from the cave on his six tiny legs not waiting around to hear any more. As soon as he was around the corner out of sight he shifted into a bird and flew out.

**

"That doesn't sound as complicated as you made it sound earlier."

It was true. Earlier she hadn't figured out what she wanted, or rather needed to do. But this was it. She had to give Ray one final push and put some distance back between them. Where was he anyway?

"I guess I should've said this town makes it complicated. We may not have a large population but it's full of nothing but matchmakers and folks stuck in a civilization that existed a hundred years ago where the only real happiness for a woman is marriage and babies."

"I take it you don't buy into all that?"

"At one time I figured I'd get married and have kids. Now that I'm pushing thirty I'm not sure that's still on the table, but I'm in no rush to rectify a change either."

Phoenix let out a deep hearty laugh. "You think thirty is official old maid status? Spinster even?"

"Around here it might as well be certifiable." She shrugged. She knew she was naïve in the ways of the real world, but she hardly considered it laughable. It rankled a little, no matter how much his teeth shown white or his brown eyes smiled at her.

He patted her leg. "Outside of these mountains the average age for marriage is early thirties. So you still have hope for a few years." His tone was bordering condescension.

Where was Ray? Was he hearing all this? It made her uneasy thinking about the fact that Ray was probably listening to every word. Even though she trusted him and he probably knew her better than anyone else, there were just some things she'd just as soon not bring to the table, especially now. At least he wouldn't laugh at her backward views like Phoenix. It wasn't like she hadn't been out of the mountains before. She'd seen a little bit of life in the "outside" world, but this was the world she'd made and chose to live in, so she set herself mostly to those standards.

Suddenly she had no desire to hang around any longer than she had to. After they ate, she was going to ask Phoenix to take her back.

"Is the food ready yet? I'm starving." Although she wasn't sure she could stomach squirrel stew, she desperately needed a change of conversation. And food.

"It should be." He checked the stew before producing two paper bowls.

They ate in relative silence. Becky Sue was in no hurry to resume the conversation and was half afraid to start any, not knowing where it would go. Phoenix was perceptive and strange. He was also hot which made awkward conversations that much worse.

"That was good." Becky Sue lied after she'd chewed her last bite and tossed her bowl into the fire. The stew had turned her stomach queasy and the taste had been as vile as death.

"Glad you liked it. Not everyone likes squirrel." His dark eyes flashed something dark and menacing lurked just under the surface. She attributed his counter appeal to her roiling stomach.

"Well, I'm a girl of the mountains, and what you kill you eat and you don't eat if you don't kill. It can be vicious cycle." She was half joking. The days of hunting/harvesting food for self consumption was past with the invention of supermarkets and commercial farms, but folks of the mountains still had a tendency to hold to old standards of living. "However, I hate to ask you, but would it be possible for you to take me back now? I have to be up early to take care of my mom."

"Do you have to go so soon? I thought we're getting along so well?" Phoenix leaned towards her, reached out a hand and brushed a stray strand of hair from her face. Chills raced down her spine. Cold chills. His brown eyes pinned her. Her heart should be all aflutter and giddy at the look in his eye and the tip of his head. He was going to kiss her. But it wasn't.

She watched in an out of body experience kind of way as his lips met hers but as soon as they did she was back to herself, all the air from her lungs evaporated. She pulled away and gasped for air. She would've liked to think that he took her breath away like that, but that wasn't it. It felt... wrong. Like the claw of death had reached into her lungs and pulled the air out.

"Are you alright? Is anything wrong?" He asked.

"You took my breath away." She didn't want to elaborate that it was in a bad way. He smiled a lazy, cocky smile. "Oh really? Do tell me more." He reached his hand around her head and pulled her back to him for another kiss. Any woman in her right mind would be crazy to resist a man like Phoenix.

As soon as their lips met again, the air in her lungs evaporated. Holy hell she couldn't breathe. She couldn't do this. She pulled back. Phoenix gave her a lopsided grin. Damn.

Why was it all of a sudden the men she kissed were giving her such wild, strong reactions? Ray with his humming and sparks. Now this. What was going on!

"If you insist, I suppose it wouldn't hurt to take you back now," he conceded sounding resigned. It must've been apparent that she wasn't putting out tonight so he was giving up trying, for now. It wasn't like she'd never had a fling before. Hell, that's practically all she'd ever had, but there was something she just couldn't name that had her waiting at the mouth of the cave for Phoenix to catch up.

This time Phoenix brought the battery operated lantern along, and tied it on the prow of the canoe for a light.

They floated down river, the lantern casting strange shadows on each side. Someone with a good imagination could easily envision demons, dragons, and all sorts of scary creatures from the bobbing light. They talked little as anything either said would be thrown into the air and whipped away by the current. Becky Sue counted it as a relief that she didn't have to try. Her thoughts were too preoccupied with Ray. He hadn't shown in some time. Now since she left early it should give him time to search Phoenix's cave.

River Hollow Landing gaped open and black like a bottomless abyss. No lights shown near the water. The nearest light was a single dim bulb hanging outside a block building Becky Sue knew was the bathroom a couple hundred yards from the river. It was a smaller campground, mostly for the canoe enthusiasts. The options for camp included twenty tent sites and five RV hookups, no cabins or other lodging.

As soon as they landed, Phoenix jumped out and pulled the canoe out of the water. Becky Sue waited as he waded into the darkness. A pair of headlights flicked on and drove up. She helped him load the canoe into the bed of the red Chevy Z-71. The color didn't escape her notice. She smirked as she remembered he was a firefighter and he drove a red truck. Wee ooo, wee ooo.

"Thanks again for dinner. It's been a pleasant evening." Becky Sue said as he tied the canoe down with a ratchet strap. Okay, so it'd been a little awkward and she might've been feeling a little guilty knowing Ray was probably ransacking his camp looking for any reason whatsoever for her not to see him again, but she'd been raised on southern hospitality and charm. She smiled.

"This isn't goodbye already is it?"

"Just for tonight. You know where to find me."

"Are you sure I can't give you a lift?"

"I'm sure. I'll be fine." She knew she was being vague, but she needed away as soon as possible.

"Thanks for coming. It was nice of you to share your stories. I'll definitely be coming by soon." He'd stepped into her personal space again. The thought of his body naked was enough to turn her blood warm.

"I almost forgot to ask, how long are you camping?"

"I haven't decided. I have a week's vacation from work so I still have a few days." He propped his elbow on the truck bed and casually took her in. "Don't worry.

I don't come from *that* far away. I'd still be back even if vacation was over just to see you."

He rose up off his elbow and leaned down, placing a short peck on her lips that were frozen in place. As soon as his lips touched hers, ice sluiced through her veins.

She stepped away and smiled wanly at Phoenix then disappeared into the darkness.

Chapter 13

From the shadows she watched as Phoenix's taillights disappeared. She waited for a few more minutes to make sure everything was quiet. No stray campers were up taking a pee break. No late night liaisons taking place.

At the edge of the campground she tucked her backpack away behind a bush and after another tentative look around, half expecting Ray to pop up out of the night, stripped her clothes and tucked them into her pack, shivering in the cool night air. An instant later she was a wolf.

Ashburn campground was only another two and half miles downriver. By road it was longer.

She'd picked the wolf figuring it had better chances with night vision and predators, and because four feet were better than two, right? Starting off at a trot she still felt winded from Phoenix's kiss. Her lungs were depleted and empty. Stopping near the river a little ways from River Hollow, she sat and inhaled a deep breath, willing the wolf's tenacity into her own. She let out a long, sorrowful howl. It felt good to cleanse her lungs.

Again, she took off at a trot, feeling better this time. A few answering yips from dogs, or possibly other wolves further up the mountain, responded to her howl. Her fangs gleamed white when she smiled. It was good to feel like the predator, not the prey. It was easier to think when you weren't the hunted.

Ray still hadn't shown himself yet and she was growing concerned. Had he gotten stepped on in his cricket form? Had he changed into something else and been killed somehow? Was it possible he'd left before she had and was already back? Nah, he was probably back at the cave searching. There were no other viable answers to his absence.

Covering the 2.5 mile trek had been a walk in the park, despite the terrain. No wonder people always used wolves in their shape shifting novels. Being a wolf was spectacular.

A light shown in the cabin window where she'd been staying with Ray. Was he there or had someone come in uninvited? She approached on quiet wolf feet. The windows were too high for her to see in. Drat. She checked the front door. It didn't look broken into.

It was late. No one else had a light on. Should she risk being caught naked outside the door in order to make sure it was Ray inside and not someone uninvited? Maybe she hadn't thought this whole thing through before leaving River Hollow. She circled the perimeter. It was quiet.

Here goes nothing. She changed back into human. The cool night instantly made her shiver. She reached for the door knob, but it was locked. That's when she remembered leaving her key in her backpack. Damn it, Ray. She didn't want to knock and wake anyone before she could get inside, but she was freezing.

She knocked and instantly began scanning the area, arms crossed against her chest, for any sign that someone might've heard her.

The door swung open. Ray blocked her entrance. "What're you doing here?" His whole countenance was standoffish.

"Can we talk about this inside?" Becky Sue pointed a shivering finger past him.

**

Ray stood in the doorway blocking her path, pissed, but a little surprised she'd had the nerve to come back at all. And what was she doing naked? Had she shifted for some reason? He felt his guard toward her lower a fraction.

He stepped out of the way and allowed her entry. As soon as the door was shut he asked again, "so what're you doing here?"

"Uh, the same thing we've been doing. Creating and keeping your cover." There was a bite to her words.

"That didn't seem to be too important to you not long ago when you went on your date with Phoenix," he shot back.

"Look, you were there. You know I didn't blow your stupid cover. Why should I put my life on hold just so you can do your damn job?" Her voice barely seemed contained from exploding. "And how did you beat me back here?"

"I left early. I didn't care to hear any more of your drivel to lover boy." It was hard to argue with a naked woman in front of him. Her hands had dropped from her chest and started gesturing instead as her temper rose. Her breast danced as she moved.

"What are you talking about?"

"I heard you plain and clear."

She let out a frustrated sigh. "What did you hear? Please tell me because I don't know what the hell's got you all fired up."

If he admitted to her that he didn't want her with Phoenix and he wanted her to himself, he'd be admitting to weakness. He was not weak, even for this beautiful, naked, pissed off creature in front of him. Weakness got you killed. But he could keep her away from someone he felt was dangerous even if he couldn't pinpoint the reason. He just had to make sure he didn't fall for her for real.

She gave an involuntary shiver. He closed the distance between them without thinking, took her into his arms and kissed her hard on the lips. Her body went rigid for a second before she relaxed, her arms coming around his body and kissed him back. Her breast pushed into his chest. He wanted to cup them in his hands, feel the fullness and weight of each one. He wanted to reach down and feel if she was wet. Every time he touched her he felt the fire. It was driving him crazy. He shouldn't be so hung up on anyone let alone Becky Sue Hocking. He pulled back before he carted her off to bed. He'd found what he wanted to know. She couldn't resist him and he couldn't decide if that made him happy or scared the hell out of him.

"Go get dressed. I can't talk to you like this."

She stormed from the room with renewed anger. He grinned. He'd forgotten how much fun it was to get her riled up. Taking up a place on the couch, he waited for her return.

Becky Sue reappeared, fully clothed. He could feel the tension back in the air, but this time he ignored it.

"Have a seat. We need to talk." His tone of voice was all business, no anger, no play. He almost checked to see if he'd grown two heads the way she looked at him.

She seated herself on the far end of the couch. Maybe keeping distance between them was the best idea.

"What?" Her voice was flat. Devoid of emotion. He kept the cringe he felt from showing.

"You're off tomorrow, well, today, right?" The clock on the wall showed ten till 1 a.m.

"Yeah, but I have to go check on Mom and probably take a trip to Harrison to pick up groceries for her." She looked confused and off guard. He wasn't ready to jump back to their pre-clothed conversation. Keep it work. Keep it business.

"Good. That should work out then." She gave him the eye. "I need to go by the office. We can ride together. You can just drop me off, do your grocery shopping then pick me up on the way out."

"Why can't you go by yourself?" Why did he think this would be so simple?

"Because if anyone is watching me, it'll look less suspicious if I ride with you like I'm helping out."

She mumbled something under her breath that sounded like she had a better way to help him out, and it didn't sound pleasant.

"Fine. Now you going to tell me what you're all head up about when I came in?"

"Nope." She glared at him. He couldn't stop the twitch of a smile. "I must've misunderstood what I heard. We're good." It didn't matter what she was telling Phoenix, he knew her better than anyone and her responses to him said she was all his. For now, that's all he needed. "What time do you think you'll be headed for groceries?"

**

"Ten, maybe eleven." She was sulking. Here she thought she'd found a way to get away and be alone for a while and he had to jump on her way out. She needed time to think. She'd thought she could fall for Phoenix, or at least use him to keep her from falling for Ray, but it wasn't working as she'd hoped. Phoenix was sexy and charming, mostly as long as he wasn't laughing at her small town thinking, but there was something about him that left her cold and breathless, in a bad way. It'd only manifested itself more plainly when Ray had kissed her a few minutes ago. He'd sent fire through her veins and made her feel irresistible. "By the way, why didn't you follow Jed tonight?"

"I don't think he has any direct contact with the maker, or middle man. My guess is they don't trust him enough. If it was me I'd made sure Jed was no where around when I made a drop to make sure he didn't mess it up. I need to go through his house and see if there are any clues, but have you seen that nastiness? I've been putting it off. If we get back early enough tomorrow, I may drop by and try to go through it. I forgot my gloves at Mom and Dad's when I packed so I'll pick some up from the office too."

It wasn't what she wanted to hear. She wanted him to say that he was watching out for her at the very least on her date. But he hadn't. This was business, not personal. "You going to check Phoenix out?"

"I wouldn't be doing my job if I didn't."

The next morning Becky Sue awoke to the sun shining brightly through the bedroom window in her face and a warm body to her back. It was surprisingly comfortable. And she didn't like it. They had gone to bed together, but the lines had been clear. No more. They were friends, barely, and trying to rid their hometown of a drug problem.

Ray rolled over when she got out of bed. He'd been pulling long hours the last few days. She wouldn't begrudge him a little sleep. That was until she dressed and realized she still needed a ride to pick up her truck and her things. She walked over to the bed and reached her arm out to shake him, but paused gazing at his face. She looked at him, really looked. He had a couple days worth of beard growth on his face that gave him a rugged look that she found surprisingly sexy. There were dark circles under his eyes. His hard jaw line and the way his eyelashes swept across his cheeks made her want to run her finger along his face.

"Are you going to stand there staring at me or are you going to wake me up?"

She jumped back and put a hand over her racing heart. "Shit. Don't scare me like that."

He grinned and opened his eyes. "If you find me so irresistible why don't you crawl back under the covers with me?"

"I ain't falling for that again. I got things to do and places to go today. I also kinda need your help."

"I'm offering my help now, what else do you need?" He held the covers up, his naked chest a work of art she longed to run her lips over, welcoming her into the bed. It was tempting. Oh so very tempting, but she wasn't willing to pay the price of a broken heart.

She ignored his offer. "I need a ride to my truck and maybe stop off on the way to pick up my things from last night at River Hollow."

He opened his mouth with a question on his tongue, but seemed to think better of it. Throwing off the covers, he sat up on the side of the bed. "Anything for a damsel in distress."

Ophelia Dickerson

She rolled her eyes, walked out to the living room, and waited for him on the couch.

**

It was good thing Becky Sue had left so quickly. After he'd caught her staring at him like that he didn't know if he could show the proper restraint much longer. His cock was already half mast. The need he had for her was almost palpable. He hated himself for it.

He dressed quickly before playing chauffer. After he dropped Becky Sue at her truck, he stopped at the bait and tackle shop on a whim to chat with Jed.

"Well, well, well, look who's back. You've been quiet. I take it that you got Becky Sue to loosen up for you?" Jed leered.

"Actually, that's why I stopped. I think she's immune to my charms. I was wondering if your offer of assistance still stood."

Jed's leer turned into a full blown smile. "Never thought I'd see the day, but I got just the thing for you."

"Great. Do you have it with you?"

"Sure do." He produced a key from his pocket and kneeled down behind the counter. A moment later he reappeared with a small baggie of white power. "Just sprinkle some of this in her drink and she'll be all yours."

Ray paid him and left with a sick feeling in his gut. How many women had Jed used his "magical" powder on? What about others? How many were willing and how many were unsuspecting victims? At least now he could take it to the lab when he went today and see if it was a match to Amy Drake.

Lost in thought he almost ran into a woman walking in. "Pardon me," he said walking around her.

"Anytime."

He turned his head to do a double take as that one word purred from her mouth in the sexiest way possible. How did that one word promise so much? She was stunning. Raven black hair hung long and straight down her back to her tiny waist. Her butt bubbled out perfectly. It was just the size of a man's hands. She turned to him, doing a slow blink, her long black eye lashes swooping gracefully over dark eyes. He felt the stupid grin on his face as he ogled her body. She turned away and walked inside the bait shop. Watching her ass as she walked was mesmerizing.

He shook his head to clear it. Becky Sue was driving him mad and had him so horny he was drooling over a stranger who'd only spoke one word to him. Maybe he should make an excuse to go back in and talk to her. If Becky Sue wanted to find someone else, why shouldn't he? He had physical needs too.

The only thing that kept him from following her inside was Jed. He'd just been in under the assumption that he was trying to get into Becky Sue's pants. He couldn't be seen hitting on another woman. Damn. He was sure that hot body that'd just walked in would take care his needs nicely.

There wasn't much he could do this morning so he grabbed his fishing gear and went out to the river to pass the time until Becky Sue came back. And maybe he was secretly hoping the hot as hell woman who'd gone into the bait shop would be out fishing soon too and he'd get another chance.

Fishing was one of the few things he found to be calming. He was actually able to relax a little as he baited his hook and cast it out into the water. He made himself comfortable along the bank and tried to let all the contradictory thoughts tumbling through his head drift off in the river.

A group of canoers put in a little downstream. He missed the days where fishing and anything to do with the river was part of his normal life. No, he didn't regret his job. He was needed. There were still people like Jed, and others, in the world that had no respect for anyone. As long as there were victims to drugs, rape, violence, theft and a host of other things, he would have a job to do.

He was deep in thought and almost didn't hear the footsteps behind him. He turned and as the morning sun shone over the mountains, he saw the Egyptian goddess Hathor approaching him. So it might not've been a long forgotten Egyptian goddess, but he was awed once more by her beauty. The woman from the bait shop was coming toward him, alone, carrying a fishing pole and small tackle box.

"Good morning," she called. "Anything biting yet?"

"Good morning." He tugged at his line. It was slack. "Not yet. Probably won't be till the sun comes up higher and warms the surface more."

She stopped short. "Oh, you're right. I was hoping to get in a little fishing before floating."

"Don't let me burst your bubble though, you're welcome to try. Obviously I'm not smart enough to take my own advice either."

She laughed a deep throaty laugh that promised long lingering sex. "Are you from around here?"

"Yep. Born and raised."

"So you know this area pretty good then don't you?" Something told him she wasn't really talking about the mountains and river. Her eyes seemed to feast on his body. He himself could barely keep his eyes off her breast that looked full, and firm peeking out of her low cut v-neck long sleeve shirt.

"Yeah." He was having trouble formulating words and sentences today.

"Do you think you could be my guide? I'm here on vacation and wanted to do some hiking and floating, but I know locals know all the best spots to go."

"Sure. I'd be glad to. Are you camped here? How many are in your group?"

"Yes, I'm at site 38." She pointed in the general direction. "My two girl friends are here, but I had to practically drag them out here with me. They don't love the outdoors like I do."

"I see." She was being purposefully seductive.

"By the way, my name is Benu." She held out a dainty hand.

"Ray. Nice to meet you." He took her hand. It was soft and promised to touch him in all the right ways.

He still held her hand when a slamming door drew his attention. Becky Sue stood leaned up against her truck, arms crossed with a look he couldn't read on her face.

"I'll have to catch up to you later though. My sister is here and I promised to spend some time with her today, but I'll be back later."

"That's nice of you to spend time with your sister. I'm here for a few days, but will be looking forward to meeting up with you again."

"Absolutely." He could feel the stupid grin return to his face. He was sure she could read his thoughts and all them included naked, sweaty bodies.

**

Becky Sue couldn't believe what she was seeing. Ray was moonstruck over some little prissy girl with a fishing pole in her hand. She should've been happy that he'd turned his attention elsewhere. But she wasn't.

He still had the same stupid shit eating grin on his face when they got in the truck.

"I see you found a new friend."

"Looks like it." There was no remorse, no sorry, no nothing. She hated him. She hated him with a passion that burned deeper than anything she could remember. "Stop by the cabin so I can drop my fishing gear and pick up something."

"Are you sure you wouldn't rather stay here and *fish* instead?"

"You know sarcasm doesn't really become you?"

"What the hell do you care what becomes you? You're not interested. I'm just a handy piece of ass that's such a sucker she doesn't know when to stop." She was madder than the situation deserved and she knew it. Lately her mother had become so frustrating in her meddling that it was pushing her patience out the window. This morning had been much the same. But after she'd called her bluff, she'd found her mother up and in her wheelchair today. Or maybe she was mad because just when she'd begun to feel irresistible to Ray, she found him drooling over another woman.

"Becky Sue, you know damn good and well I don't think of you like that." The frustration in Ray's voice was evident. She put the truck in park in front of the cabin. Not knowing how long he'd take, she shut it off and followed him in.

"You know, I wish you wouldn't think of me at all. I was perfectly happy before you came back and started messing with my life. And I hope you catch these sons of bitches soon so you can leave and go back to whatever hell raising you were doing before. I don't need you in my life." Tears stung the back of her eyes as she threw the words at him with vehemence.

"What do you know about my life, huh?" He threw his hand as he began to talk, fire shot out and hit the floor pulling both their attention from each other. He looked down at his fingers. It looked the same. No singe marks. No burns. He was stunned.

"Shit." She cursed and grabbed a couch pillow and beat the fire out that'd started on the floor. "How'd you do that?" She asked after tossing the pillow back on the couch, their argument temporarily forgotten.

"I-I don't know." He raised his arm like he was about to try again.

"No, no, no, no. Not here. You'll burn the cabin down. If you want to try it again, I know a place we can go. Then you have to teach me."

"I don't know what I did," he repeated, staring at his hand again.

"I know, but I bet we'll figure it out."

Chapter 14

Down a forgotten dirt road, Becky Sue drove them to an old campsite near the river. The underbrush was trampled down to hard packed dirt from local campers over the years. Back in high school it'd been the popular place to come and hang out. It's where a lot of underage drinking and early shot gun marriages had stemmed from.

"I can't believe you remembered this place," Ray said.

"I don't know how I did actually. I think I only came out here a couple of times with you and that was it."

He grinned mischievously. "Yeah... about that. I'd planned on bringing you out and wooing you that way when we're kids, but I chickened out."

"So taking me to your dad's barn was easier?"

"Uh... Can we talk about something else?" He was afraid to bring up the barn incident again. It'd been the indirect cause of their distancing for years. He didn't want to make her mad about it all over again.

"Oh that's right. You got yourself new arm candy now."

"No, that's not what I meant." Damned if he did, damned if he didn't. How was he ever supposed to catch a break?

"Whatever. Hurry up and figure this fire throwing thing out so I can get my shit done today. It's my only day off you know. I'd like to catch a little bit of a break."

"You're not the only one who's got real world shit to do," he shot back irritated at her matchstick temper. He walked away in disgust, but mostly to put distance between himself and the truck so he didn't accidently blow it up, leaving her sitting on the tailgate watching.

After a few attempts moving his arm in the same manner as before he said, "can you turn around or something. You're making me uncomfortable and I can't focus."

She spun around, turning her back to him. Somehow that small gesture seemed symbolic of failure to come or maybe it was just the way it made him feel empty inside at the thought of her turning her back on him for good. He was even more distracted now than when she was watching him.

Finally, he stopped. He closed his eyes and inhaled deeply bringing his energy into focus imagining it turning into a ball of flames. His hands grew warm. He looked down, small circles of fire burned in his hands.

"Becky Sue," he called and moved his hand releasing one of the fireballs right at her. It flew past her head, missing her nose by inches as she turned. She startled. "Look." He held up the second ball of fire in his other hand.

Her eyes grew round and a smile spread across her face. "You did it!"

He was grinning from ear to ear. His hand grew warmer. Spying a dead branch nearby, he aimed and threw. The fire ball released and caught the branch on fire.

"How'd you do it?" Becky Sue asked hopping off the tailgate.

"Close your eyes and channel your energy."

"Umm, ok." She walked away from the truck. She closed her eyes. Ray didn't get too close in case she made a jerky movement and threw an unsuspecting fire ball at him.

He watched anxiously to see if she could produce fire. Nothing happened.

**

After a minute she opened her eyes. She was disappointed to see no fire burned in the palms of her hands. "What did I do wrong?"

"I don't know. Give me a minute." Ray closed his eyes, his face a study in concentration. A few seconds later fire appeared in his palms. He threw them quickly to the ground to extinguish them. "Concentrate and think fire."

She closed her eyes again and thought of a campfire that she'd seen here years ago. She thought of the wick of a lanterns little flame lighting the night. She opened her eyes. Nothing.

"Maybe you have more power than me."

"Here let me help you," he said as he walked up behind her placing his hands on her shoulders. "Relax and close your eyes." His hands felt warm and welcoming. She felt the pull between them, the underlying connection they shared that she'd been trying so hard to ignore. Heat raced through her veins.

"Now breathe in." She was already holding her breath as his breath caressed her neck, sending the fire in her veins directly south. "Think fire." His fingers glided down the length of her arms, leading the fire to her palms. She tried to block him out while focusing on channeling her fire.

"You did it!" Ray said as he dropped his arms and stepped back.

Becky Sue opened her eyes and gaped at the flames dancing in her palms. "I did it! I did it!" Carefully she drew her arm back and threw a fire ball where it instantly dissipated when it hit the cold, unyielding ground. Her left hand wasn't as true as her right, but she still managed some wobbly accuracy.

"Oh my gosh! That was so cool!" She could barely contain her excitement. Turning to Ray, she grabbed him, and kissed him happily on the mouth.

**

He was so stunned by her reaction that when she kissed him he failed to respond fast enough. Becky

Sue pulled back, her face crestfallen. She stepped back putting space between them before he could reach for her. Call it pride. Call it stupidity, either way he refrained from following out his urge to go after her. It was nothing more than a spur of the moment, caught up in the excitement, friendly kiss.

They lingered a little longer as they both practiced bringing out their fire and using it until it was second nature.

The rest of the afternoon was quietly, subtly strained between them as they made their trip to Harrison and back. She dropped him at the cabin before going to her mom's to take the groceries and prepare a few meals.

Once he was left alone, he pulled the files he'd printed. Jed was nothing he hadn't expected. He had a couple DUI's and one drunk and disorderly that was several years in the past. Phoenix's file was squeaky clean. As a matter of fact he'd been more or less painted a local hero by his hometown of Hurricane Valley where he was a fireman. No wonder he didn't like the guy. Arrogant, self absorbed, probably saw himself as God's gift to women just because he could use a hose. Or maybe it was the ill feel in his gut knowing that Hurricane Valley was about 45miles across the mountains. Too close, especially taken into account of the proximity to Becky Sue.

He flipped through the other files he'd grabbed of some stray names he'd picked up, but nothing unusual popped out. Tucking away the files, he tossed them onto the coffee table. He was missing something somewhere. Jed was definitely connected, but as far as friends, or even acquaintances there was nothing to pursue. Had it been ten years ago, the list would've been long, but apparently Jed's behavior over the last few years had chased away any relationships he had with the civilized population. The bad part about that was it meant no other locals were in on it and everything was coming in from the outside. His hometown was being infiltrated and influenced by outsiders.

**

Becky Sue dropped Ray off at the cabin, stopped at her own house to leave a few groceries she'd picked up for herself, and checked on Sherlock. She unlocked the door and expected to see Sherlock perched on the back of the couch as was his custom, but he wasn't there. Crazy cat was probably off sulking at her absence somewhere.

She emptied her bags, put the food up, and went in search for her pet. "Here kitty, kitty." He wasn't on her bed, or in the bathroom. "Come here Sherlock." She checked under the couch and everywhere else she thought he could be. Worry began to eat her insides. "Where are you, you naughty cat?" She checked the windows and back door to make sure nothing had been left open for him to escape. He was nowhere to be found. It was then she realized how attached to him she was. He was her little buddy, her friend she talked to on long winter nights. What was she going to do if she couldn't find him? Her heart sank wondering if something bad had happened to him. She doubled checked everything again. Sherlock was gone.

Outside, she walked around the house. If he'd gotten out, maybe he was hiding under the house, or had got entangled in something outside and couldn't get loose. She walked around back and froze. There in the middle of the circle, singed by her and Ray, lay Sherlock. His body lay at an unnatural angle. No! She let out a whimper and bit her lip before she ran over to his body. When she drew closer she saw the blood. Tears blurred her eyes. She picked him up hoping some sign of life was still there, but there wasn't. Someone had slit his throat. She cradled him in her arms as tears spilled on to his grey fur. She sank down into the center of the circle holding Sherlock and crying wondering what kind of animal did this to her pet, her friend.

Time had no meaning as she grieved her loss. But finally something in the back of her mind prodded her to move forward. She gently laid him on the porch as she reached for a shovel, an occasional tear still slipping out as she dug. Once she deemed it deep enough, she tenderly placed Sherlock's lifeless body in the bottom of the hole, and after a minute hesitation, began tossing shovel full's of dirt returning him to the earth where he'd began.

In a zombie-like trance she went through the motions of covering and marking the grave. She changed her bloody shirt, locked her house, and drove to her mothers. The empty void left by Sherlock's passing was a gaping wound in her soul.

She arrived at her mother's house and began performing her ritual she'd been doing for years. Putting away groceries and cooking a few meals to be frozen and taken out for use over the course of the week. She'd been working for over half an hour when her mom rolled into the kitchen.

"You're quieter than normal today," Kate stated.

"Yeah."

"Want to talk about it?"

"No." She knew if she did the tears would flow again. They were barely contained now. She could blame it on the onion she was chopping, but her mom was too shrewd to buy that.

"Did something happen between you and Ray?"

"No." Instead she was going to play the "yes and no" game.

"Are you pregnant?"

"No!" Becky Sue exclaimed turning to her mom.

Kate looked nonplussed. "Are you sure? Because I keep telling you, if you continue running around with that boy all the time you're going to end up with a baby."

The anger had breached the sadness to dry her tears. "It's not like that I keep telling you. If you must know, Sherlock died today."

"I'm sorry honey. I know you liked that cat." Kate patted her hand. "I think Maggie Ann's little spaniel is due to have pups soon. Maybe you should talk to her about getting one."

Becky Sue ignored her mom's comment. She didn't want a dog, she wanted Sherlock. However, she did need to talk to Maggie Ann. They were over due on catching up even though she'd dropped by the shop a few days ago with her little whirlwind of kids. It'd been near Christmas the last time she'd been over there. She promised herself then to reach out to Maggie Ann after Ray's assignment was over and she had time to call her own again.

**

Ray was stumped. He didn't like being stumped, but he was. The only way he knew to solve a hurdle was by exercise. He'd figured out the link in more than one case while worked out at the gym, but since a gym wasn't an option right now he'd have to settle for a run.

The sun was lowering in the sky when he opened the cabin door and took off for a few loops around the campground. Somehow he'd almost forgotten about Benu until he came to the section turn off for campsites 20-49. He was tempted to change his course and go check out her camp site, but reminded himself he was on the job. There was no frolicking. No matter how unlikely it was for a random female he met to be linked to whatever it was he was investigating to be involved, it could happen. He'd watched enough old spy movies as a kid and heard enough tales from the older generation to not be wary. Besides it was just bad practice to play when he was working, the only exception withstanding being Becky Sue and he didn't count her as playing exactly. It was more like a friendly entanglement. No, entanglement still held too many strings attached to it. It was more like a friendly exploration than anything.

He'd made his first loop and was starting his second when he noticed Sam's canoe rental truck with trailer attached near the water. A group of floaters were lined up to turn in their canoes. A lone figure stood off to the side and waved at him as he passed. It was Benu. He smiled and waved back refusing to let himself be distracted. He was on the job.

By the time he circled around again and, on his last lap, the goddess Benu was nowhere to be seen. He breathed a sigh of relief. If she'd been there still waiting and watching him again, he was afraid he wouldn't have been strong enough to resist.

He returned to the cabin without further incident, showered, and put a frozen meatloaf in the microwave for his dinner. As he ate the tasteless meat mush, he wondered what kind of mouth watering food Becky Sue was making for her mom. Could he bum some of it off her to have a real meal while he was here? He could just go home and eat with his parents, but he was unwilling to have them snooping in his business right now so he shoveled another bite of tasteless mush into his mouth and washed it down with a pint of milk.

Becky Sue came trudging through the door close to 8p.m. head down, looking like she'd lost her best friend in the world.

"Did you get your mom squared away?" He asked hoping nothing had happened to Kate. It would devastate Becky Sue if and when something did.

"Yeah." Her voice was dull and she was purposefully avoiding looking at him.

"What's wrong?"

"Nothing."

"Liar." She shot him a look then. Her eyes were red and puffy. She'd been crying. He couldn't think of a time he'd ever seen her cry, with the possibility of one exception. "Come here."

She dropped her bag where she stood and obeyed him without fight, fuss, or sarcastic comment. Something was definitely wrong. She stopped near where he sat with no indication she intended to sit.

He stood and put his hands on her shoulder as he tried to look into her face. She kept her gaze averted. "Look at me."

She blinked hard as she obeyed yet again.

"Are you going to tell me what's wrong or am I going to have to call your mother and ask her?" He threatened.

A tear leaked out of her eye. Shit, he hated tears. He was no good with them. "Sherlock's dead. Somebody killed him."

"What!"

She nodded. More silent tears streamed down her face as she blinked rapidly fighting against emotions.

"Did he get out and get hit by a car?" She shook her head no. "Are you sure he was killed then? Was it another animal?"

She bit her lip before taking a deep breath, and with voice shaking said, "someone slit his throat and left him in the backyard."

Ray sank onto the couch as he tried to digest what she said.

"I don't think he got out by himself. I checked everything when I was looking for him. I think someone purposefully broke into my house, and killed Sherlock. They left him in the middle of the singed spot where we… ignited our powers. I think someone knows about us."

He felt like he'd been dealt a blow to his abdomen with a bat. First, how could someone kill an innocent cat? Two, who and why would someone break into Becky Sue's house? What were they after? And three, who and how had found out about their powers, and what did they intend to do about it?

Becky Sue turned to walk away while his mind reeled to grasp at the sudden change of balance. He reached out a hand to stop her. She had no fight left in her because she stopped. He hated seeing her so vulnerable and weak. This wasn't his best friend he knew. This wasn't his Becky Sue.

He wrapped his arms around her, holding her tight, willing his strength into her. She burst into tears. This time he wasn't bothered by them. This time he just let her cry.

Chapter 15

The next morning Becky Sue struggled against the sunlight through gritty, puffy eyes. She wanted to bury under the pillow and pretend today didn't exist. She was in no mood to work. An arm came around her and pulled her close to the thick muscled chest. A gentle pair of lips kissed her neck behind her ear.

"It's going to be alright. You can make it." Why did Ray have to always confuse her? One minute he was dragging her through piss ants making her scream, the next he was being all sweet and gooey, cuddling and coddling her like a baby.

"Yeah." Damn it if she didn't want to stay curled up to him all day and just hide from the world. But she couldn't. She threw back the covers and started her day.

It wasn't until she unconsciously thought about stopping by her house to check on Sherlock that the reality of his being dead hit again. She shook off the looming depression the best she could and threw herself into working at her mom's house.

While Kate showered, Becky Sue vacuumed, took out the trash, rearranged a stack of magazines, emptied the dishwasher, and was just about to reload it when her mother reappeared.

"You're awful energetic this morning. Must've been a good night, huh?" her tone held a wink, wink, nudge, nudge quality to it.

Becky Sue ignored the connotations. "I slept good, yes, despite what happened yesterday." She didn't want to worry her mom with the details of Sherlock's death, disturbing as they were, but if her mother continued to pester her she was going to say things she didn't mean. "Anyway, I have a lot do today so I have to go."

She pecked her mom on the cheek and fled from the house. Slipping in the back door of work, she hoped Cindy wouldn't appear first thing this morning as she was likely to do. As soon as Cindy found out about Sherlock's death she was sure a special smelling candle would appear on her counter. Because specially scented candles cured the world. She rolled her eyes.

Going through her morning opening routine was automatic. The sun was shining happily. She pulled out a book of quilt patterns looking for ideas for her next project, but nothing was grabbing at her. Normally, she'd been sitting there making a list of ideas to choose from, but not this time. All she could think about was Sherlock and his little furry bloody body. That's what she would do. She'd quilt a memorial for Sherlock. A window pattern with a cat silhouette in it.

The bells of the door jangled.

"Good morning Becky Sue."

"Morning, Cindy."

"I heard about your kitty so I brought you a little something over." She produced a small basket of cookies and a candle.

"Thanks, Cindy. I appreciate it."

"I know he was special to you. I guess whatever was making him act strange the other day when he was in here got to him. Animals have a way of knowing when they're going to die, you know."

She nodded. Sure, that sounded good. Whatever got her out of here faster.

"Well, you let me know if you need anything." She turned to go. "Oh, I was going to tell you, Iris's cat just had kittens a few days ago. She'll be happy to let you have one when it's time."

"Thanks. I'll keep that in mind." She didn't really want a replacement cat. She wanted Sherlock.

With the same bluster that she came in with, she left. Becky Sue breathed a sigh of relief. She'd just picked up the candle to see what kind of strange scent Cindy had sent her this time when the bells above the door jangled again.

**

Ray followed Becky Sue out of bed. He couldn't let daylight keep burning. He'd given up on following Jed. He needed to explore other avenues. Today he decided he needed to take a float trip and maybe stop at the site where Amy Drake's body had been found. He didn't expect to find any evidence or anything, but maybe he'd get some ideas on where to look.

His first stop was Sam's to rent a canoe. Before he'd left for the morning he'd packed an extra set of clothes in his truck in case he found himself shape shifting for some unforeseen reason, or if he got tipped into the water. He'd packed a small cooler since he'd planned to be out for a while, which he loaded into the canoe when he set in at Elk Point Landing. As he did, it occurred to him that he would pass Phoenix's camp. Would he be able to spot it in the daylight? How would Phoenix feel if he just dropped by for a visit? Would it be that obvious he'd followed him the night before last if he did? Phoenix gave him an uneasy feeling already. If he showed up unannounced it might not go over well. Besides it'd probably just piss Becky Sue off when she found out about it too. In the end, he decided against the detour.

He'd started out earlier than the first drop of tourists making him the only on the river. It was quiet. The canoe glided smoothly across the water. The quiet splash of the paddle and drip of the water as it came out again created a gentle rhythm in sync with the nature around. Sunlight danced across the water, reflecting brighter than it felt. The whole scene was calming. He felt at peace and as one with nature.

Floating along, he scanned the riverbanks for anything that might appear unusual. A few birds lingered in the air above him at one point. A fox peeped out of the woods, took one look at him and ducked back into the underbrush. He made a mental note to get out and do this more often. It was doing him good to get out and back to nature.

The rock wall where Phoenix was camped loomed ahead. Ray stared up at the behemoth and again wondered how an outsider had found the cave. If he hadn't been shown it, he wouldn't even have known of its existence. Even if Phoenix had been raised in Hurricane Valley, it would've taken lots of exploration or someone who already knew about it to find it. What other hideaways did he know about?

Looking up at the cliffs as he passed below gave him no answers. He needed answers. Knowing things was his job.

A couple hours later, he stopped at River Hollow Landing to take a break and grab a snack. He'd forgotten how hungry paddling made a man. People were starting to gather near the water, probably waiting for Sam to bring their canoes. He lingered for a little while, walking around, chatting up the tourists trying to see if he could pick up anything of interest. They all seemed like ordinary folks.

Sam's canoe truck pulled in with a load of canoe's on the trailer. Ray took that as his cue to get ahead of the flock. He'd already seen a couple other floaters pass from further up while he'd been stopped. He didn't want to get bottle necked at some point.

Ray rounded a bend and watched as a small herd of deer spooked at his sudden appearance. The vegetation in through here was dense allowing the deer an easy cover. On the other side of the river was much the same. A flash of unnatural color caught his attention. He turned to drift over for a better look.

The closer he got the more he felt the sinking in the pit of his stomach.

A body lay face down half in the water not moving. Ray hurriedly pulled up and landed awkwardly on bank, only having about two feet before the land began to rise and fill with thick thorns and bushes. He jumped out and went to the body. He could tell he was dead before he touched him. It was a good size man. A familiar looking man in well worn clothes. He rolled him over.

Jed's blank eyes and beat up face stared back at him. A slit mark across his neck gave evidence of the cause of death.

"Fuck." His voice echoed across the water. A whole slew of canoers were due any minute. He didn't need a bevy of onlookers hanging around and trampling any possible evidence in the area, not to mention he didn't want any of the kids to see the body.

He quickly dug a small camera out of his pack and took a few pictures to capture the original scene. It was a good thing he lifted often because Jed was not an easy move. He pulled him the rest of the way out of the water, grabbed some loose leaves, branches and ground debris for camouflage until he could send a crime scene unit down here. He took a few more pictures of how he left things and was just getting back in the water when the first canoe came into view.

He pushed off hoping to draw attention away from the bank. Paddling with more vigor now, he pushed ahead of the group meandering downstream. He cast one last glance over his shoulder at Jed's covered form. The first two canoe's had passed by. He could only hope the rest would too.

Why had someone gone after Jed? Was it related to the drug ring? He'd just seen Jed yesterday morning and he'd seemed normal Jed, drunk and perverted. Was it a coincidence that Becky Sue's cat had its throat slit yesterday too? It felt like a little too much throat slitting to be just a coincidence, but how were the two related? How had Jed's body got where it was? Had someone taken him to that exact spot or had he floated down from upstream somewhere?

He channeled the frustration of so many unanswered questions into his paddling sending him flying down the river like a champion rower. By the time he pulled into Ashburn, he was breathing hard. He hurried to his cabin and put a call in to his chief to send a crime scene crew out. He gave as detailed a description as he could so he wouldn't have to meet them and risk blowing his cover.

A knock at the door sounded just as he hung up. Who in the hell? He was tempted to ignore it. He had shit to do, but he also needed to get rid of whoever was there so he could shape shift, although he was torn between what he should do first, let Becky Sue know about Jed or go watch over the crime scene.

In a huff he swung open the door, ready to read the intruder their rights. He paused. Benu stood on the other side. She wore black spandex pants and a pink shirt with a zipper neck unzipped giving him a teasing view of her perfect full breasts. Her long black hair was brushed out straight and flowing around her shoulders, her dark eyes round and luminous as she looked up at him in an unassuming way.

"Hi, I hope I didn't come at a bad time." She glanced behind him, but he didn't respond immediately as he was distracted by her body. "I just saw you coming up from the landing and followed you here to ask about being my guide." She shifted on her feet. Her breast seemed to press into his face. He thought about reaching out to touch them to see if they were real. Somehow he didn't think she'd mind.

"I'm not being too presumptuous, I hope?" She asked when he didn't respond because he was too busy wrestling with what he should do and what he wanted at that moment. Those big, innocent, dark eyes that stared up at him held temptation and promise.

**

Phoenix walked through the door. Becky Sue brightened a little. If he was here that meant the other night hadn't been so awful and bad after all.

"Hi."

He saw her and smiled back with his dark, malevolent eyes. "Hi. Did you have a good day off yesterday?"

Did she answer that honestly? Yesterday had been rough. The only highlight is that she and Ray had figured out how to work their fire powers after that it'd all gone downhill, fast, topping it off with Sherlock's death.

"I'm sorry you had a bad day," he said before she could speak.

"Are you a mind reader or something?"

He smiled softly and lifted her chin with his fingers to look up at him. "No. The look on your face says it all."

"I look that rough, huh?" Was he going to try to kiss her again? She almost hoped not. Her lungs instantly remembered the last kiss and she was surprisingly in no hurry to repeat it.

"Not rough, sad. You want to tell me about it?"

"Yes and no." He dropped his hand from her face. "Yes, because you're so nice and thoughtful. No, because I don't want to cry right now, especially here at work." It was inevitable that she would as much as she hated it. Sherlock had been like a part of her family to her.

"What about this then, tonight when you get off work, I'll pick you up and we can go have a nice dinner together."

"Where?" She didn't really want to get dragged out to his camp again. It'd taken so long and she felt so helpless and stranded out there that just thinking about it made her slightly uncomfortable.

"A restaurant."

"There's only one here. Claire's." She pointed out the window across the square.

"Not here. We'll go to Harrison. I'll take you to the city and treat you like a queen. How's that sound?" The way he said it was dramatic and silly, making it sound fun. For a moment she thought it might be another subtle jibe at her small town back woods ways, but decided it was probably just his way of trying to make things right.

She grinned. "Alright. You got me. Give me thirty minutes to get home and change out of these clothes after I close later." She wasn't about to go into the city in her homespun antiquated clothes she wore to the shop.

"So about five thirty?"

"That should work." If Ray had other plans, that was just too bad. He should've told her this morning before she left. She hadn't left herself enough time to leave Ray a message. She didn't know the number to the cabin either, not that he'd even be near the phone. He'd just have to deal with it. She had her own life to live. She couldn't be jumping at his every beck and call.

"You know what. I don't think I'm going to wait." Becky Sue looked at Phoenix curiously. "I have a confession to make."

"Oh?" He was being cagey and weird making her skeptical.

"I like to pilfer through antique and junk shops. Yesterday I was out roaming and I stumbled across something I thought you would like. I was going to wait to give it to you for a few more days until just before I left so you won't forget me, but since you had such a bad day yesterday I think I'll give it to you today."

Her eyebrows rose, curious and intrigued. It'd been years since someone other than Cindy and her mother had given her anything.

"Let me go get it." He strode out of her shop before she could stop him.

He was back a minute later holding a small paper bag. "Here, I hope you like it."

Tentatively, unsure what to think, she took the bag from him and peeked inside. Something small, green and shiny was at the bottom. She dumped it out into her hand. The green stone reflected the sunlight streaming through the window turning it a vibrant mixed green.

A pendant about the size of half dollar hung on a chain. Upon closer inspection the pendant had a carving on it. It was a griffin, wings spread, mouth open, a snake ensnared in its claws. A small stone of gold, or maybe copper, was held in the griffin's mouth. The ensnared snake was attempting to fight back, its mouth open, tongue out, to no avail. It was all very intricate.

"It's beautiful. Thank you. But you shouldn't have. It looks expensive."

"I hoped you'd like it. When I saw it I thought of you and your stories. And those little junk shops aren't really that expensive, but maybe I shouldn't have told you that."

Typically she wasn't an impulsive person, but it'd been such a long time since anyone had been so thoughtful without an underlying motive she reached out and hugged him.

"Will you wear it for me tonight?"

"Absolutely." She ran her finger over the stone one more time. "What kind of stone is it do you know?"

"Malachite. The lady who sold it to me said that people used to carry malachite stones to get rid of negative energy."

"Well, just having you around is easing the negative energy around me." He smiled, his white teeth a perfect contrast to his tanned skin. She didn't believe in the drivel people made up about rocks and gems carrying certain energy and power. They were just natures little pretties to be appreciated and traded.

She wanted to wear it now, but if anyone caught her with a gift from another man it wouldn't sit well. As far as the town was concerned, she and Ray were an item and if she accepted a gift from someone else she'd be proclaimed a slut, a gold digger, and a slew of other unpleasantly connotative words. She slid the necklace back in the bag to protect it, and set it on the shelf under her counter until she wore it tonight.

"I better be getting out of here. I was going to squeeze in a hike before tonight. Build up my appetite." He winked.

"Okay, see you then. And thanks again, the necklace is beautiful."

Phoenix left. Becky Sue walked back to her work table and started working on her design for her cat quilt.

Chapter 16

Ray inwardly sighed. He knew he was going to regret this later. "Sorry Benu. I was just on my way out. I have some stuff to do that may take up most of my day." The fact that Becky Sue had been so cold toward him the last few days only made his struggle harder turning her down.

She took a step up to him and placed her tiny hand on his chest. "That's too bad. I was really looking forward to it." She ran her fingers down his torso and stopped at the waist of his jeans, pressing her firm breast lightly to him, and batting her eyes seductively.

"I should be free tomorrow. We can shoot for then." To hell with his self imposed rules. She was practically throwing herself at his feet. He could have one of the guys run a check on her later, just to give him peace of mind, and tomorrow he would allow himself some pleasure because if he didn't he'd be too distracted to work.

"I don't know if I can wait that long, but I'll try," She purred. With that she turned and left as he stared dumbly after her watching her perfect ass in motion.

He shut the door and groaned. If he was this weak over a stupid woman, he needed to reconsider a different line of work. First he'd lost control with Becky Sue, and now, because she'd left him blue balled, he was letting the first floozy that shook her ass at him sway him to bed. Maybe that's what he needed was a good fuck to distract him from Becky Sue.

Locking the door he stripped off his clothes. It was the quickest way back to get where he needed going. If Benu hadn't been so tempting he'd have asked her for a ride to his truck instead, but today called for work, not play.

As a lizard he slid out the kitchen window and into the woods. Once out of sight, he changed to a crow. He flew out over the river and upstream on the lookout for a group of people huddled around Jed's body, but all he saw were canoers and kayakers floating downstream, occasionally pulled off on popular sand bars taking a break.

By the time he made it to his truck, he'd decided to let Becky Sue in on what was happening just in case she was able to pick something up. He landed on the bed of his truck, which was parked in the farthest corner he could find earlier. After doing a quick scan of the area, he hopped to the ground nearest the trees and changed back into a human. He hurriedly retrieved his keys out of his hiding spot, unlocked the door, and pulled on his clothes.

On his way into town, he didn't pass any vehicles that were official in nature. Had he missed them or had they not made it yet? The readout on his truck said it'd only been about thirty minutes since he'd put the call in. They weren't out here yet.

He parked behind Becky Sue's shop and walked in the back door.

"Holy crap you scared the hell out of me sneaking in like that." Becky Sue exclaimed holding a hand over her heart.

"What are you so nervous about?"

"I'm not nervous. But I'm the only one who uses that door. It scared me for a second. Hanging around you has me seeing boogey men everywhere."

"Good. I'm glad you're being alert. You should be." Even in her homespun with her sharp tongue, there was something that pulled to him and made him forget everything Benu had to offer. "Jed's dead."

She was reaching for her pencil she'd dropped when he'd scared her but froze. "Dead? Like accident dead or murder dead?"

"Looks like murder. I don't think he had it in him to slit his own throat. Found him out in the river earlier. He's been dead less than twenty four hours because I saw him myself yesterday morning."

"Shit. Think there's any connection between Sherlock and Jed?"

Connecting two dots on such flimsy evidence of just a slit throat was risky, but was a possibility he couldn't rule out, although killing a cat and a human were vastly different. He shrugged noncommittally. "Too soon to tell. Not sure what the connection would even be to tell the truth. Anyway I called the chief. He's sending a crime scene team out to work on it so I can keep my cover. I just wanted you to know what was going on in case you hear something."

"Alright, I'll keep my ears open." He really could fall into those blue eyes if she'd let him. She blushed then as if she could hear his thoughts.

"Whatcha working on?" He'd noticed the grid sheet paper in front of her.

"It's a design for my next quilt. It's kinda like a memorial to Sherlock in my own little way."

He felt his heart squeeze a little knowing her pain, even if it was just an animal, he'd seen how badly it'd affected her last night when she'd come in with blood shot eyes. She still looked a little ragged today, but seemed to be rallying. Walking over to her, he gave her shoulders a reassuring squeeze. She tensed for a second, but then relaxed and seemed to droop into his hands.

He felt criminal for leaving Becky Sue to sew up her tattered heart alone.

"I have to go now. I'm going to drop my truck at the cabin then head out to the crime scene."

"I thought you said you couldn't because it'd blow your cover."

"Oh I'm not going like this." He stepped away heading to the door. "I'm going naked." He winked at her, drawing out a wan smile.

"Just so you know, I don't know when I'll be back tonight." He stopped. "Phoenix invited me to dinner. He's taking me to Harrison."

Ray gritted his teeth. He was afraid if he opened his mouth it would turn ugly in a flash.

"Look, I know you don't like the guy and I have no idea why, but this is my life. I get to live it as I choose. He's actually very nice. He brought me a present. He was going to wait for a few days and give it to me as a going away gift I guess, but when he found out Sherlock died, so he gave it to me today."

He couldn't believe what he was hearing. What an ass wipe. He could feel his blood boiling. How could he spell it out for her that Phoenix was bad news. Should he pretend to throw himself at her and make her promises he probably couldn't keep just to keep her away from him? Would she fall for it or see right through his lie?

She reached for something under the counter, and pulled out a small brown paper bag. Dumping it upside down, she held up a shiny green necklace. It looked old, but he was far from an expert. Phoenix was playing hard ball. Well, he could play hardball too.

Taking two steps to cover the distance between them, he inserted himself into her space.

"It's pretty, but not as pretty as you." And then he kissed her like his life depended on it. Only it was her life that depended on him. She couldn't ruin it by throwing herself at some shady character. It'd been a weak line, but he didn't need words with her. He knew and understood her on a level that didn't require words.

She melted into his arms and kissed back with as much ferocity as he gave. His head was spinning as his tongue dipped into her mouth, tasting her like it was the first time all over again. She parried back, exploring his. She was breathless. Her hands were groping him like a dessert drinks in rain. He squeezed her against him willing her to change her mind about Phoenix, nearly crushing her in his embrace.

He was hard against the zipper of his pants with need and was going to bust something if he didn't breathe soon. He pulled back. They were both breathing heavily. Good, that was a good sign. He still had part of her and could call her back to him. He smiled.

"I'll see you after they wrap up the crime scene tonight." He kissed the tip of her nose.

"I'm still going to dinner with Phoenix."

He glared at her, wanting to rage and shake her and beg her to tell him why she was so stubborn against him. But he didn't. Instead he turned on his heel and walked out.

Becky Sue had to be the most stubborn, hard headed woman he'd ever met. Why did he have to be the one cursed with being her protector? It wasn't something he chose. It was something he'd been given to do by some invisible force. If he tried to walk away and leave her to her own devices he knew he'd never be able to live with himself again if something happened.

Long ago he'd tried to distance himself from her when she'd left him for college. He'd said to hell with it and married – thinking he'd be able to forget her. He'd almost succeeded until he'd been sent back here on assignment. Now that they'd reunited and explored previously untouched terrain, there was no turning back no matter how much either of them fought it. He just hadn't figured out how to get her to see it.

He parked his truck at the cabin, grabbed a quick lunch, shifted into a common crow, and flew out for the crime scene trying not to worry about Becky Sue.

The river traffic was at an even flow, not crowded, but rather a steady stream of canoers. Ray landed near Jed's body and pecked around making sure nothing had been tampered with. It appeared secure. Where was the crime scene crew? He flew upriver to check for them.

The crew was easy to spot. They all wore official uniforms and looked like little clones of each other, even from the air. Their canoes were loaded with equipment. The first canoe was roughly half a mile out. Good. He thought about going a little further up and poking his beak into a certain cave, but decided he needed to make sure the crime scene crew found their body. Circling back, he made it before the others. Carefully he began pulling leaves, twigs and other small debris off of Jed with his beak.

It was a good thing they came when they did, Jed was becoming rather ripe. Ray's stomach was getting queasy even as a crow. He was no stranger to a crime scene, but normally didn't have this much proximity to dead bodies. Mostly what he dealt with was drugs, rape, non death shootings. There'd been a few bodies, but not enough to become accustomed to the stench.

By the time the first crime scene canoe came into view he had enough of the body uncovered for them to find. He flew up into a nearby tree and waited. The lead paddler pointed. Good. They'd found it easy enough. Ducking behind the tree he transformed into a small lizard. Now he was small enough to get in where he could hear well and not get spotted and shooed off.

**

Becky Sue watched as Ray left out the back door trying to still her racing heart and just a little pissed that he was trying to turn her away from Phoenix. But she couldn't be pissed at anyone except herself, especially after that kiss. He'd kissed her like he was a dying man clinging desperately not wanting life to go. It'd taken her breath away, not in the way where her lungs hurt and craved oxygen because they were being sucked dry, but rather because she'd forgotten to breathe. Hadn't cared if she drew breath because all she'd needed was him. The feel of his body pressed hard against hers, the touch of his lips crushing down. All conscious and subconscious body functions stopped just to feel him, drink in every shred of essence in him.

She stamped her foot like a petulant child. That man was so infuriating the way just his presence laid claim over her very soul. He wouldn't distract her. She wouldn't allow him to pull her away from the path she'd chosen. It was her choice and nobody else's.

Returning to her table she threw herself into her work, occasionally chatting with the tourists flitting in and out of her shop.

It was near close before the first hint that Jed's body had been found and crime scene techs were on scene. A group of early twentyish tourists had come in after floating and had seen the uniforms on the bank. None of them had actually seen the body, so their versions of what had happened varied from a drug bust to a kid drowning by accident to a drunk and disorderly fight.

It'd been unclear to her why exactly Jed had been killed. It made her uneasy. Coming so close on the heels of Sherlock's demise was suspicious, especially considering the location her poor kitty's body had been found. Was Jed's death connected to the drugs he'd sold Ray? Or had he somehow found out about her and Ray's shape shifting and had sold that information to someone who'd then quieted him to keep him from a double cross sell out? Jed the drunk? No, that was impossible. There was no way for him to know about the Sparker power she and Ray possessed.

She gave up trying to connect the dots and turned her attention to her upcoming date. It'd been so long since she'd been on a real date. Most of her dates had consisted of Claire's diner, or a campfire considering she hadn't dated any locals since high school and the tourist she met were more like playmates than anything.

By closing time, Becky Sue was giddy with excitement at the prospect of getting out. She locked up shop and went home to look for something to match her new necklace from Phoenix. Her closet was not conducive to real dates, instead it held a full array of jeans, t-shirts, and antiquated style clothes. She sighed wishing she could be a little more exciting at times. Then she remembered she was a Sparker and had magical powers. She also had a friend named Ray, knew a dead guy named Jed, and maybe she didn't want to be more exciting after all. Her life was becoming quickly more complicated than it ever had before and it had all started when Ray came back to town.

She chose a black button up long sleeve shirt that she tucked into her nicest pair of jeans. The vibrant green of her new necklace contrasted nicely with the shirt. Her shoe options were worse than her clothing. She brushed the dirt off her boots and wiped them down with a damp rag. They'd have to work. Time was running out. She yawned. Too bad she didn't have time for a nap.

For once she left her hair down, long and straight, where normally it was either in a ponytail or braid. But not today. Today was special. She yawned again as she put down her brush and did one last check in the mirror. All the stress and keeping different hours was suddenly catching up to her.

Walking back into the living room she sat on the couch and absently reached out to pet Sherlock. Her hand stopped mid air. Sherlock was gone. Dead. She yawned again. He'd been her calming cat. Whenever she'd felt nervous or afraid or angry, anything, he'd been there and let her pet him, purring as she did, calming her. Now he wasn't. The pain of his loss hit her again. Now she was depressed and tired. Some company she'd make for a date.

But she had to go. She had to stay away from Ray.

Phoenix pulled into her driveway precisely on time. Not wanting to give herself a chance to back out, she hurried out the door and jumped into his red truck, covering another yawn as she did so.

"I'm so glad you made it. If you'd been late I'm afraid I'd have fallen asleep and missed our date."

He smiled at her as he hesitated before putting the truck in drive. "I'm glad you made it too, but if you're too tired we can stay here. We don't have to go to Harrison."

"No, no, no. I'm good. I want to go. It sounds kinda small town, but I don't get out much. I need this."

"Then out you shall get." He shifted into gear and pulled out the drive. "How was business today?"

She yawned again.

He was trying to make small talk, which she was grateful for. It would help keep her awake if she was engaged in conversation. "It's picking up being Spring Break and all."

They kept up small talk for the next few minutes, but Becky Sue's eyes were growing heavier. She leaned her head up against the passenger door to rest. The last thing she saw was the Hilltop Bed and Breakfast six miles out of town.

**

Ray watched the crime scene crew work. Some of them had come to collect Amy Drake's body a few weeks earlier and made comments like "rednecks need to leave the drugs to the professionals" and "this guy could preserve himself with his drinking habit". They'd found a small flask tucked into Jed's pocket, empty. It was no news to Ray. The estimated time of death was the night before.

After they'd collected what evidence they could, they rolled Jed's body up and put him in a canoe to send him downriver. Ray waited till everyone had left before returning into crow form and flying back to the cabin. Just before he landed he saw Benu coming out of the woods off a hiking trail. Alone.

What on earth was she thinking? Didn't she know it was dangerous to go out alone, especially being a woman? Didn't she know what could happen? What was it with women these days and thinking they were invincible? He wasn't anti-feminist. He was a realist. He'd seen enough in his career to know the possibilities.

He circled above. She left the woods and went straight to his cabin. What did she want? He watched as she knocked on the door. When he didn't answer after two more tries, she walked the perimeter peeking into the windows. He did a mental high five for not banging her. She was stalker crazy. Landing on a nearby branch, he watched as she pulled something out of her pack and with experienced hands opened his door.

His birdie beak dropped. What was she looking for? Was she going to rob him? Was she `a gold digger? If so, she was on the wrong track. He was able to make a living, but it wasn't the high life by any means. He flew to the ground, checked to make sure no one was watching, then changed into a lizard.

He ran up to the door, arriving just in time to see her tape something inside the cuff of his pants. She was putting tracking devices on all his clothes! Taking a deep breath he was about to change back into human form to catch her and call her out red handed, then thought better of it since he'd be stark naked. That wouldn't go over well at all. She could easily tell someone he'd tried to force himself on her and who would he be to say differently when he was standing there naked. Secondly, he didn't trust his body to respond appropriately despite the fact she was a crazy bitch. And being naked, there was no hiding anything. She could easily manipulate him to do as she bid.

Benu turned to leave, her job done. Ray raced to the corner of the cabin to hide. Who was she working for? Was it the drug runners? Surely she couldn't be that crazy on her own. Was it something else that had followed him here?

She left and walked in the direction of her camp. He followed the best he could on his little legs. Then noticed he was also in the middle of the road. He ran to the edge of the grass and tried to keep up, but was quickly falling behind. This wasn't going to work. He turned and scuttled his way back to the cabin.

The last batch of canoers for the day were beginning to land. It'd be dark soon. He could see the first two from his cabin. The line of sight was too direct. He couldn't risk being seen naked by kids as he snuck into the cabin. He was stuck.

He cursed as he watched another canoe dock. Sam wasn't there with his trailer for pick up yet, so it would be a while before they left. The only thing left for him to do was change back into a bird and go see what Benu was up to when all he wanted to do was go rip out the tracking devices, put some real clothes on, and go surprise her with a visit.

Just as he changed and took flight he saw her behind the wheel of a red truck exiting the campgrounds. Now what was she up to? He lazily followed her up the river to River Hollow.

Benu turned into the small campground and parked beside an identical truck, only with a canoe in the bed. She got out with her pack she'd carried out of the woods and jumped in the passenger side of the other truck. Something told him she wasn't going out canoeing with her girlfriends he'd yet to see.

The other red truck ambled through the curvy roads to Elk Point Landing. Ray perched in a tree far enough away to watch and not be easily seen when the truck parked. The parking lot had a few cars in it. Most likely the group that had landed just before he left would be back after dark to pick up.

Phoenix exited the driver's side. What in the name of blue blazes hell was going on? Where was Becky Sue? Didn't they have a date tonight? Why and how did he know Benu?

Daylight was quickly fading into dusk as Benu and Phoenix took the canoe out of the truck. That's when he saw it. They were siblings. They had to be. They both had the same dark shiny hair, the dark eyes, the same shaped nose and mouth. How had he not seen it before? Why weren't they camped together? Something about this whole thing seemed very fishy.

They took the canoe to the edge of the water and made another trip loading a cooler and another bag. Maybe Benu's camp site was set up and she was actually staying with Phoenix for safety. Again they returned to the truck. This time they opened the passenger side door. After a quick look around, Phoenix reached inside. Whatever he was trying to get wasn't being cooperative.

Ray watched Phoenix tug and pull as Benu looked on. A limp hand flopped out the door.

The body Phoenix pulled out of the truck was Becky Sue.

Chapter 17

Ray flew to the next tree to get a better look. Was she dead? He felt his pulse quicken at the thought. In the dimming light it was hard to tell. He didn't see any blood, which was a good sign, right? In that instance, it didn't matter. He wanted to kill them both. He wanted to change into a bear and maul them to death for whatever they'd done to his best friend. But he didn't. He sat and watched.

Phoenix carried Becky Sue's limp body down to the canoe. The way he laid her in it, not just dumping her directly, gave Ray a small spark of hope that maybe she wasn't dead.

Just before the canoe slipped into the water as the last of the light faded from the sky, Phoenix cast a look over his shoulder in Ray's direction. There was something seriously up with this character. It was almost like he could sense when Ray was nearby, especially in animal form.

There was no sense in risking being spotted when he knew where they were going. For a minute he contemplated trading the bird for a wolf, but in the end decided the bird was easier and faster and less likely to miss the cave.

On the way there, Ray debated on how to confront them. It was inevitable. There would be confrontation. But he couldn't do it naked. He could do it as an animal, but the problem would be his normal skills he relied on would be hampered by the animal he chose therefore creating more risk. Shit. Shit. Shit. There was no way to win this. But he had to. There was no losing either. He didn't have the time to return for his truck and get his hands on a canoe to follow them. It would take too long. Whatever he did, had to be done soon.

The cave was dark and he almost missed it. He flew in and immediately changed to a wolf where he could access the wolf's excellent hearing for when they approached. Then he waited.

The waiting was excruciating. He paced. Sat. Paced some more. How long would it take them to get here? Had he miscalculated? Was there another place they had before here? Would he hear them if they passed without stopping even with the wolf's keen hearing?

He was plagued with doubt as the darkness crowded in.

The first voice he heard was Benu's. He couldn't make out what she'd said, but there was no mistaking the sound. He poked his nose out of the cave and saw the dark shadowy outline of the canoe floating low in the water. That's when inspiration struck.

He hurried out of the cave and down to the water as quietly as he could on his padded feet. The canoe landed a few yards away. He took his gamble, changed into human form and charged Phoenix from behind, effectively catching him partially off guard.

The charge knocked them both into the water. Ray found his footing and stood waist deep on the slippery cold rocks as the icy water pushed at him, trying to force him down again. He threw a punch at a recovering Phoenix. He heard Benu cussing behind him. Phoenix took the blow easily and came back with one of his own. Ray blocked it and got in a shot to Phoenix's stomach. But the icy water was taking its toll. They were both shivering.

Ray grabbed Phoenix by the jacket and pulled at him to get out of the water. He wasn't done by a long shot. As soon as they stumbled out of the water, Benu came flying at Ray with fury, nails out, screaming and clawing. He tried to reach around and grab her. She was everywhere at once. While she had him distracted, Phoenix recuperated enough to kick him in his cold, shivering balls. Ray struggled to breathe through the pain. A hard fist connected with his jaw and he crumbled to the ground.

He only saw stars for a few seconds but in that time Phoenix had pinned him face first and Benu tied his hands. The cold was taking its toll on him as well. He was shivering and shaking.

After they had him trussed up like a Christmas goose, Phoenix half prodded half dragged him up to the cave. He struggled against him every time he got his footing. When they reached the flatter part where the rock began to protrude out, Ray made one more attempt to free himself from Phoenix, but something hard whacked him on the head making him see stars again. He stumbled the last little bit, still dazed and dizzy. Phoenix dropped him to the floor. With a flick of the wrist Phoenix lit the campfire.

If his jaws hadn't been chattering with cold, he'd been staring open mouthed at Phoenix when he lit the fire without a match. Why hadn't he thought to use his fire power when he was springing his little naked surprise on Phoenix and Benu? Was Phoenix a Sparker? That was impossible. Sparkers only had blue eyes. It was a genetic anomaly. Had it managed to mutate somehow over the years? Could Phoenix shape shift? It might explain some of his strange behavior and why he could spot Ray so easily when he was in animal form.

That was it. He'd shift into a bear and when Phoenix came back he'd maul him without mercy. He visualized the bear. Nothing happened. He tried again. Still nothing happened. Why wasn't it working? Did the mental stress have anything to do with it? Was it the fact that he was still freezing?

Phoenix walked behind the curtain, grabbed a blanket and threw it unceremoniously over Ray.

"If you so much as budge from that spot I'll kill you," Phoenix said before he ducked back out of the cave, presumably to go help Benu with Becky Sue. He had no aversion to personally being killed if it was for the greater good, but he had to save Becky Sue first.

Ophelia Dickerson

Ray was still pondering what in the name of blue fire was going on when Phoenix reappeared, Becky Sue slung over his shoulder. Phoenix laid Becky Sue on the cold rock floor opposite Ray on the other side of the fire. She was limp, pale, unbound, and unresponsive.

"What did you do to her?" Ray growled, struggling against his restraints.

"I haven't done anything, yet. She's just... sleeping." The malevolence that crossed Phoenix's face boiled Ray's blood and made him see red.

"You bastard!" In his struggling to free himself, he'd managed to knock the blanket Phoenix had so carelessly threw over him off.

"Look. I didn't really put the blanket on you to keep you warm, because really, I could care less if you freeze to death, but please keep it covered. I don't care to see your teeny, shriveled weenie flapping all over."

"Fuck you." Ray shifted and shook his cock the best he could at Phoenix, who promptly walked up and threw the blanket back over him, turned his back and went behind the curtain against the wall.

Benu had been standing in the shadows the whole time watching the exchange. When Phoenix stepped behind the curtain, she walked over to Ray and put a dainty finger under his chin, forcing him to look up at her.

"Don't worry, Ray. I'll fix you here soon," she purred. What the hell was she going to fix and how? He doubted she meant she was going to set him free, not after the way she'd attacked him. After watching her break into his cabin earlier, he only had a bleaker outlook on the situation.

Phoenix reappeared in dry clothes, tucking a knife half the size of a machete into a back sheath. Unless he missed his guess, the hard blow to his skull earlier had been dealt with the butt of that knife.

"You! You're the one who did it. You killed Jed didn't you?"

Phoenix shrugged like it was no big deal as he walked over and poked at the fire. "And Becky Sue's precious cat. Jed had become a bigger liability than asset. He should've known better than to sell to an undercover cop. I wasn't quite ready for you."

Ray stared in shock. "How did you know I was an undercover cop?"

"I've known for quite a while actually. Why do you think you were sent back here to begin with? It was no accident."

"What about Becky Sue's cat? Why kill it?"

"I needed to send her a message. I know about-"

"Shut up, Phoenix," Benu hissed at him. "If you say too much you'll get us both in a bind."

"Don't worry sis, if he survives hypothermia tonight, I've got the perfect plan."

"You and you're plans. It better work this time."

"It will." He walked over to Becky Sue and lifted a glowing green orb from her neck. "It's almost ready. By the time you get your part done it should be finished."

"What're you doing to Becky Sue? What's that around her neck?" He thrashed around on the ground trying to get into a better position.

"Shh, shh, shh, shh." Benu came over and put a finger across his lips. His first instinct was to bite it, but with him being tied up decided it was a bad idea. "She's just... sleeping."

Ray glared at the beautiful witch in front of him. "Sleeping as in forever, or sleeping as in you've drugged her and she doesn't know what the hell you've done to her?"

"Neither. We're not barbaric. We're only extracting the Spark power from her."

Ray let out a harsh laugh. Barbaric didn't even begin to describe what he suspected they were capable of.

"Now," Benu continued, "it's time for you to do your part and we'll leave you alone."

"Somehow I doubt that."

"You're so unpragmatic. Are you warm yet? You took quite a dip in the water." She sat there crooning over him in her sultry voice.

His blood was roiling with anger enough he'd finally stopped shivering. The blanket and fire might've played a small part in it too. "What does it matter to you? And how exactly are you taking Becky Sue's Spark power? Are you killing her? Mutating her? Wait, you must be Quell." The light bulb in his head finally went off, flickering but lit.

"It matters a great deal to me. You see, what I need you to do will require you being warm because yes, we are Quell. And unfortunately we cannot allow you to hang onto your powers. We've been working on this a long time and it would be a great disappointment if we didn't succeed after all the hard work we put into this."

"You're not getting my Spark from me."

"Why not?" She leaned in pressing her perfect cleavage against him. "No one knows about it but us. It's not like you're really losing anything since you just figured it out. And the extraction will be fun." She leaned in close to his face and ran a hand down his chest under the blanket, stopping at his waist.

He looked over pointedly at Becky Sue's limp form. "I doubt that."

"Quit worrying about her. She had more options than you."

"What do you mean?"

"The necklace works with most people, but there are exceptions."

"Shut it, Benu. He's just stalling." Phoenix called harshly from his seat near Becky Sue. "Just do it and get it over with. Since he showed up here we're going to have to move our plans forward faster."

It was true. He was stalling, but he also wanted to know what exactly they were doing and how. Knowing could mean the only chance of survival.

Benu stood and began taking off her jacket, her shoes, and slipped her shirt off her head revealing the perfect body he'd thought she had.

"What're you doing?" Ray asked.

"We're going to have a little fun." She shimmied out of her pants, kicking them to the side, leaving her only in a matching lacy pair of bra and panties. Had he not been beaten and known what kind of psychotic bitch she was he'd have been hugely turned on. But not this time. His body didn't even flinch in response.

She took the blanket off him, folded it in half and laid it out a little closer to the fire, patting it like he should come join her. He stared at her like she'd grown two heads. Was she out of her mind? Did she really expect him to do her bidding as she chose? Was she planning to fuck him here, tied up, in front of her brother?

"Don't be so cold. Come join me. I promise to make it a pleasurable extraction," she purred.

"How can I when I'm trussed up like a Christmas goose?" His arms were tingling and trying to go numb beneath him.

She shot a quick glance at Phoenix who nodded. "Turn," she ordered.

Ray rolled to his side. A moment later his hands were free. He sat up and rubbed his wrist trying to get the circulation back. If he played it right, maybe a different kind of surprise attack would work.

Benu took his hand and pulled him toward her and led him to the blanket. He decided to play along for a minute while his aching limbs came back to life. She turned her small, ripe body into his, running tiny hands across his chest, down his thighs, and in. Her eyes were trained on his face.

"This isn't so bad, is it?"

"You want me to fuck you here? In front of your brother?"

"Yes. He insists. It's the only way to your powers." She purred into his ear, hooking her leg around his knee and rubbing herself across his body.

He opened his mouth to tell her how sick he thought they were, but reminded himself that he needed to play along for another minute or two to catch them off guard.

"Well, I guess there's worse ways to be robbed than by a beautiful woman." He grabbed at her firm breast. She gasped. The anger boiling just below the surface prevented any rise in his cock.

He scooped her up, intending to kiss her hard and make her pay for what she'd done if he had to beat it out of her, but as soon as his lips met hers he struggled to breath. Ice filled his veins and the air seemed to be sucked out of his lungs with an icy wind. He pulled back, holding her at arm's length, gasping for breath.

She smiled a wickedly at him "Pack quite a punch don't I big guy."

"What the hell?"

"It only gets better. Before it's over your head will be spinning." He had a feeling it was going to be spinning right off his shoulders.

He'd caught his breath but continued to fake it as he glanced at Phoenix who'd just lifted the glowing green orb from Becky Sue's neck. He watched as Phoenix placed it in a pendant that looked like a sun. Immediately the sun began to glow as he slipped it over his neck. What kind of voodoo ritual was this?

Before he could wrap his mind around what was happening, Benu was against him again. She'd ditched the rest of her lacy under things and pressed her hard nipple firm breast against him, and ran her hand over his cock, rubbing it gently trying to bring it to life.

Without thinking, he pushed her back off of him. Play time was over, he went to make a run for it but before he could take another step, Phoenix was there, his hands like a vice on his wrist. When he let go, glowing rings held his wrist with a line going straight into Phoenix's hand. Was this how he'd been bound before, with magic? Is that what kept him from shifting into animal form or throwing fire?

He wanted to fight, but this was all new and strange to him. He needed time to observe and learn before fighting back. The only problem was he didn't know how much time he had. Becky Sue still lay motionless on the ground even after Phoenix had lifted the necklace from her.

"It would be wise of you to do as the lady says," Phoenix said.

Ray spit at him and was rewarded with a back hand across the face from Phoenix.

"Lay down. On your back." Phoenix didn't let go of the line to Ray's tied hands. "Benu, chair." He barked.

Benu retrieved Phoenix's chair and set it behind him. He sat holding Ray's line as he lay on the ground.

"Please continue, Benu." Phoenix said in a friendly voice, like this was just run of the mill every day stuff.

Without hesitation, Benu dropped to her knees and went straight to the point. She lifted Ray's cock in her dainty hands and began suckling it with her mouth. Ray closed his eyes and willed himself not to go hard. If Benu couldn't get him up, she couldn't fuck him and take his powers, for whatever they were worth right now considering he couldn't even shape shift at the moment.

Phoenix kicked at Ray's shoulder until he opened his eyes. He knew what he was trying to do. Ray looked over at Becky Sue, his heart constricted at her lifeless form. Rage began building deep inside him.

"I can't get him up," Benu said to Phoenix.

"Get the powder."

Powder? Now what were they going to do to him? He watched as Benu walked naked and lithe as a cat around the curtain. A moment later she reappeared with a water bottle and something else in her hand. She dumped most the contents of the bottle, only leaving a small amount, and poured the contents from a small baggie into the bottle then shook it up.

"Here, drink this." Benu sat beside him, offering the mixture in the bottle. He glared back at her. She put the bottle to his lips, he allowed some in, then spat it back out at her. His reward was a swift kick in the ribs by Phoenix. Ray groaned.

Benu straddled his chest, naked, her knees on his shoulders, a delicate hand pinched his nose shut forcing his mouth open. She poured the remaining concoction into his mouth despite his efforts at turning his head. He tried to hold his breath as long as he could and not swallow, but Benu was patient. He choked and gagged as the strange tasting liquid went down his throat.

Benu stayed seated on him, waiting. What was she waiting for? He glared at her. She smiled back serenely. He would make this bitch pay if it was the last thing he did. Bracing his shoulders he went to throw her off, but before he could, he was hit with such a strange sensation that he paused instead. His head was buzzing. He felt like he was floating. A small fire of desire started in the pit of his stomach. His skin tingled. He wanted to be touched.

"He's ready." Was that Phoenix's voice?

The weight on his chest lifted. He was so light and happy. Something touched his cock. It felt good. It was warm and inviting. He had a happy little cock. It twitched and bounced. It was ready to play. He heard his heart beating faster in his ears as he stared at the ceiling wondering if he reached up, could he touch it?

A weight was bouncing up and down on his hips, in a good way. It felt good to his happy little cock. It was being stroked with something warm and wet. He looked to see what it might be. Long dark hair fell across the face, but the perfectly round boobs were bouncing in a nice rhythm, up and down, up and down. Benu? Was that Benu on his cock? She felt so good. She shouldn't be doing that. Why shouldn't she be doing that? He didn't know. Just something far back out of reach in his mind told him she shouldn't be there. He tried to speak and tell her she shouldn't, but nothing came out when he tried to move his mouth.

The room began to spin slowly, lazily. He watched as the walls slowly began to move and followed them up to the ceiling. What a strange ceiling. It was so dark and uneven.

Oh, his cock was feeling so good. He closed his eyes to block out the spinning room and let the pleasure his cock was feeling romp through his body. If whatever it was on it wasn't careful, he was going to explode. He tried to reach up to get it to stop, but his arms felt like leaden weights.

And then he burst. His cock erupted in a glorious explosion of delight. Then everything went black.

Chapter 18

Darkness began to close in on her. It wasn't the sleep kind of dark. It was the kind of dark where you were aware of the dark and it was coming after you, trying to take something from you. Its fingers reached out and touched her. She pushed it away, but it came back. She pushed again, but it wouldn't leave.

Icy tendrils seeped into her heart slowing it. The same icy fingers reached into her lungs and plucked at the oxygen, picking one tiny piece at a time, leaving her struggling to breathe. Her skin crawled with fear. She tried to fight it, but it surrounded her, it touched her soul leaving a cold, stark fear in its wake. She had no sense of time or space. She fought and fought, but resistance was useless. The darkness was slowly claiming her. She fought anyway pushing back.

She hung there gasping for breath for an eternity. Suddenly, the darkness retracted. Its icy fingers left her weak and exhausted. She gasped for breath. Sweet oxygen began to fill her lungs, but she was just so tired she couldn't move. Fighting the darkness had worn her out. She drifted off into a troubled sleep.

Waking with a start, she opened her eyes grateful not to be in the darkness anymore. A low light flickered from somewhere nearby. Her eyes were still heavy with exhaustion, but she was too scared to let sleep claim her again. She turned her head to the side towards the light. Moving any other part of her body seemed like too big a task.

Two people were naked near the fire. She blinked. They both had dark hair. The girl was half the size of the man. She blinked again. Phoenix? He was having sex with some other girl. She blinked again. Sparks were flying from them both much the same at they had from her and Ray. He was a Sparker? That wasn't right. He had brown eyes. And who was she? Why was she herself laying on the floor watching them fuck?

She had more questions than she had answers. She fought the exhaustion trying to claim her again. The sight in front of her helped, even if she tried she couldn't quite tear her eyes from watching. Then she noticed another body across the fire. It was unmoving. Was someone else watching too? Where was she? Her eyes pressed closed. She forced them open, refusing to let the darkness come back.

The rock walls looked familiar. The cave where Phoenix camped? The haziness of her hard fought battle was fading. Why had Phoenix brought her here just to screw another woman? It didn't make sense.

Groaning noises reached her ears as the sparks around the two figures increased. At last they stilled. Somebody was finished. The weight of her eyes was too much. No matter how hard she tried, she couldn't open them again. But this time she didn't drift off to sleep immediately. She heard the voices and strained to hear what they said.

"Did it work?" It was the girl's voice.

"I don't think so. There was supposed to be some kind of blue halo that engulfed us," Phoenix said.

"Shit. Seriously? After all that and we still can't shift into animals?"

"Let me try." There was a minute of silence. Sleep threatened. Becky Sue tried pushing it away, wanting to know what happened. "Nope. Still can't do it."

"Damn. Now what?"

"We have to go after more Sparkers," was the last thing she heard before the sleep of the exhausted claimed her.

**

It was cold. He was freezing. He reached for his blanket to pull around him, but nothing was there. His head was pounding and felt like a fifteen pound bowling ball. Blindly he patted around him, trying to find his cover. All he felt was cold floor. No wonder he was cold, somehow he'd come to sleep on the floor.

He cracked an eye open to crawl back in bed. Something was off. This wasn't the cabin or his room at his parents. With a moment of clarity, everything came tumbling back to him. Benu. Phoenix. Becky Sue.

Becky Sue! Ray pushed himself up on an elbow and opened his eyes a little more. A hammer cracked in his head. The fire had burned out. Grey light was coming from the cave opening leaving most of everything in the shadows. The blanket Phoenix had covered him with was lying a few feet away. He reached for it with shaking hand. That's when he saw her. Becky Sue was still there.

He felt weak and drained as he tried to stand. His head was splitting so he grabbed the blanket and crawled on all fours to Becky Sue. He wrapped the blanket around them both, curling up to her trying to share what body heat either may have, before passing back out again.

**

Her eyes fluttered open. Bright light hit them. She snapped them shut and tried to open them more slowly. A heavy weight was across her stomach. A small wave of warmth came from her side. She was feeling more awake now. Almost rested. The weird visions and nightmares of the night still danced in her head.

Ray was lying next to her, his arm across her. Where had he come from? She didn't remember seeing him anywhere in the long night. Then she remembered the other body across the fire from her. Had that been Ray?

She pushed his arm off her and sat up. He moaned and reached out for her again. His hand caught her foot and he stopped moving. What was going on? What had she missed?

The curtain was missing from the back wall. Some stray things were strewn about, but it looked as if Phoenix had cleared out after his little escapade last night. It was a good thing, because she was tempted to give him a piece of her mind before she punched his lights out. What kind of crap date gives you a date rap drug only to let you wake up to see him screwing another girl? Wait, had he raped her her while she was unconscious?

She was still clothed. Her panties were intact. She didn't feel wet and nasty. Maybe she hadn't been drugged, but then why had she passed out and not known what happened?

Ray stirred beside her again. He moaned as his eyelids flickered struggling with the light. That's when she noticed he wasn't wearing a shirt. How had he gotten here? Why was he shirtless? He had to be cold. His face looked worn and rough. Two day old stubble covered his face. Unconsciously she reached out a hand and stroked his head, the short military cut had softened in the time he'd been in town as it grew out. She'd never seen him look more vulnerable than he did right then, hand on her foot like he was cleaving to a handhold hanging over a cliff, dark circles around his eyes, hair slightly askew, unshaven, at least half naked.

"Are you alright?" He croaked out in a rough voice.

"I think so. What about you?"

"I feel like death."

Images and feelings from wrestling the dark most the night came back vividly to her mind. "Don't say that. I think we walked a narrow trail past it last night."

**

His eyes had finally adjusted to the light, but the pounding in his head was still there. The only way he was going to move was if he had to. "You don't know the half of it."

"We're you awake the whole night? What happened? I only had brief moments of consciousness."

"I was awake most of it." He paused as he took in the emptied cave. "I think."

"Tell me about it. The last thing I remember was getting in the truck with Phoenix and falling asleep."

Her voice changed when she said Phoenix, enough to let him know she knew something wasn't right. How could he tell her how bad he really was though? And Benu? How could he tell her that another woman had him after drugging him? How could he tell her that even though he himself was a big strong guy, he'd let those two get the best of him? Robbed him of his power... and hers?

His head spun and tipped crazily. A hammer pounded in the back. "My head hurts."

"What happened to it?"

"They drugged me." He wrapped the blanket up tighter around him, despite the sun warming the day, the cold rock under him and the thoughts of the night events left him with a deep chill.

"They drugged you?" She asked incredulously, her blue eyes growing large. He met her gaze and held it. In that single look, he begged forgiveness, willed her hurt away, promised they'd find the strength together to survive. "Who's they exactly? Why did they do that?"

He looked away, partly because his head was pounding so hard, it felt as if it would fall from his shoulders at any minute, partly because it made him sick to think about it. "It's a long story. Is there any water left in here or a way to get any?" His mouth was cotton, dry, scratchy, and rough.

Becky Sue walked around the cave and through the camp debris that'd been left behind returning with a bottle of water.

"Thanks." He hesitated as he took it from her, checking to see if the seal had been broken, the visual of Benu dumping the water and pouring the contents of the rest in his mouth danced through his mind. His stomach recoiled. He guzzled over half before he stopped. "Do you need a drink?"

She accepted the bottle, took a small sip, and handed it back.

"Is that enough?"

"I'm good." She watched as he downed the rest of the bottle. For a second he thought he was going to puke as the nausea returned with vigor. He focused on breathing steady and it went away, leaving only the pounding in his head to deal with. He sat up slowly, making sure the blanket stayed wrapped around his lower half.

"Got caught with your pants down, huh?" Her smiled cocked to one side. She was trying to be funny in light of their situation. He might've laughed at himself had he not known the truth.

"Some days I don't like you."

She laughed out right. The sound was music to his ears, despite the hammer in his head. It gave him a spark of hope and a tweak of motivation to get going.

"Are you really naked?"

He nodded. She put her hand over her mouth, but he could see her shoulders shaking with laughter.

"I was flying around as a crow when I saw you and came to try to help. As you can see it didn't work." She stopped laughing, her expression serious again.

"Tell me Ray, I have to know. All jokes aside. What happened? I was only awake for a few moments."

He plucked at invisible lint on the blanket. "I'm not sure if you're ready to hear all of it yet."

She knelt down in front of him, leaning in where he had no alternative than to look her in the eye. "I have to know. Tell me. You're not laying in here naked for not reason."

He exhaled, dreading the words he must speak, all the while the hammer banged away in his head. "When I left you yesterday I went out to the crime scene in shifted form. I stayed until they wrapped up. When I got back to the cabin I saw Benu, that girl you saw me talking to the other day, which also happens to be Phoenix's sister, came up and broke into the cabin. She was putting tracking devices inside my pants. Which of course made me wonder what she was up to. I followed her. She met up with Phoenix and they came out here, with you. When I saw you, you were limp. I thought you were dead." He swallowed down the lump he felt rising in his throat remembering the fear he felt at the thought. Her blue eyes were unflinching as she waited for him to go on. "I flew and got here first. I tried to spring a surprise attack, but got sucker punched. I forgot about our fire throwing abilities, but I doubt it would've helped much. They bound me with some kind of magical rope and brought me in too. My shape shifting powers were useless. All my powers were useless." He looked down not wanting to tell her the rest.

"Then what happened."

"They took our Sparker powers."

"What? How?" It was the first time she'd flinched.

**

She sank back on her feet. She'd barely had to time to use and experience her new powers and here Ray was telling her that Phoenix and his sister had taken them. She remembered how it felt the night she and Ray had ignited their spark, fiery, wild, insatiable. Did their powers go the same way they'd come? "Ray, did he rape me?"

"No." He wouldn't meet her gaze.

"Are you sure? Are you telling me the truth?" He lifted his sad blue eyes and nodded. She believed him.

There was no room for lies in the pain of that simple look.

"How did it happen then?"

"It was that necklace he gave you, I'm pretty sure. It was glowing green around your neck. When he thought it was finished he took it and put it in some kind of locket shaped like a sun, then hung it around his own neck."

She remembered wearing the necklace. It was after that she'd started feeling tired. She reached for it now. It was gone. "Who else was here? I distinctly remember seeing three people. Two of them were getting it on."

"It was just us four. I'm almost a hundred percent sure." The look on his face was bitter.

"There had to be another one, a female. Phoenix wouldn't have sex with his own sister."

"That was me you saw then, not Phoenix. She drugged me then stole my powers by fucking me. Literally." The hang dog expression on his face squeezed her heart. He felt so bad. She just wasn't sure if it was because he screwed up and fell for the wrong girl or because he failed his mission.

"It wasn't you I saw. I know it was Phoenix. The girls face was covered with her hair and she was turned away from me."

"You're sure? Because if you are that means Phoenix was banging his own sister."

"Seriously? What the fuck? You mean you didn't see it?"

"No. After she drugged me and fucked me, I passed out. Phoenix already had taken the necklace from you."

"That's it then." She stood and snapped her fingers. "They're stealing our powers and becoming more powerful by sharing. They had sparks flying from their bodies and I heard them say something about not having enough yet and they had to go find other Sparkers. But why didn't they use the necklace on you or the sun thingy you said Phoenix wore?"

"I don't know. Benu said at one point that something wouldn't work on me. Maybe she meant the necklace? But I wonder why?"

"I don't know either, but we're not going to figure it out sitting around here yapping all day either." She reached out a hand to him to help him up. He stood, the blanket falling to the ground when he did. Glancing down when he didn't immediately let go of her hand, she felt a spark of desire kindle in her chest. She let her gaze linger on his body as it travelled upward, forgetting for a moment where she was only thinking about the pleasure he could bring her.

"If you keep looking at me like that we won't be leaving for a while," his voice was sexy husky. He dropped her hand in lieu of wrapping his arms around her waist.

She leaned into him. As soon as she was in his embrace, the walls of insecurity tumbled down. A huge wave of relief washed over her as she sagged with relief and pulled him in tight. They'd avoided death. They'd made it and they still had each other. The relief was so great that tears threatened to spill over any second. He held her tighter. If she had nothing else in this world, she had him. That's all that mattered.

"We made it. We're alive," she whispered.

"I love you Becky Sue." With those soft spoken words she startled, but didn't get a chance to respond as he brought his lips down to hers. His kiss was that of a man full of relief and need. A man given a second chance and not wasting any time. Familiar warmth flooded her veins. She felt so alive again.

His cock pressed hard against her leg. She fought against her need for Ray right at that moment and a killer instinct to go find and take care of Phoenix and his sister.

"Becky Sue I'm so sorry. I didn't mean for any of this to happen." He said around kisses.

"It's okay. We made it. We're going to win." His fingers found their way down to her wet spot. She couldn't deny him again. She needed him with every fiber of her being.

And he took her there, on the rock floor of the cave, locked in passion that only two matching souls could know.

When they finished, they lay on the ground, out of breath staring up at the blue glow around them in awe. Slowly it burned out, leaving them in wonder.

"Did… we just rekindle our Sparker power?" Becky Sue asked.

Ray flicked his arm, fire shot from his hand and hit the rock wall, instantly diffusing. "Yep. Looks like they didn't get all of it. Now let's go find those mother fuckers and take them down."

Chapter 19

After a long awkward hike, with Ray only wrapped in a blanket, they made it to the cabin. He hid in the woods while she retrieved his clothes. He put in a call to his chief to get all the information he could rolling in on Phoenix and Benu before he made the drive up there to pick up the file since receiving a fax or email was out of the question.

Afraid her mother would be worried sick about her, Becky Sue left to check on her mom while he drove to Harrison and back. She was half surprised her mom hadn't sent a posse out scouring the hills for her.

"Mom? I'm here." She called out.

Kate rolled out of the kitchen. "There you are. I wondered when you were going to get around to coming by today. So when are you going to tell me?"

"Tell you what?" Becky Sue looked at her confused, all the more so because her mom actually looked happy and gleeful when she expected her to be either raging mad at her tardiness or worried sick.

"That the reason you're late is because you and Ray ran away to elope this morning."

"Mom." She was at a loss for words. On one hand she didn't want to worry her, but on the other she needed to know they hadn't married. "We didn't elope." There she said it.

"Then why are you so late today and not at the shop?"

"We…" She couldn't tell her mom they'd been hijacked, drugged, relieved of magical powers, hiked through the woods, Ray naked in a blanket, or any of it. "Alright, yes we did elope." It was the easy way out and one day she'd try the truth again, but today it wasn't working for her.

Kate squealed. "I knew it. I'm so happy for you." She reached out for a hug from her daughter. Becky Sue felt like a fraud.

"So when are you going to bring Ray by so I can congratulate him too?"

"Umm. I don't know. He's kinda busy right now," she hedged.

"He must be, now that's he's married. He needs a job. Good. I knew you'd give him the motivation he needed to restart."

Becky Sue turned her head to keep her mom from seeing her eye roll. "Go shower Mom. I can't stay long."

"Of course not dear. Not with a young husband waiting." She squeezed Becky Sue's hand one more time and wheeled off. It was going to break her heart when she had to tell her it was all a lie.

**

He couldn't remember a time when he'd felt so focused and satisfied with his personal life. But he did and it was all because of Becky Sue. He'd never really been one to believe in soul mates before, but if she didn't fit the bill, no one would.

At the office he collected the files they'd prepared for him, promised the chief he was hot on the trail, although it looked like it could just be a front for something far more dangerous, but he'd soon have the drug runners in custody.

On the way back home, he started thinking about marriage for the first time in years.

There was no more use for the cabin so when he got back, he cleaned and packed up. Becky Sue arrived just as he was finishing stripping the bed.

"Whatcha doing?"

"Checking out. I think it's safe to say our targets," because he refused to use their names as pissed as he was about everything still, "have fled. I was thinking maybe we could work the rest of the operation from your house, since everyone thinks we're together and all that anyway."

"Yeah, about that…. Mom thinks we've eloped."

"Whatever gave her that idea?" He grinned. It wasn't a bad idea.

"I was late and have been with you so much, she just assumed we just up and eloped this morning. At first I tried to tell her we hadn't, but when I went to explain I knew I could never tell her about what actually happened. So I lied."

He laughed. He wasn't exactly sure why, but he did. It felt good to be able to laugh again. Becky Sue quirked an eye brow at him.

"I'm glad you find it so amusing."

He picked her up and spun her around before kissing her lightly on the lips. "Let's go finish this job so we can spend some real time together and see where to go from here."

They finished packing and drove their own trucks to Becky Sue's. He dove into the files trying to pin down where exactly to look for the Quell siblings while Becky Sue fixed them some food.

"Are you up for some more adventure tonight or do you need to rest?" Ray asked after their plates were emptied and they sat talking at the kitchen table.

"Does it involve bringing down a certain person and his sister?"

"Yep."

"I'm game. Let's go."

Hurricane Valley was located about halfway to Harrison and a few miles off a side highway, population: almost double Thunderhead. Night had fallen. An occasional porch light dotted along the road.

They took a turn down a dirt driveway and pulled up short at a small ordinary house that was listed as both Phoenix and Benu's home address. Outside the house an over abundance of animal statues were scattered around the yard, many of them had dark splotches on them near their throats, heads, and chests.

A few of them looked singed, like they'd been through a fire.

"Stay here for a minute." Ray put the truck in park and got out. The windows were dark, the porch light was off. Walking outside the beams of the headlights he crept into the yard and took a closer look at the animals. It was either blood or red paint making the blotches on them. A cold chill that had nothing to do with the cool night air ran down his back. They were at the right place. It was creepy.

He tread softly around the house looking for any sign of life. There was none. He motioned Becky Sue to get out and join him.

"What is this?" She asked motioning to the animal statutes when she approached.

"Long thought out revenge, or just evil imagined. Take your pick. Just don't dwell on it too much." She visibly shivered. He took her hand and led her to the door.

He knocked. Nothing stirred. He tried the door knob. It turned. Either they weren't returning or they weren't worried about visitors. Considering their yard décor, he leaned toward the latter. Flicking on the light, he blinked twice at the sight that greeted him.

The living room was a conglomeration of strange and disturbing. On the wall were framed newspaper clippings, some with pictures, many of them with fire engines, some without. Between the pictures hung objects with strange designs carved into them, horoscope charts, and over the couch one lone woman's picture hung. She was clothed in garb of the late 19th century.

"Becky Sue, come here." She was still standing in the doorway, mouth agape. "Look at this picture. Does it look legit or is it one of those mock up things people do on vacations?"

She studied the picture for a minute. "It looks legitimate to me."

Was it some relative of Phoenix and Benu or some hocus pocus person they looked up to? Why was she the only person singled out on the wall? He fished a small camera from his jacket pocket and took a picture as it was, then pulled on a pair of gloves and took it down to examine it closer.

"What an egotistical maniac," Becky Sue's voice pulled him away from the picture.

"Why do you say that?"

"All these newspaper clippings are about Phoenix. Apparently the local paper thinks he's a hero. These three here are about him rescuing someone from a burning building. This one is for some good citizen award he got," she was pointing to various clippings framed and hung on the wall as she went. "These people really don't know what kind of creep he really is."

Ray hung the picture back on the wall and moved to examine the newspaper clippings Becky Sue had pointed out. "Here's one where a couple people died in the fire and he was injured trying to save them."

"I still don't like him."

"Me either, but something tells me we better tread softly in this town or we may ruffle some feathers and get thrown out."

They moved out of the living room and into the kitchen, which turned out to be the most normal place of the house. At first glance, the first bedroom seemed to be average, but on closer inspection the knick knacks and collectibles scattered about were ancient Egyptian in origin. A small book case in the corner was full of ancient Egyptian mythology and lore. A single book on genealogy stood out. Ray pulled it out and flipped through it. A few things were highlighted here and there, but nothing was written in it. He opened the closet to see whose room this was. It was Phoenix's.

As an afterthought, Ray opened the dresser drawers one by one. Most of it was typical, socks, underwear, long underwear, t-shirts. He opened the last one. Junk drawer. An old wallet, loose change, screws, nails, and other odds and ends floated in it. He was about to shut it when something caught his eye. He pulled the drawer out further. It was an old book. He picked it up and opened it. Correction. It was an old diary in a feminine script. The page he'd flipped to was dated June 23, 1871.

**

While Ray searched the first room they came too, Becky Sue wondered down the hall, past the nondescript bathroom to the other bedroom. She flicked on the light and immediately felt like she'd entered the twilight zone. Posters and charts with stars, planets, and all things astronomy littered the walls. Some books were stacked on a dresser. How to Read Tarot Cards, The Complete Guide to Stones and Their Healing Qualities, Advanced Astronomy, Horoscope Reading, and other variations of the same subject matter.

She moved to the closet to see who the astronomer was. It was Benu. Clothes littered the floor of the closet, but near the bottom a piece of paper stuck out. She pulled it out. It was a picture of Ray standing with a group of policemen out on a job. Reaching down she threw the clothes aside. At the bottom of the pile was as small stack of photos. They were all of Ray in one capacity or another. A few he was in uniform, but more often he wasn't even though he was in the presence of those who were. They'd been watching him for a while. What about her? Had they been watching her too? But why?

We have to go after more Sparkers. The words echoed in her mind. They were after other Sparkers, but how did they know who they were? She and Ray didn't even know they were Sparkers themselves until they lit the flames by accident. How many others were there out there? How did they find them?

Becky Sue walked out of the room to check on Ray when he exited the other room. "Did you find anything?"

"Did I find anything? You mean other than these two are total whack jobs? Maybe. I found a book about genealogy in his room. I'm betting that's how they found us. They tracked us by our ancestors. That's probably how they'll track the others too."

"How are we supposed to know who they've gotten too already and who's next? There's no way we can cram in that much genealogy and track people down when they're so far ahead of us. We don't even know where to start!" She felt over whelmed and defeated.

"This might help point us in the right direction." Ray held up an old book.

"What is that?"

"It's an old diary. It dates back into the 1800's and was written by a woman named Elizabeth Downs."

"That was the Quell I told Phoenix about from the war!"

"What?"

"You obviously haven't been listening. Have you not heard any of the stories about the Sparkers and the Quell from the Civil War?"

"I never really paid attention. I always thought they were fake and they didn't interest me." He shrugged. At least one of them had been listening though.

"You're useless."

"No I'm not. I gave you your powers back." Ray stepped up to Becky Sue and wrapped his free hand around her, kissing her lightly on her lips.

"You dummy." She kissed him back. "You didn't give me nothing I didn't already have. You just helped, a little."

"Stop distracting me, I'm supposed to be working," he mumbled into her lips as he kissed her again.

Becky Sue stepped back first. "Alright then, let's work."

Ray made a play pouty face at her. "All work and no play make you boring."

She rolled her eyes. "Is there anywhere we haven't looked that might point us in the direction we need to go?"

"I think we've checked everything. We covered both bedrooms, the kitchen, the living room. Did you check the bathroom?"

"Not closely." Ray ducked into the bathroom.

Becky Sue wondered back into the living room, walking around, taking in all the pieces and trying to patch it all together. She knocked her shin into the coffee table in front of the table. "Ouch." She grabbed at her leg and rubbed it.

What's this? A small drawer was inconspicuously hiding under the lip of the table. She pulled it out and picked up a hand sized notebook. The pages were filled with writing, mostly names and lines, some had dates. This was some of their research! Ray walked in and came to stand beside her, looking at what she'd found. She flipped to the front again. The first names on the page were Phoenix and Benu.

"They were tracking their own ancestors. Do you think this will help us find other Sparkers?"

"I don't know, but it's worth a shot."

Ray grabbed the picture of the woman off the wall from behind the couch and they left with just the diary, notebook, and picture, leaving everything else as untouched as possible, just in case Phoenix and Benu returned.

"Home?" She asked as they got in the truck to leave. She was anxious to get back so she could dive into the diary and notebook more.

"Not yet. There's one more place I want to stop tonight."

They turned out of the dirt driveway back onto the main road and headed into the middle of downtown Hurricane Valley.

The fire station was easy to find, a block off the main highway that ran through town. Three trucks were parked out back.

Ray knocked on the door. A large man that had a few inches on Ray and a mustache that'd have made Hulk Hogan proud answered the door.

"Can I help you?"

By the time Ray explained who he was and that he was looking for Phoenix another man had joined the first at the door. This one just a little over half the size of the first, shaggier hair and a sharp nose.

"What's this guy want Bo?" His question was directed at the bigger man in the doorway, but his eyes never left Becky Sue. She squirmed.

"He's looking for Phoenix and I was just about to tell him he's on administrative leave."

"What for? How long ago was this?" Ray asked.

"It's been close to a week I imagine. It put us in a little bit of a bind with covering shifts and all, but just as soon be rid of him." The one referred to as Bo said.

"He's being investigated for arson," the other fire fighter said.

"Arson?"

"Why don't you two come in where we can talk more comfortably? This could be a long conversation," Bo opened the door wider to allow them entry.

Inside Bo led them to a room with two couches, a large coffee type table in the middle with a large TV against the wall, and a small kitchen off to the side. One last man was sitting on one of the couches flipping channels, apparently taking advantage of the remote while his companions were absent.

Bo made the introductions, and they shook hands all around before offering them a seat. The man who'd joined Bo at the door was named Wayne. The one taking advantage of the remote was Lonnie.

"Ray's here looking into Phoenix," Bo told Lonnie. "You're the one that first put us onto him why don't you tell him what got your hair up."

"Don't believe a word of what the papers tell you about him. Phoenix ain't nothing but trouble. He's got the whole town in an uproar thinking he's a hero."

"I don't read the papers so tell me your side of it," Ray said.

Lonnie's eyes slid over to Becky Sue and sized her up. "Phoenix joined the force about five years ago. At first he was all gun-ho and played everything by the rules. Then his sister came back to town after having left for college and things changed shortly after that. The number of fires we got called to increased. Sometimes they were nothing more than an old barn burning in someone's pasture, or a little grass fire that started near the road. But sometimes they're bigger."

"Houses started burning more. Most the time it was when folks weren't home, but last year we had a family not make it out of one. Phoenix wasn't on duty that day, but he was on the scene. Said he was passing by and saw the smoke so came to help. We got there just as he ran out of the house, coughing and soot faced. He acted all sad to us and made a big scene. Benu showed up right after. I'm sure he didn't realize I could hear him, but I overheard him tell his sister that he'd succeeded and there was one less to worry about. Since I didn't catch all that was said, I didn't think about it much at the time. I was too busy making sure the house fire didn't get out of control."

"Later, I started thinking about what he said and it made me curious. When we started investigating that fire, there was evidence of arson. Now around here most the kids that like to burn stuff don't target houses, especially houses with folks sleeping in them. Phoenix had been declared a hometown hero for trying to rescue the family before we could get there, but when he found out that it was ruled an arson, he argued vehemently it wasn't. Some of the evidence was tampered with, but I wasn't able to prove who done it although I had my suspicions."

"About two weeks ago another family's house burned. This time they made it out, barely. Phoenix was off duty, but he was there again. The woman said she'd seen him skulking around before the fire started. He swore up and down it wasn't him. That he'd arrived just before us. A neighbor confirmed seeing him, but no one actually saw him start the fire. We had to rule it faulty wiring with inconclusive proof."

"Phoenix was always a bit of an odd duck. He always acted like he was God's gift to women too," Wayne interjected.

Becky Sue rolled her eyes. Didn't she know. She felt stupid for falling for it. Ray squeezed her hand giving her a little reassurance.

"He was always talking about Ancient Egypt voodoo too. When we had slow nights he would bore me to tears with it," Wayne continued. Ray perked up. "I could probably tell you more than what you wanted to hear about their mythology. I think Phoenix thought he was half way to mythological legend level and claimed he possessed a special stone that made his special gene he had more powerful. I kept telling Lonnie he needed to send him for a psych eval. That dude was off his rocker some days with it. It only seemed to get progressively worse after his sister came back."

"What do you know about his sister?" Ray asked.

"Not much. She's as strange as her brother if not more so. She's hot I'll give her that, but she also seems to be quite the slut and I've heard is into that super kinky stuff." Wayne volunteered. "Not that I know on a first hand basis mind you."

"Their folks died in an accident when she was sixteen. I was one of the ones who worked the scene. They're hit by a logging truck," Bo said. "Still, she managed to find a way to go to college, or at least that what she told everyone when she graduated high school and left for four years. The only one who might've heard from her in that time was Phoenix. Then one day she showed up out of the blue all grown up and filled out. It wasn't long after her reappearance that rumors started circulating about her. Let me tell you, once the rumors start flying, it don't take long to get out of control around here. I think the worst I heard about her was that she and Phoenix were lovers. That's just sick. But like I said you can't trust the rumor mills so I only gave it a grain of truth."

Becky Sue knew well what the rumor mills of small towns were capable of, but this time she knew there was truth to what he said about Benu and her brother, sadly.

"Nobody's seen them in about a week. Some folks in this town are kinda hoping they've moved on. Some of the women folk may even throw a party if they have. Benu's been known to turn more than one husband's head."

This time it was Becky Sue's turn to squeeze Ray's hand knowing how close he almost came to falling for her pretty face, even though he tried to resist her in the end.

"Well, we appreciate ya'lls time. If you see either of them or hear of their whereabouts I'd appreciate it if you'd give me a call." Ray scribbled down the phone number to Becky Sue's house and shop.

"Well this is getting more interesting as it goes," Becky Sue commented as they drove back to Thunderhead.

"It does. I just hope we can get to their next victims before they do."

Chapter 20

The next morning Becky Sue went to check on her mom still living the lie that she and Ray were married. It was easier now that he was staying with her while the investigation unfolded. She should've felt guilty, but didn't.

She was still pondering her lack of guilt when she unlocked her shop and let herself in. She should've been working on her cat quilt, but Elizabeth Downs' diary piqued her interest more. Putting her quilting pieces aside she opened the thoughts of a long dead woman and began to read.

April 18, 1863

I have been recognized for my service to my country. Tomorrow I travel to the capital. It is unclear as to the purpose of my visit other than to congratulate me and possibly give me a new mission.

I do not mind serving my country in the capacity I have, although sometimes the men can get rough. I have learned how to deal with them.

I sincerely hope that this war ends soon. I'm tired. The troops are tired. We all just want to go home and rest. I hope I'm given a new mission soon, or at least no longer need rely on my beauty as I fear it has faded in these harsh conditions. Last week I was held as a possible spy. My charm fell on deaf ears. They searched me, stripped me naked, and humiliated me. But I prevailed. Those fools of the South think women have no brains, but again I have outwitted them. Sometimes I almost pity them. Especially those I've known all my life.

Last week I had to seduce poor James Brown. He's had a crush on me since we're ten years old. The poor sap will go home to Victoria, useless. I almost wish I could see her face when he can no longer conjure fire for her simple entertainment. The twit.

I must be careful what I write now before I travel. If anyone were to get their hands on my books, I would surely hang.

Becky Sue grabbed a piece of scratch paper and wrote down James and Victoria Brown. It sounded like he'd been a Sparker, whether he survived the war or not was yet to be determined. Did he have children that had inherited his trait before he left?

April 29, 1863

The journey to the capital was exhausting. I'm just now recuperating thanks to the dear lady who has offered me lodging.

Tomorrow I've been invited to a grand social gathering. I've been told the president is expected to attend as well as several foreign dignitaries.

She scanned through the next few pages as Elizabeth Downs described the social season and the political figures she met. Had Becky Sue missed all the important stuff? There'd been reference to more than one book. Had the others been lost or destroyed? She hoped not, but she also didn't know where to find them without returning to the house of horrors as she now referred to Phoenix's house after their visit.

Last night when they'd returned to her house it'd been late. They'd taken the back off the picture to see if held any clues. It turned out to be a picture of Elizabeth Downs herself. Their current pet theory was that she was an ancestor of Phoenix and Benu.

Becky Sue had the notebooks with their genealogy in it to try to make heads and tails of while

Ray was supposed to be making some calls to get more hands on deck to start tracing back both his and her genealogy to see who else might be targeted.

A foreign name caught her attention as she flipped pages and saw it for the third time.

May 17, 1863

Tewfik comes regularly to call now. I think the man's intentions are good, but I do not know if I want to become the wife of an Egyptian prince. I have never left this soil and in the midst of this war have no intention to. He is handsome and dashing and pledges his country's allegiance to the Union, but still, I ask myself where my duty lies. It lies here on this land.

The bells above the door jangled interrupting her reading. She greeted the tourist.

"Do you know when the shop next door opens?" The woman asked.

"She's not open?" Becky Sue looked perplexed. That's what had been missing from her morning, Cindy.

"The door is locked."

"I don't know. She's usually open by now. She could be home sick."

"Okay. I was really hoping to get some good homemade soap."

"Here, this is one you can sample. If you like it next time you come I'm sure she'll be open." Becky Sue handed the woman the bar Cindy had given her to use to catch Ray. She didn't think she'd need it.

After the woman left, Becky Sue was concerned. Usually Cindy called her and told her if she was staying home sick. She picked up her work phone and dialed her mom.

"Hi, dear. This is a pleasant surprise," Kate answered.

"Have you heard from Cindy today?" Becky Sue couldn't explain the panic that was rising in her.

"No. Is something wrong?"

"She hasn't come in to open her shop and she usually calls if she's home sick. I haven't heard from her."

"You're right. I hope the poor woman hasn't fallen or had a stroke or something. I'll call give her a call and if she doesn't answer I'll have Cletus check on her."

"Alright. Let me know when you hear back."

Becky Sue hung up and paced around her shop. She went out the back and checked the back of Cindy's shop. Everything was locked up nice and neat. The woman may annoy her but she didn't wish harm on her.

She sat down and tried to read more of the diary, but not knowing what happened to Cindy kept her distracted. Opting to use her nervous energy, she walked around her store dusting a shelf here and there.

The phone finally rang.

"Hello."

"I'm so glad you called me. Cletus just called me back. He found Cindy unconscious at her house. She's still breathing and he has help on the way."

Becky Sue breathed a small sigh of relief. At least she was still alive. "Does he have any idea what happened? Was she robbed? Was she attacked?"

"Where are all these morbid questions coming from? Have you been reading too many books again? Whatever happened to she's old with medical conditions?"

"I guess I just don't think of her as having health problems." The lies that rolled off her tongue these days were getting easier. Sometime she might have to address that. "At any rate keep me in the loop and let me know how she is later."

Was it possible Cindy was a Sparker? She had the blue eyes, but that didn't necessarily mean she carried the gene. Either way she'd put her name on the list for Ray to look into.

She sat back down to the table and picked up the diary again. The next several entries were all about the Egyptian prince name Tewfik and their courtship.

June 8, 1863
I have missed my first cycle. I'm afraid I must be carrying Tewfik's child. All these times I have always been so careful, but this time I wasn't and should have been. I have no one to

blame but myself. I'm afraid this spells disaster for me.

I'm afraid I am faced with the choice of marrying the prince or be sent back to the front lines, working the small men again if they do not throw me out of society all together. I have maybe three months before I am forced to run. I cannot tell Tewfik. He would order me to become his, or own my child. I cannot do either. He is a passionate lover, but he is not mine to command. I shall have to send him away soon.

August 12, 1863

Yesterday I informed Tewfik that we can longer be together. We were not meant to be. He does not know the babe that grows inside of me. It will come in the dead of winter and I am afraid of where that will find me.

This morning I received a gift from him, two actually. One necklace is a beautiful green malachite stone, carved with a griffin and a snake. The other is brown, sunstone he calls it, *carved as a locket of the sun. The sunstone is mine to keep. The green is for me to give to the one who holds my heart. If the receiver returns the malachite stone to me, I am to place it in my sun locket and their heart will be captured as mine.*

It sounds like witchcraft so I dare not repeat it. I'm not sure if I believe it or not, but I will cherish it anyway as a reward to loving a prince. I'm sure if I need some monetary help some day it can be used as a trinket of value.

Trinkets of value, something about that phrase made her think of her best friend Maggie Ann. The vision of a house full of antiquity came to mind. A shelf of old books, trinkets and pictures on the wall. Maggie Ann's grandma's house. She'd been there only a couple times over the years growing up. She lived in Hurricane Valley. If anyone, she might've heard stories, or even know some genealogy to help. Was she even still alive?

She picked up the phone and dialed the number she knew by heart.

"Hello. Tucker, get that out of your mouth," Maggie Ann answered sounding tired.

Becky Sue smiled trying to imagine what Tucker had gotten into this time. "Hey Maggie Ann. Sounds like you need a break."

"Tell me about it. But that's not why you called is it? So are you finally going to tell me that you and Ray eloped?"

"Oh no, not you too! I swear. Was it my mother?"

Maggie Ann giggled. "Yes. She called looking for you when you didn't show to check on her at your normal time."

"We didn't elope. That's Mom's version of the story. I tried to tell her we didn't, but then it got too complicated so I just let her believe it. Now I may be rethinking my alibi."

"Well, if you didn't elope what happened?" If nothing else Maggie Ann was perceptive. She knew there was more than what was being said.

"Like I said it's complicated. I actually called to ask you if your Grandma Virden was still alive?"

"Your life got awfully complicated awfully quick when Ray came back to town. And yes, Grammy is still alive and full of spit and fire. Tucker! Give me that. "

"Tell me about it. Does she still have all that history stuff about the area around here?"

"Yeah..." Maggie Ann's interest was clearly piqued.

"Do you think maybe we could go visit her? Soon."

"Let go of the dog's tail. Now," she scolded Tucker. "What's with the sudden interest in the history stuff... soon?"

"It's too long to explain over the phone and besides that you probably won't believe me either unless I show you. So would you call Grandma Virden and see if we can drop by tonight after I get off work?"

"Sure. I'd be happy to get out of here and take the kids for a ride. I'll give her a call and let you know. Are you at the shop?"

"Yep."

Maggie Ann promised to call her back as soon as she was able to set things up. Becky Sue was no closer to figuring anything out than she'd been before. Instead of pacing like she wanted, she put her hands to work ironing fabric and cutting out cat silhouettes for her quilt. Somewhere along the way Maggie Ann called her back letting her know tonight was set.

The afternoon passed with tourists flitting in and out. The phone rang late in the day. As Becky Sue reached for it, she hoped it was news from Ray.

"Hi honey, how's work?" It was her mom.

"It's ok."

"I just called to give you an update on Cindy. They're not sure what exactly happened to her. The working diagnosis is heart attack, but when she finally came too she was talking some gibberish about a necklace and some salesman who'd stopped by. The other possibility is she hit her head somehow and has a concussion."

"Okay. Thanks, Mom." Just as she was hanging up, Ray came through from the back door.

"What's going on?" Ray walked up and gave her a peck on the lips.

This was comfortable in a strange way Ray coming in and giving her a welcoming kiss. She kissed him back.

"Well, quite a lot actually. How about you? Did you get any leads?"

"Got both of our family trees ran back to the mid 1800's. Aside from the obvious cousins we know, there weren't any surprises. As far as we can tell none of them have been targeted, yet. So I'm not sure how they're determining who's Spark and who's not. I feel like we're missing something."

"Yeah, well Phoenix and Benu, or should I call them the Dark Duo? They've already struck again."

Ray's eyes darkened. "Not here, right?"

"No. They haven't been back. I'm not even sure if they knew if we survived or not. They got to Cindy though. Mom just called, long story short, Cindy was found unconscious earlier. She was taken in. When she came too apparently she was trying to tell them about the necklace so now they think she might've gotten a bump on the head, otherwise the diagnosis is heart attack. I think Phoenix must've gotten to her through the guise of a salesman."

"Oh shit. Is she alright?"

"Overall, I think she'll come out okay. Might be a little rough for her for a little while though."

"But how did they take her power? Do you think she knows about it? Wouldn't she have to have her spark ignited first before they could take it?"

"Don't look at me. I don't know any more than you do there."

"Well now we know they're moving faster that's for sure. Let me call the chief and tell him to check the hospital for heart attacks and head concussions coming from this area, maybe we can spring a lead there."

"One more thing, I'm going to go visit Maggie Ann's Grandma Virden tonight because she's as good as a walking history book. You got things to do or you wanna tag along?"

Ray smiled, his eyes glittered. "Tag along of course. How could I miss such an exciting adventure with my new wife?"

Becky Sue rolled her eyes and handed him the phone. "Here, go make your calls."

They killed the last hour discussing genealogy and who the most likely candidates were that they could think of to be targeted. The list was sketchy at best. She filled him in on the parts of the diary she'd read, but the relevance was undetermined.

An hour and half after close they pulled in behind Maggie Ann and parked in Grandma Virden's driveway. Levi and Violet bailed out of the car and ran in before Maggie Ann got the back door open to let Tucker out.

A minute later Grandma Virden came to the door awaiting her visitors. Becky Sue didn't think she'd aged a day since the last time she saw her several years prior. She still reminded her of the National Geographic pictures of the little old ladies who're the back bone of the society, even if they barely cross five feet tall. Steel grey hair, wrinkles, hunched shoulders, but more speed to her gait than looks indicated.

Grandma Virden greeted Maggie Ann and Tucker with hugs. "Becky Sue it's been too long. I was so pleased to hear you wanted to come see me."

A faint prick on conscience hit her. She felt like she was here under false pretenses. All she could do was hope Maggie Ann clarified that this was a visit for a history and possibly a family tree lesson. She hugged the old lady like she was one of her own family. She'd always felt like part of the family anyway. "I know it has."

"And who is this handsome young man you have with you?" Grandma Virden eyed Ray like she might already know, but out of politeness was forced to ask for introduction.

"This is Ray Burnett. He's…" How did she explain his presence here?

"I'm her boyfriend." Ray reached out to shake the frail hand, looking like a giant.

Becky Sue shouldn't have been surprised since that was their cover, but hearing him say it aloud caught her off guard with her mouth starting to gape.

"It's about time that girl settles down. It's taken her too long. You look like just the man to do it too."

There was something about older people who never minced words.

She risked a glance at Maggie Ann, who was snickering silently behind her grandmother and mouthed the words *I told you so* to her. "Come on inside. No point in standing out here so all the neighbors can gossip."

The house was just as Becky Sue remembered. It was like stepping into a time capsule that smelled like cedar and apple pie. None of Becky Sue's grandparents were still alive, at least on her mom's side. She didn't know about her dad's. It'd been too long since the divorce for her to keep up, or care.

"I baked an apple pie when I found out ya'll were coming by. Why don't we go light in the kitchen and you can tell me what you're up to."

Becky Sue's stomach rumbled in appreciation since they'd skipped dinner to come over. The kids were nowhere in sight, but she thought she heard noises down the hall in one of the rooms. The kitchen was peaceful and homey. Despite the fact Grandma Virden lived alone, she had an eight chair dining table set in her kitchen. The proffered apple pie sat in the center with other baked goodies in little dishes to the sides.

After everyone was served dessert, Grandma Virden took a place across from Becky Sue, crossed her hands in front of her and waited. Becky Sue shot a look to Maggie Ann then Ray. She didn't like being thrust into the center of attention, but here she was. They were waiting on her.

"What can you tell me about the history of Thunderhead?" Becky Sue was struggling with where and how to start, hedging on how much she should actually say.

"We'd be here a week, at least, if I told you everything I know. Be more specific."

Becky Sue glanced at Ray. He nodded the go ahead. "I need to know about some genealogy."

"If you're looking for your father's family, they're not from around here. They never made it into my books."

Thrown off guard at the misconception, Becky Sue paused. "No. I gave up on him and them years ago. No, I'm looking for..." How did she say this without sounding crazy? She looked at Ray. He met her eyes the silent conversation between them clear. It was time to let their secret out. "I'm looking for people who might be related to those they thought were Sparkers years ago."

Chapter 21

"You know that's myth. Why would you ask Grammy about such a crazy thing?" Maggie Ann piped in slightly put off by the request. Grandma Virden didn't flinch.

Becky Sue took a deep breath and told the highlights, without going into too much detail, about how she and Ray had discovered they're Sparkers, how they'd been bushwhacked and stolen from, and now where trying to keep from further instance where others lives might be in danger as the Dark Duo became more desperate.

When she'd finished Maggie Ann sat there mouth agape, eyes round as saucers. Grandma Virden just nodded like she knew everything and nothing about this surprised her.

"It was bound to happen. I always thought there was more to those stories than just legends. My mother was always convinced the powers would be rediscovered and show up one day. She'd be pleased as pie to know she was right. It was that belief and the stories that fascinated me that got me piecing together the genealogy books I've fiddled with over the years."

"Why didn't you ever tell me any of this?" Maggie Ann asked her.

"You didn't believe. All the stories I told you when you were a wee one, my mother passed down to me. I believe most the ones she told me held fairly true to fact. But you can't see if you don't believe. You, Maggie Ann, carry the Spark within yourself as well. I believe I do to. We just never got our powers because we didn't find a Sparker to love. We loved and married ordinary men."

"You're telling me that if I slept with a man who carried the Spark it would ignite and I'd have Sparker abilities?" Maggie Ann's whirling mind was visible across her face. Grandma Virden nodded. "That means my kids... have magical powers they could potentially unleash?" Her face was a mixer of horror and glee. Grandma Virden nodded again.

Becky Sue watched the exchange, fascinated to know that her best friend carried the same magic as she did, but sad she was unable to unleash it.

"Maybe you should check into the genealogy books your grandma has and bring back arranged marriage. I bet little Levi would love to come into the Sparker power." Becky Sue elbowed Ray in the side. He'd been silent until now letting the women talk, but Becky Sue took that as it was time to get back to business as the conversation was getting out of hand.

"What about the Quell? Do you have genealogy on them as well?" Becky Sue asked.

"Some, though not as extensively as the Sparkers. The Quell never really had any power before. The only reason I kept up with some of them was to see who'd they'd permanently deactivated."

"What about Elizabeth Downs? What do you know about her?" Becky Sue didn't know how she and Ray had kept, or reignited, their powers after being hit by the Dark Duo of Quell so left it a mute point to come back to later if it felt needed.

"She was a slut plain and simple. She heralded herself a spy for the Union, but was nothing but a camp follower. Mother was convinced she targeted our boys during the war and took their powers out of revenge. Her husband joined the army, for the Union, and was killed in the first battle. No one at home treated her unkindly. She was a widow after all, but she was a witch all the same. I came across an old clipping where she was courting an Egyptian prince, or something like that at one time during the war, but after that she disappeared. No one knows if she went with him back to Egypt or if she stayed here and continued her *war efforts.*" Her words were spoken without malice, but rather as stated fact.

"You've lived here in Hurricane Valley for quite some time. Did you hear about the fireman they just recently put on administrative leave?" Becky Sue asked. Her mind was reeling. She needed to get back to the diaries and read more towards the end. It might give her a direction to search and possibly other familial connections to Phoenix and Benu.

"I did. I didn't know him personally."

"He and his sister are Quell. They've found a way to pull the power from us Sparkers and use it for themselves."

"Interesting. I didn't realize they could do that." Grandma Virden said thoughtfully.

"We didn't either, until we experienced it first hand and let me tell you, it was not a pleasant experience." Underneath the table, Becky Sue felt Ray's hand on her leg. He gave it a gentle squeeze. Her heart bubbled happily knowing he was there for her. She smiled at him. Despite the war surrounding their lives right now, she felt at peace with this part.

They talked a little while longer before Grandma Virden went to pull out her genealogy books. With a promise to return the books when it was over, Ray and Becky Sue left.

**

Ray was still mulling over what he'd learned when they left the old woman's house. "What do you think about going by Phoenix and Benu's house one more time?"

Becky Sue shrugged. "You're the boss. Lead the way Napoleon."

He grinned at her. Why had he ever thought he should leave and there'd be any other woman for him?

They pulled up to the house of horrors. It was still dark and looked empty. Not taking their chances, they approached the house on panther feet, quiet and stalking. No one was home.

The house looked untouched from when they'd been there before. This time they switched rooms and searched. When neither turned up anything new they turned to the bookshelves. There was a reason they were so interested in Egypt and horoscopes.

He sat in the floor and started pulling horoscope books off the shelf in Benu's room, flipping pages and scanning to see if anything was marked. He'd gone through three with no luck and was beginning to think they'd struck out again when a line of yellow highlighter caught his attention. He flipped back to it.

The word Capricorn was highlighted. The sign was for those whose birthdates were December 22-January 19. He was a Capricorn. His birthday was January 12. But what did it mean? He stared at the page waiting for something to jump out at him. He didn't believe in the zodiacs. Wait didn't Benu say something about the necklace wouldn't work on him? Did it have something to do with when he was born? What was Becky Sue? He couldn't remember her birthday off the top of his head.

He flipped a few more pages. Leo and Libra were also highlighted in the same manner. This book was going with them. He set it aside and flipped through more. Time was wasting and nothing was turning up. He was about to give up on the books and almost didn't pick up the book on stones. Once he did, he found more highlights. He'd read it later and put the book on his short stack to take with in hopes they'd figure out something between the two of them.

Becky Sue was propped up against a wall in Phoenix's room thumbing through books on Egypt. He stopped in the doorway and watched her for a minute. Sometimes she took his breath away in the most unexpected ways. Seeing her sitting cross legged in the floor brushing a loose strand of hair from her face turned out to be one of those times. He smiled. She caught him.

"What?"

"Nothing. Just standing here watching you." She blushed. He'd never known her to be the blushing sort, but she did and he liked it.

"Did you find anything?" She asked trying to draw his attention away from her.

"Not sure how it fits into the picture, but there's some highlighted stuff in these books. What about you?"

"Not really. There was something highlighted about 'the Khedivate of Egypt'. It was something with the power between 1867-1882 before the British came in to rule. Elizabeth's diary mentions something about an Egyptian prince. I'm thinking it might have something to do with his family. At this point I figure the Dark Duo are descendants of hers since we know she was carrying this Tewfik's kid. Think they have any contacts in Egypt, distant family? As in, if they run would they go there for asylum?"

She had a good point. "Maybe. Grab that book and we'll read more on it. Are you ready to go?"

"Yes. This place gives me the creeps."

"Ok, this sounds bad, but remind me again when your birthday is?" He asked as he drove them back to Thunderhead. The zodiac stuff was troubling him.

Becky Sue quirked her eye brows at him. "September twenty-ninth. Why?"

"Do you know what sign that is?" When she looked at him quizzically he elaborated. "Zodiac. Your horoscope thing."

"Oh! I'm a Libra, I think. Why are you suddenly interested in horoscopes?"

"One of the books in Benu's room had three signs highlighted in it, Capricorn, Leo, and Libra. Do you know when Elizabeth Downs was born?"

"No, but it might be in one of the genealogy books Grandma Virden sent with us."

"When they were trying to take my powers, it sounded like the necklace wouldn't work on me so thought it might have something to do with the zodiacs. I'm a Capricorn and you're a Libra, both were highlighted, but the necklace worked for you, but not me. What if it has something to do with them and not us?" He was musing aloud, mostly.

The first thing he did when they returned to Becky Sue's was dig out his file on Phoenix and Benu to look up their birthdays. Phoenix was born March 28th. Ray checked the horoscope book. Aries. That didn't fit in anywhere. Benu was born August 13th. She was a Leo.

Ok so she fit, but he distinctly remembered Phoenix wearing the necklace... after he placed it inside the locket. He rubbed his temples trying to make head and tails of it all.

Becky Sue walked up behind him and began massaging his shoulders. He relaxed almost instantly. She leaned down and kissed his neck.

"Why don't you take a break? You're super tense."

One look at her full inviting lips and he didn't need more convincing. He grabbed her hand and pulled her down into his lap, kissing her as he did. When he thought she'd cry for mercy he picked her up and carried her off to bed trying to decide what animal it would be fun to shag as.

**

Becky Sue woke up feeling like a million bucks. She thought about going for a morning run. It'd been so long. But hesitated remembering the Dark Duo was out there on the loose still. She could wake Ray and he'd go with her, but he looked so peaceful sleeping there beside her she couldn't bring herself to wake him. He'd wracked his brain half the night trying to put the pieces together with no luck.

Instead she slipped out of bed and went outside to the back porch to enjoy the dawning of a new day. She stared at the singed circle where she and Ray had made love for the first time and brought their Sparks to life. It seemed like after that the whole world had tilted crazily.

She was still sitting there lost in thought when Ray came out the back door. "There you are. I didn't know if you were even still here."

Becky Sue stood and kissed him. "Good morning sleepy head. What time is it?"

"A few minutes till eight."

"Crap. I gotta get going. I need to go check in on Mom before work."

Ray blocked her path. "Are you sure you have to go?" His voice was husky. His face still had a day's worth of stubble on it, his hair stuck up in places. His eyes held a hint of promise of promiscuity. It was tempting. Very tempting, especially when his hand circled her waist and the fire in her veins carried the heat through her body at his touch.

"Yes. Quit tempting me."

He kissed her.

"Don't you have work to do?"

He sighed loudly. "Yeah. I suppose so."

For once she felt like she could take on the day as she pulled up outside her mom's house.

"Mom, I'm here," she called out.

Kate came rolling out of the kitchen. "Good morning dear. You're looking rather refreshed and glowing. It's the new bride look. Have you checked to see if you're pregnant yet?" She paused for a second as she realized what she said. "Wait, are you pregnant? Is that why you eloped?"

"Mom, no! Neither. None of the above. I'm not glowing. I'm not pregnant." She was about to say she wasn't married too, but though better of it in light of the current situation.

Kate gave her a knowing look, smiled and started to the bathroom for her shower. Becky Sue walked into the kitchen, exasperated, and checked on the leftovers. Nothing needed to be cooked for a couple more days. She moved some laundry around and changed the sheets on her mom's bed.

Breathing a sigh of relief when nothing else was said about babies or marriage, she left to go to her shop completely forgetting to ask about Cindy. Instead of picking up the pieces to work on her quilt, she opened the genealogy books to begin looking for familiar names, and potential targets of the Dark Duo.

She was fully engrossed in reading and making notes when her store phone rang.

"Hello."

"Hi Aunt Becky Sue, this is Levi." His voice sounded shaken and scared. Levi never called. He was only eight year old. Something was wrong.

She bit down her own panic and responded as calmly as she could. "Levi? What's going on?"

"Some people just came and took Mom."

"What?"

"Yeah, some people came up in a red truck and knocked on the door. They grabbed her and took her. I tried to stop them, but the man threw me off the porch. I might have a broken arm."

"Oh no. I hope not. You're a brave boy for trying to help your mom. Are you home alone now?"

"Yeah. Dad's still at work. I couldn't find his number. The only one I could find was you." She heard him fight back a sniffle.

"Okay. Keep your brother and sister inside with you and don't let anyone in unless its family. I'm going to make some calls and send somebody over."

"Thanks Aunt Becky. I hope Mom gives those idiots hell." She could hear the tears he was trying to hold back in his voice. Now wasn't the time to tell him to watch his language.

She'd already grabbed the phone book while she'd spoke with Levi, her mind reeling. There was no way to chase down the Dark Duo from that far out alone. She needed to call in some help from the gossip mongers.

As quickly as she could, she made calls to people she knew around the area Maggie Ann lived, letting them know to be on the lookout for Phoenix's truck and send word back to her shop. After the first few calls, making sure they understood to pass the word down the line, she called Ray and filled him in.

He arrived at her doorstep in under three minutes, walked directly to her, and wrapped his arms around her. She only allowed herself to cling to him for a minute before she pushed him away.

"We have to find her."

"I know. We will." He rubbed her back in a comforting gesture.

"We're running out of time. What if they're on the run now?"

"We'll catch them."

"But when they left us alive, they knew they were taking a chance. It's not like they'll be able to go home after they get all the power they're after. They have a bigger plan... or an escape plan."

"You're right. They wouldn't leave loose ends unless they thought they could get away with it. Phoenix has already proven he's capable of murder."

Becky Sue quirked her eyebrows at him in an explain yourself look.

"He's the one who killed Jed and Sherlock."

"That bastard."

"Maybe they think once they get all this power they'll be untouchable. But why leave us alive?"

"As a recurring power source, maybe?"

Before Ray could answer her phone rang.

"Becky Sue, this is Verna. That red truck you're looking for just passed us a minute ago."

It took Becky Sue a minute to remember which road Verna lived on. "Ok. Send the message down the line for me. Thanks."

She gave Ray the highway number and he phoned it into his chief to put the police departments in the towns near where they were headed on alert. They were headed out further into the mountains. But where? She paced as she tried to think, knowing that soon they're luck with the gossip chain would run out and the Dark Duo could disappear.

Chapter 22

After Verna's call the phone rang every few minutes, providing them tracking information on Phoenix and Benu. Then the calls stopped. Had the chain been broken or had the Dark Duo stopped? Out in the mountains there weren't a lot of side roads and such. Folks didn't try to fight the mountain often, but if they did it was usually a gradual take over starting near the highway, that's why it'd been so easy to track them early on.

Low thunder rumbled across the mountains. Chills ran up her arms. It was like the storm was bringing a grim prophecy of what was to come.

The phone rang again. Becky Sue's face lit with hope renewed, but it turned out to be Maggie Ann's Grandma Shirley letting her know that she'd made it to the house and the kids were okay.

"Do we wait for more calls or should we go after them now?"

Ray had been pinning points on a map of the area as the calls came in and was now studying it carefully in the area where the last call dropped off. "They got a good head start but if they've stopped our time is getting shorter. Let's go."

While Becky Sue locked her shop, Ray called his chief and gave him the last known location. They jumped into Ray's truck. He threw it in gear and peeled tires pulling out of the parking lot. With white knuckles, she gripped the door handle while he flew down the road at a clip that made her teeth clench and body stiffen.

It felt like hours before they passed the last house that'd called in a location of the red truck while the clouds overhead grew darker. Ray slowed a little to watch for the truck. It was a good thing because when he hit the brakes a short time later because he missed a turn off, they'd have been thrown through the windshield.

He parked on the side of the road not knowing what they're getting into following the dirt track. "We need to shift to get this done. Crows work pretty good for surveillance."

She didn't hesitate, despite the looming storm. She had to trust his instincts as well as her own. They shed their clothes quickly, leaving them in the truck. It took her a minute to figure out how to fly. Mostly it was getting herself to calm enough to tap into the crow's natural abilities.

The wind beneath her wings would've been a pleasant experience had she not been worried sick about her friend. They flew just above the tree tops, weaving in and out with each other trying to cover more distance faster.

Ray spotted the truck first. It was parked outside a decrepit, abandoned building. They made a circle looking for anyone outside before landing in a nearby tree. Muffled sounds came from within. Becky Sue looked to Ray for the plan.

**

He didn't like the sounds that reached his ears from the inside of the ramshackle old house. It sounded distressed. There was no time for planning surprises. This called for brute strength. He motioned Becky Sue to land on the ground.

"Shift into a bear and follow my lead. Oh, and watch out, don't let them grab you. They have some kind of ability to bind you and it prevents you from using your powers," he said remembering the glowing ropes Phoenix had held as Benu had forced the drugs into his mouth.

She did as he bid without hesitation. He knew the fear she must be feeling for her friend. The feeling he was getting in his gut about this wasn't so good either.

Ray shifted into the biggest, meanest bear he could imagine and charged the door, hoping it would give as easily as it looked.

The first drops of rain from the storm touched his fur just before he crashed through the door. Someone screamed, possibly two some ones. Ray didn't halt his charge as he took in the scene before him. Benu had Maggie Ann tied much the same way they had him, glowing magical blue ropes. Phoenix was in the floor on top of her, naked, pulling at Maggie Ann's clothes. He went after Phoenix first, swatting him off Maggie Ann with his large paw, sending him sprawling across the floor.

Ray felt a ball of fire singe the hair on his neck as it grazed him from the side. He glanced over just in time to see Becky Sue the bear go after Benu, knocking her down. Maggie Ann shrieked and cowered on the floor, drawing the clothing that had already been ripped from her close to her chest.

In the second Ray had taken his eyes off of Phoenix, the Quell had managed to get to his feet, his eyes dark with anger. Ray stood on his hind legs for a better position. Phoenix let loose a fiery ball aimed at his heart. Ray dodged it, throwing his large hulking body off balance. This wasn't working quite as well as he'd planned. It made him mad. He swatted at Phoenix again with his claw, but was too far away. Phoenix threw another fire ball. It singed his arm as it passed.

Think fire, he scolded himself. He glared at Phoenix as he channeled the fire into his paws. He threw one blazing ball at Phoenix who ducked. The ball hit the wall, sparks rained down to the floor. This place was a match box ready to go up at any minute.

**

Becky Sue followed Ray the bear into the fallen down house, feeling the first cool drops of rain touch her thick coat of fur. The sight of Maggie Ann on the floor struggling against these two monsters sent a spark of anger coursing through her that she'd never felt before. Fire raged through her veins. Benu had seen Ray enter and had thrown the first fire ball at him, but then she'd seen Becky Sue. She'd released her hold on Maggie Ann's tie to be able to defend herself against Becky Sue. But Becky Sue didn't slow a step. She plowed straight into Benu bowling her into the wall. Dirt fell from the ceiling like a sprinkling shower. Benu somehow landed on her feet, crouched in an attack stance, her eyes ablaze.

Standing on her hind legs, trying to look as menacing as she felt, Becky Sue called the fire from her raging veins to her paws, and threw the flames at Benu. She ducked at the last second. The fiery ball hit the tinder box wall. Maggie Ann shrieked again as flames rolled down the wall, catching and climbing back up.

She heard a snarl behind her coming from Ray. Benu came at her. She narrowly dodged a swift kick to the gut. Becky Sue swatted at Benu again, knocking her to the floor. This time she didn't hesitate to follow and pin her beneath the weight of the bear, roaring into her face, feeling the saliva drip from her sharp teeth. She felt the first shiver of fear run through Benu. The bear grin maliciously, but it also smelled the smoke beginning to float away from the walls.

**

He had to end this fast or they'd all end up as barbeque. Ray went after Phoenix with a vengeance, but the flea had nerve and speed. Phoenix dodged and ducked, trying to sucker punch, kick, and throw fire with every movement he made.

The fire was beginning to crackle as it ate the walls in a hell of a hurry.

"Becky Sue! Outside!" He roared as he managed to get in one last good swipe at Phoenix. He scooped up Maggie Ann awkwardly and headed for the door. The fire was just starting to eat away at that corner of the house.

He turned as soon as he was clear of the door. Becky Sue galloped out with an angry Benu wrapped around her neck. Rain drizzled lazily from the heavens. Ray dropped Maggie Ann gently to the ground just out of range of the fire, hoping she could get herself further away and went to pull an angry Benu off of Becky Sue just as Phoenix came stumbling from the burning building clutching something in his hand.

Before Ray could help relieve Becky Sue of her tick that was Benu, she flopped over on her back, knocking the wind out of Benu and managed to subdue her. That left him with Phoenix.

Their eyes locked. Phoenix glanced at his truck. He was going to run for it. Phoenix shot out to the side, but Ray knew where he was going and cut him off. The weight of the bear finally came in handy, as he wrestled Phoenix to the ground. He pinned his arms and opened his mouth to Phoenix's neck as a warning not to move.

Ophelia Dickerson

Phoenix screamed like a girl as soon as he felt the sharp teeth of the bear on his neck, saliva dripping, and dissolved into uncontrollable blubbering.

Ray let up to get a good look at the sniveling man beneath him. With one good backhand he knocked him out to shut him up.

**

Becky Sue watched as Ray the bear tried to open Phoenix's truck. His paws were too cumbersome, so he shifted into human form. She could only see part of his body from where she sat on Benu, but it was a sight she didn't think she'd ever get tired of seeing.

Ray opened the truck door and rummaged around inside. A minute later he appeared with rope in hand. Before he came into view he glanced over at Maggie Ann who was staring, mouth agape, ripped clothing still dangling from her hands. "You might want to close your eyes for a minute while I tie these two up since you're married and all."

Maggie Ann nodded and did as she was told. Ray stepped out and bound Phoenix, then came for Benu. She tried one last time to bite at him, but Becky Sue dug her claws in a little harder and she stopped. Ray dragged both siblings to a nearby tree and bound them there before shifting back into a bear.

"Alright, Maggie Ann. You can open your eyes again," Becky Sue told her softly ambling over to stand beside her friend, who she was pretty sure had peeked during the tying. Her friend of many years took in the large furry beast beside her before collapsing into tears, falling into the arms of the bear.

"I thought… I thought… They were going to rape me, maybe kill me." Maggie Ann sobbed. The rain from the sky mingled with her tears. Becky Sue sat there stroking her back waiting for her to calm down and watched as the fire broke through the roof of the house, only to hiss as cool drops of rain tickled its touch.

"We don't have long before someone sees that smoke and comes to investigate, not to mention we have people out looking for us. I'm going to go get the truck and bring it back so maybe we can get dressed before the party starts. Are you okay with those two?" Ray motioned to the Dark Due tied to the tree.

"Yeah, we're fine." With that Ray shifted into a Road Runner and ran for the truck.

While they sat there waiting for Ray to return, Becky Sue noticed a dark green spot on the ground. She walked over and realized it was the necklace Phoenix had given her. She was afraid to touch it, afraid it would send her back down the dark hole again.

Maggie Ann saw what Becky Sue was looking at. "That necklace is used for something bad. But I guess it didn't work on me, because they got angry when nothing happened. That's when…"She hung her head.

"I know what it's used for and mostly how it's used. I'm just glad we got here when we did."

Ray rumbled up in this truck, fully clothed. He angled it so Becky Sue could put her clothes back on without being on display.

Becky Sue pointed out the necklace lying in the dirt. He picked it up and walked over the Dark Duo.

"By now you two should know there's going to be a long trip to prison for you. So before you go I want to know about this necklace."

Benu spat at him.

"We know it's used to harness the Sparker power and it doesn't work on everyone, so why don't you fill me in." The sound of his voice was like an arm being twisted, waiting for the receiver to cry mercy.

Phoenix had finally stopped blubbering and looked the most resigned of the two. Ray stood in front of him and waited. "Might as well tell us a good story, because we might have to wait a while for backup."

"The necklaces were a gift to our ancestor Elizabeth Downs from an Egyptian named Tewfik. He was like a prince. It took her a little while to discover what the possibilities were with them, but once she did she came up with a plan. Every other generation since has tried to marry into the Sparker gene pool. The malachite stone doesn't work on Capricorns. That's why it wouldn't work on you. The sun stone, our receiving necklace that unlocks the magic the malachite takes away, doesn't work with Leo's and Libra's. Benu is a Leo, so she has to get her powers the old fashioned way. We hadn't planned to take her powers the old fashioned way, but the necklace didn't work." He motioned with his head to Maggie Ann. No one seemed to notice the rain pouring down on them.

"That's because I'm a Capricorn."

"The information we found had your birthday as February 7th."

"My parents might've lied to the papers about that to give me time to be conceived legally after their marriage. It's a family secret."

"Alright, but how does it harness the powers of those who's Spark hasn't been lit?"

"It automatically activates the Spark. It helps if the Spark has already been activated though. More power came from you two than any of the others we took from because you'd managed to activate the Spark already, which also made you more dangerous. That's why I killed your cat." Phoenix's face turned dark as he looked over to Becky Sue. "I wanted to scare you so maybe you'd be afraid to use your powers if you thought someone knew and had killed for it."

"Where's the sun necklace?" Ray asked reigning in hard to keep from waylaying the piece of shit tied to the tree. Phoenix glanced down to his chest. Ray reached down and pulled the pendant out and yanked it from his neck. Taking both the pendants he retreated from the group and was looking around on the ground. He found a good size rock and smashed both pieces to shards.

Phoenix hung his head. Benu snarled a rabid animal sound. Sirens sounded in the distance.

Ray picked up the shards of stones and walked up to Becky Sue, placing them in her hands. "It's over. We're free from them. We have the genealogy books to track others like them, and us. It's time to move on."

Becky Sue's heart was pounding in her ears. This was good bye. It was over. Time to move on. He was leaving. She felt as if a part of her was being ripped out from deep inside.

"What do you think about stopping by a justice of the peace on the way back and eloping for real this time?"

"What?" Becky Sue blinked back the tears she'd been fending off. "Are you asking me to marry you?"

"I guess I didn't do that right. Let me try it this way," Ray dropped to one knee and took her hands in his, "Becky Sue will you marry me?"

"Yes!" She opened her arms and knocked him over into the mud as she flew at him, smothering him in kisses.

They could work out the details of jobs and responsibilities later. This is where she belonged. This is who she belonged with. Nothing else mattered. She was going to marry her best friend.

"Well it looks as if you folks have it all under control," a voice said from the edge of the woods.

Becky Sue and Ray turned their heads. Verna stepped from behind a tree close by rollers in her hair, worn work dress, and boots holding a shot gun in her hand.

"Congratulations, Becky Sue. It's about time." With that the old woman turned and disappeared back into the woods as silently as she'd come.

THE END

About the Author:

A little bit of southern sass, a little bit of sweet tea. A little unconventional, but built on tradition. I enjoy writing and life in general with two kids and hubby in tow.

How did you like the story? Let me know! Don't forget to write a review.

Follow me on Twitter: O_Dickerson3

Email: o.dickerson333@gmail.com

Made in the USA
Middletown, DE
26 October 2022